NOVEL
PROBLEMS

George Morrison

Tennin Books ™

To Bev, with gratitude and thanks
for your endless patience and understanding.

*(When you finally get that dog you've always wanted,
I hope he's like Chaucer!)*

1

The US Government protects its secrets like a manic squirrel guarding its nuts. This was something that Jake Andersen failed to consider when, desperate to write a best-selling novel, he borrowed one of those secrets.

It was midnight in late January when he made his mistake. Jake was alone in his cubicle, one of dozens filling a room dedicated to Northwood Shipbuilding's IT department. Pursing his lips, he leaned back in his chair and scowled at his laptop. His dark brown eyes normally glowed with the shy intensity of a dreamer intent on bringing those dreams to life, but now they showed only annoyance.

The glow from his laptop's screen and the monitor on his desk barely lit the gray fabric of his cubicle's walls in the gloom. If it had been daytime, when the room hummed with quiet conversation and the chatter of keyboards, then the cinder-block walls would have appeared a dirty tan color under the fluorescent overhead lights. But they were invisible at night, as the room purposefully had no windows, both for reasons of security and to prevent the IT employees from succumbing to outside distractions. Working there was much like being the last passenger on a bus at night, alone, isolated from the world, and absent all sense of time.

Jake shrugged and zipped up his hoodie. He blew on his hands and rubbed them together to warm them before resuming typing. Northwood turned off the overhead lights and set back the thermostats in their buildings to fifty-six degrees at night in an effort to conserve energy. Located at the mouth of the Menominee River, where it passed through the town of Marinette before flowing into the western edge of Lake Michigan, the Northwood facility bore the brunt of the lake's winter fury as it lashed the Wisconsin shoreline. In January, the subzero wind coming off the lake chilled the outer walls to such an extent that the condensation on the cinder blocks occasionally froze.

He popped a handful of Cheese Puffs into his mouth, grinding them into an orange powder as the salty cheese flavor burst on his palate, then washing the slush down with a saccharine-spice slug of Dr. Pepper. The crunch of his snack resonated in the empty office, carrying further than one would have expected, almost as if the lingering scent of overworked staff and overheated electronics was helping it on its way.

Jake reread what he had just written on his laptop, and then he deleted it. *Complete garbage. Not the way to start the Great American Novel; better suited for an entry in the Stormy Night contest.* But he knew what the problem was.

I need a plot.

And there it was. Without a compelling storyline, anything that he wrote was just froth. But the ideas wouldn't come.

Jake sighed as he set his laptop aside, returning his attention to the monitor on his desk. His job as a UNIX administrator consisted of running a lot of batch programs to patch and update applications and to back up the company's files. He also monitored system processes and adjusted the priority of long-running jobs, ensuring that the company's database systems were secure and responsive. By its nature, the job had to be done when the systems were not in use, so Jake worked nights and weekends; a situation that suited him well.

With a slender build, warm brown eyes, and short, curly brown hair, Jake was an attractive young man in a geeky sort of way, although he was shy and lacked the confidence to ask a girl out. It was no surprise to anyone who knew him that he ended up working as a UNIX admin, a position where he worked nights and human contact was nil.

A tacit perk of the job was that when the systems were running well, Jake had considerable free time at his desk. It didn't take long before he started to fill the empty, unsupervised hours by drafting novels on his laptop.

Kicking off another back-up job on the mainframe, he leaned forward and watched filenames scroll down his monitor as the system sent copies of the files to a cloud-based repository. He was about to return to his laptop when he noticed something strange. The term "eschaton" kept showing up in the filenames.

Jake killed the back-up job, worried that the filenames were being corrupted. "Eschaton" wasn't a word or technical term that he was familiar with, and a quick Google search only returned references to a Greek term heralding the end of the world. *That's just the kind of thing a hacker would use. Oh, God, I hope we haven't been breached!*

He pulled up one of the files and was relieved to find that it was still readable, showing no signs of corruption. *Maybe it's just the filenames?* But as he read further, Jake realized that the term appeared multiple times within the document. It referred to one of the systems that Northwood was building into the Liberty-class destroyer currently under construction for the US Navy in the company's shipyard.

He pulled up a few more files, and then quickly closed them. *OMG!* The chill he felt had nothing to do with the temperature of the room. Northwood was installing an Eschaton control system in the destroyer, and a cursory glance through the documents revealed that it formed the core of a ballistic missile defense system. An involuntary look around reassured him that he was still alone, that no one had seen him reading the documents.

Well, at least we haven't been hacked. Jake restarted the back-up job, and then sat back to think about what he'd just read. The documents he'd viewed didn't contain any engineering info or classified specifications. *But even so, they really shouldn't leave documents like that lying around in plain text on a file system. The files should be encrypted. Heck, anybody working here could read them, and a spy would...* Jake paused for a moment. Then, before his more prudent side had time to raise an objection, his creative side came up with a grand idea for a new novel.

What if he wrote about spies trying to steal the Eschaton secrets from Northwood? But Jake was a sci-fi writer, and he didn't want to do a Bond movie knockoff. The story had to have a sci-fi twist to it. *Aliens. Aliens trying to steal the secrets of our ballistic missile defense system in preparation for an invasion.*

Winters are long and cold in Wisconsin, and with no social life to distract him, Jake poured himself into his new project. Twelve weeks and one thousand, three hundred and seventy-two cups of coffee later, his masterpiece was complete.

Jake gave a copy of the manuscript to Felipe Ortega, his friend and roommate, for feedback.

Felipe had been a devout supporter of Jake's writing efforts from the time they first met in high school. Their initial intro-duction was somewhat informal, coming together while invol-untarily participating in the swirly tradition imposed on nerds by the school's jocks. Swirlies involve shoving a victim's head into a school toilet and then flushing it. On this particular occasion, the football team's star quarterback had demon-strated a laudable commitment to water conservation by attempting to flush the heads of the two boys at the same time in the same stool. Because the boys were of similar build and hair color, the jock claimed extra points for the prank because they were 'twins.' Jake and Felipe soon formed a strong bond based upon shared misery and unfulfilled dreams.

Their friendship continued throughout college, where they both took advanced degrees in computer science. Recently, they found themselves both working for Northwood. As a UNIX admin, Jake worked nights, while Felipe worked the day shift as a web consultant.

When he wasn't working at his regular job, Jake would write and he had produced several sci-fi novels, none of which had ever been published. The two men had recently moved in together in an old, but well-maintained bungalow with white clapboard siding, two bedrooms and a shared bath that Jake had purchased on Merryman Street, just a few blocks from where they worked.

Felipe admired Jake's writing efforts, and he loyally offered moral support to the struggling author after each setback. This hobby took up much of Felipe's time, as Jake tended to spiral into long periods of depression after each book was rejected.

The two friends were in the living room of their home watching a Brewers game on a lazy Sunday afternoon in early May when the subject of Jake's latest literary effort came up.

The room was like an old shoe, with a brown leather couch pushed up under a set of double-hung windows and facing a flat-screen TV on the opposite wall. The plaster walls were medium blue, as was the shag carpet. A box of pepperoni pizza sat on the coffee table in front of them, closely watched by Jake's chocolate Lab, Chaucer. The dog considered anything on the floor to be his property and the coffee table was low enough to almost qualify, so he lurked under it watching for a chance to snatch a snack.

Ignoring Chaucer's hopeful gaze, Felipe stuffed half a slice of pizza into his mouth and then washed it down with some Spotted Cow. Taking a moment to dislodge a scrap of pepperoni from his teeth using his pinky finger, Felipe leaned back on the couch and said, "I read your new book last night. It was great, man!"

"I wish somebody else thought so," Jake said. "Remember what happened to my first novel? One of the New York agencies actually went to the trouble of shredding the manuscript and returning it to me with a handwritten note saying never to contact them again."

"Okay, that one maybe did need a bit of work."

"And my second novel? Have you forgotten what happened at the Greater Chicago Writer's Pitch Convention? How that agent had me thrown out and threatened me with a restraining order if I ever showed her a manuscript again?"

"Dude, I still think she was overreacting." Felipe fished a joint from the ashtray on the table and lit it.

"And I wallpapered one side of my room with the rejections from my third book. I put up over three hundred before I ran out of space."

"Yeah, but they didn't shred it, did they? You've gotten better with each book, and this one's legitimately great."

"Felipe, you're so stoned that your judgement's impaired." Suddenly suspicious, Jake asked, "Did you finish it or are you just saying that to make me feel better?"

"Of course, I read it! Well, most of it. Enough to get a good feel for it, anyway. Seriously, it's great, man! I mean it. Especially where you have the alien turn purple when it's in its horny male phase. Having aliens change sex based on the phase of the moon is pure dope. But don't you think it's a bit, well, clichéd to have it turn pink when it's in the female phase?"

"Maybe. Would yellow be better?"

"Nah, I'd go with something cool, like black, or red, or black and red—you know, like a flat black with red pinstripes, kind of like a whacked-out zebra."

"I'm not sure I want a horny, demented zebra trying to seduce the company's CEO in my story. That's not an image I'd care to inflict on an unwary reader. And now that you mention it, I wish I could get it out of my own mind. Ewwww! Anyway, since you didn't read all of the book, perhaps you'd like me to read some to you?"

"Is that entirely necessary?"

"Well, no. But—"

"Dude, in case you hadn't noticed, we're in the middle of the Brewers game."

Jake grabbed the remote and turned the TV off.

"Hey, I was watching that!" Felipe protested.

"Really? What inning was it?"

"Uh, the top of the sixth?"

"Nope. Bottom of the third and all the heavy hitters have been to bat and struck out. Trust me. You're not missing a thing for at least half an hour. I'll just read the first chapter. Then you can get back to the game, okay?"

"Sure," Felipe said, chugging the rest of his beer to fortify himself, "but before you do, there's something we should talk about."

"Which is?"

"Jake, I'm not sure it's such a good idea to use company confidential information in your book. You could lose your job, or even go to jail."

"Nothing in the story is secret. It's all public knowledge."

"Oh yeah? If I ask the next guy I meet on the street what an Eschaton ballistic missile defense system is, what do you think he'd say?"

"Well, nothing, I guess."

"Right. You know how twitchy management gets if you even mention weapon systems during a meeting. And talking about putting a system into one of the new destroyers that the company is building? Jesus, Jake, that's seriously hush-hush."

"But it's not secret. At least, the bits I talk about aren't secret. I don't include any technical stuff or anything that could compromise security."

"Are you sure? And what's this about a spy working in the company? How do you think they'll react to that?"

"But it's vital to the plot!"

"I don't know, I'm not a writer, but the whole thing has a bad vibe."

"How do you mean?"

"Well, it reads more like a spy's personal notes than a novel. It feels a little too real."

"Look, I wrote it like a diary in the first-person so that it would engage readers better."

"Better than what, day-old cat food?"

"Felipe, stop already, okay?"

"Dude, where did you even get the idea for doing that?"

"There was an article in *Writer's Digest* that talked about how to build interest in a story. Besides writing it like a diary, the author said to write about what I know. Other than UNIX operating systems, I don't really know much. Heck, I get my butt kicked in fantasy sports even with a ten-gig database to help with my picks."

"I told you the database wouldn't work. How much did you lose, anyway?"

"That's none of your business, and besides, we were talking about my book. Don't change the subject."

"Okay, but I still say it's a bad idea."

Jake sighed as he leaned back on the couch. "You might be right, Felipe. But I'm going crazy! I just can't get anybody to look at my books. I'd do anything to get published!"

"Does that include going to jail?"

"I guess not. Maybe you're right, but what else can I do?"

"Start something new that doesn't include national defense secrets. And look at the bright side of things."

"What bright side is that?"

"You haven't gotten a single rejection letter for the book!"

Jake stared at his friend for a moment and then threw the manuscript on the floor in frustration.

"I could use another beer!" Felipe said hopefully as Jake stalked from the room.

When Jake didn't return, Felipe got up and hit the kitchen for a brew and a snack. While he was out of the room, Jake's dog Chaucer saw his chance. Slipping out from under the coffee table, he snatched up the manuscript and bounded out of the back door before anybody noticed what he was up to. It took only a few minutes for the dog to bury Jake's latest manuscript in the vain hope that it would never be found.

The next morning, when Jake let Chaucer out, the dog rushed to the back yard to make sure that the recently interred manuscript was undisturbed. Something about the book woke that canine sense of caution that responds to ghosts, muggers, and traveling salesmen.

Chaucer spent the day patrolling the yard on high alert. When Jake woke and got ready for work that evening, the dog contrived to slip out of the house and return to his post, like a French Legionnaire returning to his fort. The night was mild, and other than an inquisitive squirrel that needed shooing off, passed without event.

But nobody can stay vigilant forever, not even the most devoted hound. When morning came, Chaucer, convinced that the danger had passed, abandoned his post and went to the sidewalk to watch for his favorite person in the whole world, Jake's eight-year-old niece, Daphne Andersen, who lived next door.

Thus began a chain of events that would change Jake's life forever. His niece, whom he adored, was destined to play a key role in this, although the term "destiny" had not yet been covered in her third-grade reading class.

School had not yet let out for the summer, so after a quick bowl of cereal, Daphne left the small, light-green bungalow where she lived with her mother and headed down Merryman Street toward her school.

To Daphne, the morning was like a flute solo played by a Buddhist monk. She paused to twirl on the sidewalk in exuberance at the glory of the day, the normally serious expression on her oval face replaced by one of sheer delight. Her long brown hair swung wide as she pirouetted on her skinny legs, grinning up at the sky. The budding leaves of the ash trees lining the streets caught the morning sun with a shimmer of pale green, and the sound of the waves from nearby Lake Michigan served as gentle background music for the scene.

After being joined by Chaucer, Daphne sat down under one of the ash trees to rummage through her book bag. This was a mistake that was soon to have serious consequences for both her Uncle Jake and a delightful woman named Claire Miller who Daphne hadn't yet met. With the natural curiosity of a third-grader, Daphne wanted to know what was in her lunch box. Not a peanut butter sandwich, she hoped, at least not on a Tuesday. PB&J sandwiches were Friday fare, giving her something to look forward to all week. So she piled her books and papers next to her as she rooted around in the bottom of her bag till she found the box. She set it next to her on grass still damp from a recent rainfall. Overhead, cardinals sang their "pretty-pretty-pretty" song from the treetops and were answered by the soft raspberry of chickadees who didn't believe a tweet of it.

Moments later, the universal quietude was dispatched with great energy as Daphne chased the dog down the sidewalk shrieking, "Give it back! Chaucer, let go! Let go!"

Chaucer often tagged along when she walked to school. Jake's house was right next door to Daphne's place, and Chaucer had been waiting for her when she left for school that morning.

But Daphne had forgotten about Chaucer's long-standing policy of taking anything not nailed down and burying it in Jake's back yard. There, under the dappled shade of an oak that was old before the town of Marinette was founded, the items found a stately repose beneath the rich Wisconsin loam. When Daphne caught up with the dog, he was busy with the excavation phase of his current project. A foot-high pyramid of moist soil had already formed behind Chaucer's hind legs as he worked the job with great energy.

"Chaucer, you ruined it!" wailed Daphne as she retrieved a slimy scrap of paper from his jaws. "Ms. Eliot will kill me!"

"Hey, what's this?" she asked, noticing some other paper that had come to light at the bottom of Chaucer's big dig.

Brushing back her long brown hair and tucking it behind her ear so that she could see better, she left a broad smear of dirt on her cheek that would have caused real distress if she hadn't been so excited by her discovery. It took only a moment for her to pull a masticated manuscript out of the pit. It was several hundred pages long. More, she figured, if you added back in the pages missing from the front of the book. And it was a book. She could see that. Unca Jake had been writing again and it looked like Chaucer had done to this manuscript what he had done to Jake's last three books.

Daphne thought that was sad. Bad enough that her uncle kept getting rejected by publishers. But by his own dog? Sad.

Frowning, she wiped the dirt off the stack of papers and tried to read some of the book. She was an advanced reader for a third grader and understood most of it. Of course, her uncle was a smart guy and so used a lot of big words, but she could still figure out a lot of what he'd written.

"Wow, this is his best yet!" she exclaimed. "It's got an alien living right here with us. And he's got a cat named Tom. Gee, I hope they publish this one. That'd make Unca Jake happy!"

Daphne reached over to scratch Chaucer in his favorite spot behind the ears while she explained the situation to the attentive dog. "You know, he's got such a tough job. Up all night, every night. And he's so lonely. He says girls don't like geeks, they just go for the flashy jocks. But if I was grown up I'd date him. If he wasn't my uncle, of course."

Daphne gave the situation several minutes of deep consideration before she made her fateful pronouncement, "Chaucer, we got to do something."

Half an hour later, she was standing in front of her teacher's worn oaken desk.

Daphne's classroom at La Follette Elementary School had seats for twenty students arranged in rows facing the teacher. A terrazzo-patterned linoleum floor supported low bookcases filled with encyclopedias and dictionaries that were arranged along a wall filled with windows facing out onto the river. A large blackboard covered the wall behind the teacher's desk, while poster boards featuring cutouts of whales, bears, cows, and other animals covered the other pastel-yellow walls.

Daphne watched with apprehension as her teacher unfolded the crumpled sheet of paper on which she'd done her homework, smoothing the paper out as she laid it on her desk.

Eliot stared at the paper for a few moments before taking out a red pencil and marking up the text. "Daphne, this is not your best work," she said as she slid the paper back to the girl. "And if I didn't recognize the tooth marks from previous occurrences I wouldn't buy your story about a dog chewing it. But this is Chaucer's handiwork again, isn't it?"

"Yes, ma'am."

"Well, I can only give you a C for this paper. You can do better, and I expect you to make your best effort on every assignment. Now return to your seat. We'll talk more about this after school. You've got a half-hour detention for being late this morning."

"Yes, ma'am," Daphne said, picking up the offending document and then returning to her desk.

As the day wore on, Daphne felt as if the time was passing both slowly and quickly, a sensation that often comes from the mingling of terror with a sense of normalcy.

Not that she had anything to be particularly afraid of. Although stern, her teacher, Ms. Eliot had never laid hands on a child or even raised her voice to one. It was just the thought of letting down such a God-like figure in so public a manner. Daphne felt deeply ashamed, but when the bell rang and the other students bolted from the classroom, it occurred to her that getting detention might actually present an opportunity.

As soon as they were alone, Daphne raised her hand and asked, "Ma'am, may I please ask a question?"

"Of course you may," Eliot said, setting down the well-thumbed copy of *The Canterbury Tales* that she had been reading. "What would you like to know?"

"How hard is it to publish a book?"

"To publish a book? Why, that depends on how well the book is written and whether it's about something interesting or important."

"If I wanted to publish a book, what would I do?"

Eliot was caught off guard for perhaps the first time in years. She blinked several times as she brought her complete attention to bear on the subject. "Well, Daphne, first you would have to write a book. Then you would have to send a copy of the manuscript to a publishing agent along with a letter telling them a little bit about the book."

"What's a publishing agent?"

"An agent is a special person who reads books that people would like to have published. If the agent thinks that the book is worthwhile, then they send it on to a publisher."

"Wow, so agents have a lot of power. How do you find one?"

"Most agents work in either New York City or Los Angeles, although some have offices in other parts of the country. There's even a small agency right here in town called the Marinette Masters Literary Agency."

"Gee, so how does an agent decide if a book is good?"

"Daphne, please don't use the term 'good' in that context. Books can be worthy of being published, but they cannot be good or bad. I believe we've discussed the misuse of the word 'good' in class, haven't we?"

"Yes, ma'am, I'm sorry."

"That's quite all right. To answer your question, there are two general types of books. Fiction books contain made-up stories. They are fun to read but aren't usually very important, unless the author is able to make the story relevant to a significant issue such as immigration. Non-fiction books relate facts and tell us about the world around us, just like the history book that you're reading for class. They're very important."

"So if I wanted to publish a book, it would have to be about something important?"

"Yes, that would be best."

"And non-fiction books are the most important?"

"Usually."

"Thank you, ma'am!"

Daphne sat back in her seat with a smile. Helping her uncle was going to be easier than she had expected.

That night, Daphne borrowed her mom's laptop and took it to her room along with a brown paper grocery bag and some tape.

Her room wasn't very big, barely large enough for a small bed with a worn wooden headboard and an Amish quilt featuring cows and goats, but like a mother's pocket, it was big enough for all the important things. It was decorated with a tan carpet and yellow daisy wallpaper covered with posters of horses and pictures of her uncle. Dark wooden bifold doors opened onto a small closet, and there was a double-hung window over her bed.

There was no room for a chair. The only furniture was a birch nightstand and matching dresser, so Daphne plopped down on her bed to work.

She switched on the sparkly-pink, unicorn-shaped lamp on her nightstand and smiled. A pair of pictures framed the lamp, one of her dad in his army uniform, and one of her with her parents at the Wisconsin Dells. Then she frowned, tugging at her chin.

She wasn't sure what to put in a letter to an agent, so she googled it. There were lots of examples online, and she soon found one for non-fiction books. She copied the text into a blank document and then laboriously typed in Jake's name and address. Changing the title of the book in the letter, she picked through the rest of it until she had changed as much as she could manage.

Printing the letter off, she put it on top of Jake's manuscript and then wrapped the bundle in the paper from the grocery bag. When asked, Google politely provided her with the address of the Marinette Masters Literary Agency, which she wrote on the package in all capital letters so that the Post Office would know that it was important and give it special attention.

The next morning, Daphne put the package in the mail. Hugging herself with delight, she wondered how long it would take before somebody came looking for Jake. The possibility that the people who showed up might not have Jake's best interests in mind never occurred to her.

It took a few days for Daphne's package to reach the Marinette Masters Literary Agency. When it did, it lurked innocuously beneath a pile of unsolicited manuscripts like a crocodile waiting underwater for an innocent deer to come to the pond for a drink.

Indeed, if the literary agent Claire Miller had known what was waiting for her at the agency that morning, and the impact that it would have on her life, she might have just stayed in bed. But fate, and her neighbors, had different plans.

It must be Saturday, she thought, burying her head under her pillow in a vain attempt to muffle the noise of her neighbors having sex. She wasn't a prude, and she was sympathetic to the fact that the couple worked nights. Saturday mornings seemed to be the only "alone" time that they had. But it was impossible to sleep when the wall-thumping started. Without meaning to, Claire began counting down in her head; *three...two...one...here it comes*. A whoop was followed by a series of lusty grunts and moans. *And it's always the same.*

Giving up on the idea of sleeping in, she tossed her pillow aside, swung out of bed, and headed to the bathroom.

After a quick shower, Claire gave herself a critical look in the mirror. Her blonde hair, parted in the middle, was still wet and hung limply to her shoulders. She'd worn it that way since she was a teenager. She kept telling herself that she should get it styled, that she would do so at her next hair appointment, but she never did. At twenty-three, her round face still had perfect skin, with dark blonde eyebrows over clear brown eyes. That was the good part. Looking down, she frowned. She was of average build and height, and she kept in pretty good shape, but she couldn't dismiss the idea that she needed to lose a few pounds.

When she was finished in the bathroom, she dressed for the office. Then she worked some lavender hand cream into her hands, pausing to take a deep breath of her favorite scent when she was done.

Before leaving for work, Claire took a minute to tidy up her apartment, dusting the almond-colored countertop in her galley kitchen as well as the oak shelving unit in her living room with lemon-scented spray wax. She ran the vacuum cleaner over the beige carpet in her living room and bedroom, dusted the nature-scene art prints hung on the peach-colored walls, and then straightened the quilt on her bed. The quilt was old now, and the stitching between some of the blue and white panels was starting to come apart, but she couldn't let it go. She ran her fingers across the worn fabric and smiled. She'd had the quilt since she was a child. Her mother had helped to pick it out at a church raffle, and it was one of the few things that she had left to remind her of her mom.

After she put away her cleaning supplies, Claire headed for the door.

Technically, she didn't have to work on the weekends, but she was so busy helping other people with their projects during normal working hours that Saturday morning was the only time that she could focus on her own assignments. She also didn't have to dress up, but she thought it was important to present herself in a professional manner just in case a client happened to drop in. On her way out, she stopped in front of the door mirror to adjust the seam of her ivory blouse and to pin a topaz broach on it. Her sneakers didn't go with her brown tweed skirt, but once she got to work she'd change into the pair of kitten heels that she kept under her desk. Her hair was still wet from the shower, but it would dry on the walk to work.

Locking the door behind her as she left, Claire held her breath as she scurried down the hallway to the stairs. The apartment building's owner had recently cleaned the brown shag carpet in the hallway, and the smell of industrial disinfectant was nauseating.

Stepping out of the apartment's wooden entry door, she paused for a moment to enjoy the morning. A cool, moist breeze was coming in off Lake Michigan to the east, and it was so quiet out that she could hear the sound of waves breaking on Marinette's shoreline. The soft scent of the lake mixed with the aroma of coffee and baked goods that was coming from

Wilson's just up the street. The sky was that steel blue color you only see early in the day; it would deepen as the sun rose further. While she stood taking in the morning air, two cars passed by. *Rush hour in Marinette.* She grinned. Cars were a newfangled invention for a town that dated back to 1830, and she liked to imagine that the small, well-maintained cottages lining the town's streets were still withholding judgment on such innovations.

"Perfect day," Claire said as she looked around. "Too bad I have to work."

She decided to stop at Wilson's to pick up breakfast. She noticed a couple of homeless people hanging around the café's back door as she went past. Each one had a steaming bowl of soup cupped in their hands. "Pay it forward" had been Gretchen Wilson's motto since she opened the coffee shop. She'd been homeless for three years herself after completing a master's degree in philosophy. Unlike Diogenes, she had had no barrel to sleep in, and she still carried the scars both inside and out from those years spent on the streets. When she got a break and was able to start her own business, she made up her mind that she would never turn away anybody in need, so she gave out soup to anybody who asked. Claire hoped that she'd be able to do the same someday.

Gretchen was at the front counter and waved to Claire as she came in.

"Up early today, Claire? What can I get for you?"

Pendant lamps hanging from an old-fashioned, black-tin ceiling lit the dining area and reflected off the knotty-pine paneling to provide a warm glow to a room filled with small square faux-marble tables and black hoop-back chairs. A raised counter with bar stools ran the length of a window facing Main Street.

Claire's sneakers squeaked on the freshly-scrubbed black-and-white checkered flooring as she made her way across the room. A glass display case to the left of the counter held a tempting array of pastries and a chortling espresso machine hulked to the right. Claire's resolve to have something light and healthy proved no match for the intoxicating aroma of cinnamon and vanilla.

"I'll have a black velvet grande and a power muffin," Claire replied, deciding to indulge herself. The black velvet was a latte made with chocolate milk instead of regular, and it was scandalously good. "Wait a sec," she said, "as long as I'm being bad I might as well go all the way. Change the muffin to a cinnamon crunch bagel with cream cheese."

"You got it!" Gretchen grinned. "Special occasion?"

"Nope, just heading to work."

"On a Saturday morning? That sucks!"

"I guess, but it's all for the best."

"In this best of all worlds." Both women laughed at the reference to *Candide*. "God, I hope it's not that bad."

"No. I just wish I could make some headway. I keep getting all the cruddy assignments. This week the boss asked me to go through the agency's entire slush pile. Those are all the unsolicited stories that wannabe writers send to us. There must be at least twenty manuscripts to read, and he wants it done by Monday!"

"Yikes! And he gave that to you for the weekend? What a jerk!"

"Actually, he gave me the assignment on Wednesday, but Tina asked me to help with her presentation for the next writers' conference, which took up all my time."

"Girl, you have to stand up for yourself and stop doing other people's work for them. It's not fair."

"I know, but Tina said she was in a jam and that she'd make it up to me."

"How?"

"Well, she didn't say."

"She didn't say the last time she torpedoed your career either, did she?"

"Well, no, but—"

"No ifs, ands, or buts about it, girl! If you don't start being more assertive, people will walk all over you for the rest of your life."

Claire sighed. "I hear you, but it's not that easy."

"It's a lot easier than working Saturday mornings!"

"Hey, you're here too."

"Yeah, but I own this place. Do you own the agency where you work?"

"No, of course not!"

"Why not? You're just as smart as the stuffed shirt that runs the place and you work much harder. Why not start up your own agency?"

"Who'd want me to represent them? I'm a nobody in a business where you have to be a somebody to succeed."

Gretchen took a moment to gather her thoughts as she fitted a lid onto Claire's coffee cup. Looking up, she said, "Claire, I don't believe that. You're a somebody, and if you just gave yourself a chance, then you'd see that, too."

"You're not wrong," Claire said as she picked up her coffee and bagel. "But I just don't feel it. Know what I mean? Anyway, gotta scoot. Thanks for the pep talk and for the extra cream cheese for my bagel!"

"Take care, kid," Gretchen said with a sigh.

After leaving the coffee shop, Claire turned left and headed down Hall Street, which housed most of the businesses in Marinette that weren't associated with Northwood. The agency where she worked was located on the second floor of a low, buff-colored brick building in Marinette's Oakwood Office Park. When she reached the building, she found a small black cat with white paws waiting for her on the stoop.

"Hey, Boots, what are you doing up this early?" she asked, crouching down to pet the kitten. It had a collar and appeared to be well taken care of by its owner, but for some reason it always seemed to be hanging around when Claire arrived at the office. The treats that she gave it when she saw it might have been part of the reason why, but then she'd always been good with animals. "I hope you're not looking for a snack," she said, opening the bag containing her breakfast, "because I don't have a thing for you." The warm scent of cinnamon wafted into the air as she scooped some cream cheese off the bagel with her finger and held it out for the cat. "Nope, not a thing." She grinned as Boots licked her finger clean.

"Now, I have to go in to work, so you'll just have to fend for yourself," Claire said as she stood up.

A loud meow from Boots made it clear that he was certain to die from malnutrition if she left.

"No, there's no more. I shouldn't have given you that. Now there won't be enough for me."

With some difficulty, she made her way past the cat, which threw itself at her ankles in a determined effort to keep her from leaving.

Finally making her escape, Claire headed up the stairs to the second floor and then down a long, narrow hallway to the office, which consisted of a large, off-white room filled with two rows of gray fabric cubicles for employees. There was an office for the manager at one end of the room, and a meeting room at the other. Windows filled the wall opposite the entrance.

Once inside, Claire settled down at the desk in her cube and sipped her coffee as she stared at the stack of manuscripts piled in front of her.

She'd barely cracked the cover of the first manuscript when she heard a cheery greeting for the doorway. "Hello! Thank God you're here, Claire, I'm up against the wall and I need your help."

Oh, God, it's Tina, Claire thought as she forced a smile. *There's no escaping this woman.* "Hi, Tina, what brings you in today?"

"It's that presentation. The boss said I need to flesh it out with a few more examples of successful books we've promoted. You know our sales better than anybody, so I was hoping you could be a team player and lend a hand."

I should say no, Claire thought, even as she found herself saying, "Sure, I'll be happy to help, Tina."

"Awesome! I'll be in my office when you've got the data. And as long as you're deep into it, you might as well do the last little bit and draft the slides. If you don't mind, of course."

Of course I mind! the voice in Claire's head screamed, but she said, "Sure, I guess. But I need to get these manuscripts done for the boss, so I can't spend too much time on it."

"Whatever. I figure I'll have to polish anything you give me anyway, so if you could just step up and get it done quickly, I'd appreciate it. I've got a dinner date tonight and I don't want to be late."

I'd like to polish you off! Claire thought as she set aside the manuscript she'd just started reading.

It was mid-afternoon before Claire could get back to her own work. Using an old agent's trick, she just read the first paragraph of each chapter from a given manuscript. If the plot wasn't clear from that, and if the lead-ins didn't pull her into the text, then she crossed the book off her list.

When she noticed it starting to get dark outside, Claire took a quick break for supper. Set in a small alcove at the end of the hallway outside the office were three vending machines, one offering soft drinks, another displaying a tantalizing assortment of candy bars and chips, and a third presenting supposedly "fresh" sandwiches that were day-old a week ago. Claire scowled at the meagre offerings, finally selecting a sandwich optimistically labeled as "roast beef" that appeared to be less dry than the others, or at least less so than the papers on her desk. She bought a Coke to wash it down with and then returned to her desk.

While she gnawed on her sandwich, Claire considered the manuscripts in front of her. Three of them were resubmissions, which she was able to immediately cross off the list. Agencies don't waste time looking at books they've already rejected.

Even so, it was well past midnight by the time she reached the bottom of the stack. *Another weekend shot in the ass*, she thought as she leafed through the final manuscript. This one baffled her. The cover letter stated it was non-fiction, but the story was written like a first-person novel. And what real-world spy would publish their own diary? But she was familiar with the company, living as she did just half a mile from

Northwood's shipyard, and when she googled Eschaton, the info matched what she read in the book.

Time to punt. Riffling through the contacts in her address book, Claire pulled up the listing for her fact-checking contact in the Navy. *Commander Jim Solomon, I hope you can make sense of this, because I sure can't.* The officer's duty assignment was listed as the Great Lakes Naval Station, just north of Chicago, but there was a comment in the file stating that he was on detached duty at Northwood. "Sweet!" Claire exclaimed, feeling as though she'd just scored a victory. Working with somebody local was always easier than dealing with someone via email. It meant that she didn't have to scan in the whole document so that it could be attached to an email.

It took a moment for her to type a cover letter, attach it to the manuscript, and then stuff it all into an envelope. She grabbed a sweater that she kept in her desk before heading out the door. The temperature had been in the sixties when she got to work that morning, but it had dropped into the fifties after sundown. At least she didn't have to worry about walking home alone in the dark. Like most small towns in Wisconsin, Marinette was the kind of place where people didn't lock their doors at night or worry about leaving their wallet on the car seat when out shopping.

The post office was on the way to her apartment, so she decided to drop the manuscript in the mail on her way home rather than waiting until morning. She slid the package into the letter box in front of the post office and then pulled her sweater tight around her neck. Smiling, she hustled through the chill night air back to her apartment. *That's the last I'll see of that one. Not my problem anymore.*

While Claire dusted her hands of his manuscript, Jake went about his daily life, unaware of the events that Daphne had set into motion.

It was Sunday, and after an afternoon thunderstorm, the evening sky had cleared to the west, revealing a velvet sunset. The air was filled with the smell of the lake mixed with a lingering tang from the lightening. The remnants of the storm drifted away to the east, coloring the sky like Kahlua and cream. Soft white clouds floated over a darkened lake that brooded like Manitou contemplating what modern man had done to his pristine shoreline.

Jake had picked up a couple of large pizzas for dinner and was sharing them with Felipe and Daphne in his back yard. They sat in a circle on a ground cloth that he had spread out on the damp grass, using paper towels instead of plates as they munched away.

As a writer, Jake would have appreciated the irony of Daphne's visit on that afternoon, if he had been aware of the tidal wave of misfortune instigated by the innocent-looking cherub sharing a pizza with him and his roommate. Not only was she a good reader, for a third-grader, but she was also quite skilled at reading people, though perhaps not measurably better than any other precocious little girl, that being an activity that adolescent females of the species had raised to a form of art.

Sitting across from Daphne, who was plopped on the lawn next to Chaucer, Jake was so wrapped up in his own sense of failure that he failed to notice Daphne's expression. While none would contest her advanced reading skills, her performance as an actress lacked subtlety, and only the most uncasual observer (or the average man) would fail to notice her exaggerated expression of innocence.

While Jake stewed in his funk, his niece quietly made sure that he got the largest slice of pepperoni, working in league with Felipe, who was also concerned for his friend.

Halfway through dinner, Felipe handed Jake a check. "Here's this month's rent, bro." Felipe smiled, hoping the rent payment would cheer Jake up.

"Thanks!" Jake did perk up at the early rent payment, something rare in his experience with Felipe.

"No problem. I appreciate your letting me squat here while I'm on assignment with Northwood. It's a great chance to get caught up again. Not to mention, the consulting company doesn't give me much of a per diem for housing and this really helps me save money."

"So you can spend it on Clash of Clans? How much did you drop on in-app purchases this month?"

"Less than you did on your fantasy football league!"

"Possibly, but at least I have a chance to win it back."

"Yeah, when pigs fly!"

"Pigs can't fly," Daphne said firmly. "They don't have wings."

"What about if one was in an airplane?" Felipe grinned as he took a sip of Coke.

"That's different."

Before Daphne could continue, Chaucer nudged her arm with his nose, reminding her that he was there for her should she find that there was more sausage on her pizza than she could eat. "Sharing is caring" was the dog's motto, though he rarely found any people who wanted to share what he had in his own food bowl.

Jake finished his pizza, then said, "It's too bad we're on different schedules at work. Otherwise, we could team up during lunch hour to run a campaign in League of Legends."

"Do you mean with company equipment? Jake, we'd never get away with it."

"I have been for nearly a year." Jake grinned, revealing a morsel of sausage wedged between his front teeth. "Or have you forgotten that I'm a UNIX admin? Dude, I have root control over every piece of hardware in that shop. Let me tell you, running an op with the full resources of a server grid is awesome. There's zero latency and I'm able to dedicate two servers just to process the graphics. And you should see it on the eighty-four inch monitor in the conference room!"

"How is it you never mentioned this before? I've been here since February."

"If you recall, we work different shifts. The only time we get together is on weekends away from work. In fact, I doubt if anybody there is even aware that we know each other. Besides, I've been buried in my latest project."

"Yeah, what happened to that, anyway?"

"Well, it's odd, but I seem to have lost the manuscript. I thought I left it on the coffee table, but I can't find it anywhere."

Jake was looking at his friend as they spoke and failed to notice Daphne's reaction. Eyes wide, she made a quick shushing motion to Chaucer, giggled behind her hand like a Japanese schoolgirl, then took a quick bite of pizza to cover her actions.

"Could you just print out a fresh copy?"

"Yeah, but what's the point? Like you said, it's got issues with some of the Eschaton info I used. After you pointed them out, I started having second thoughts about mentioning it at all. When I get some time, I think I'll tone that down a bit."

"Good plan! If anybody ever saw that, you'd be in the pokey so fast it'd make your head spin."

"Yeah, well, the manuscript's gone now, so that's not likely to be an issue, is it?"

"Nope. I think you dodged the bullet on that one."

5

Claire's decision to boot the problem manuscript down the line to somebody else had the same effect as pulling the pin from a hand grenade and then handing it to somebody else with instructions to "think quick." Commander Solomon's mail rarely held anything as perplexing as the document that arrived from her on Monday morning.

Solomon was a short, pudgy man of such average appearance that he faded into the background wherever he went, a situation that suited him well. He was currently working on-site at Northwood. This made it possible for him to review classified material right away instead of waiting for the weekly courier to bring it to his office at Great Lakes Naval Station in Northern Illinois.

Northwood management had provided him with a "managerial grade" office to work in, which meant that it was an actual office and not a cubicle. An effort had been made to dress up the room to "executive" standards by adding scuffed oak paneling from the floor up to the worn chair rail and painting the walls a color optimistically called "eggshell" but bearing no resemblance to the eggs of any known creature. Regardless of the time of year, the air in the office smelled like somebody had used the room as a welding shop, and the age-etched window in the cinder-block outer wall allowed only weak light to enter. The flooring was the same gray linoleum used in the rest of the building, albeit a little less worn.

Most of the documents on Solomon's gray, Steelcase desk dealt with the company's naval projects. While these projects formed the bulk of his responsibilities, he did have other duties, including reviewing manuscripts and technical papers for research workers and publishing houses.

Normally, all he had to do when fact-checking a document for a literary agent such as Claire was to verify that the tonnage, dimensions, and number of guns listed for a warship were correct. That, and making sure that none of a ship's more advanced weapons systems were discussed in the amount of detail that would give aid to a potential adversary. But the manuscript in front of him was unlike any that he had previously dealt with.

He reread the cover letter from Claire and half-smiled. She was one of his favorite literary agents, always thorough and reliable in her work. It was rare for her to send him something that she hadn't vetted herself first. As he turned the cover page, the paper made a soft crinkling sound and he caught a faint hint of lavender. He surmised that it was Claire's favorite scent; he had noticed it on some of the other manuscripts that she had sent to him. *Nice to smell something besides welded steel and industrial cleaning solutions. This room could use some windows.*

After a few minutes, Solomon stopped reading, perplexed. He rubbed the short gray bristles on the back of his neck with one of his weathered black hands as he tried to make sense of the text and then gave up. Setting the manuscript to one side, he sorted through the rest of his mail. Memos and vendor contracts were placed in a pile at the center of his desk, while documents with cover sheets identifying them as classified material went straight into his briefcase. A quick glance confirmed that they were related to the new Eschaton control system that Northwood was building into their destroyers.

Pretty sharp move, he thought, leaning back in his chair as he scanned one of the Eschaton papers. The Liberty-class destroyers didn't carry the Eschaton ballistic missile defense weapons, so they weren't regulated by any international treaty. But with the control systems already built in, the actual Eschaton missiles could be added to the destroyers in less than a week. Doing so would double the size of the US missile defense system without needing Senate oversight or budgetary approval.

Just the sort of thing I was sent here to watch for. Solomon put the document in his briefcase with the others and locked it. Then, he put his briefcase in the credenza behind his desk and locked that.

He spent the rest of the morning reading and commenting on the contracts and memos that had arrived with the morning mail. A couple of the company managers that he worked with grabbed him for lunch and they headed out to Rhodes Beastly

Burgers. Solomon forgot to ask the waitress to hold the onions, which had been deep fried in grease, and by the time he returned to his desk, he had a case of heartburn that would put a hole in the hull of one of Northwood's destroyers; and they could stop a three-inch naval round.

Solomon picked up the manuscript in need of fact-checking and then leafed through it in a half-hearted way, pausing as he did so to rub his distressed stomach with a sigh. *I was warned about some of the food on this planet. But it tasted so good!* After about twenty minutes of that, he stopped to rummage through his desk drawers. He'd left his antacid tablets back at the Budget Inn where he was staying. Ten minutes and two trips to the men's room later, it seemed prudent to work from his hotel room instead of his office. Taking his briefcase from the credenza, he threw the manuscript into it without looking and then bolted for the door.

His hotel was located just off Highway 41 on the outskirts of town. It was a well-marked route, and on such a bright, sunny day Solomon should have had no problem driving the short distance to get there. But his growing distress from the onions prompted him to drive with a greater urgency than might have been advisable. As a result, he was going well over the posted speed limit when he approached the Y-shaped intersection where Highway 41 parted ways with Highway 64 on the outskirts of town. Worse, his distracted state of mind led to a brief moment of confusion as he tried to decide which branch of the intersection that he needed to take.

Coming from a civilization that exclusively used self-driving cars, he lacked the ingrained safety habits of native drivers, and so without giving it a thought, he looked down at the car's navigation screen to verify the correct route. When he looked up again, both options were behind him, leaving him with one brief moment in which to ponder whether Detroit steel was up to the challenge posed by Wisconsin concrete. An instant later, his car plowed into the road divider, spun in a full circle, and then slammed to a halt with its front grill embracing a steel light pole.

That's one hell of a well-made pole. Pinned to his seat, Solomon felt himself slipping in and out of consciousness. Time seemed to move forward like a travelogue in a slide show, jumping from one scene to the next with no connection between them. He opened his eyes for a moment when he heard the screech of metal as the first responders pried the car door open. The tang of spilled gas made him retch. He felt himself being lifted up, up, and then fading away as the sound of sirens dwindled into the darkness.

Within minutes of Solomon's accident, his superior officers at the Great Lakes Naval Station had been notified. They dispatched intelligence officers to the scene to investigate what had happened and also helicoptered expert medical staff to Solomon's aid. Some of the medical staff were less happy about that than others, among them the neurologist, Dr. Wilbur Hansen.

A lifetime at sea and in space, and not a hint of motion sickness. But five minutes in a chopper and I've got my head in a barf bag. If it were anybody but Solomon, I'd turn around and let the locals handle it.

Hansen felt miserable and trapped. Even though he was a man of slight build, the passenger compartment of the Black Hawk felt cramped and hot. There were four seats arranged back-to-back so that there were two facing out of each side of the chopper. A rack on the back wall of the compartment held three stretchers for carrying wounded soldiers. The stretchers were folded down when not in use. Everything was olive green, a color that Hansen was sure the Army had selected because it was the most nauseating shade available.

The sweat running down his sides had already stained the armpits of his khaki work uniform, and his soft ginger mustache glistened with droplets of perspiration. His skin had the kind of pallor that made morticians reach for a tape measure.

Hansen bent over in distress as the chopper performed a dainty dipsy-doo through an air pocket. "How long till we're there?" he asked the copilot.

"We just took off, doc. Sorry, but you've got another forty-five minutes of misery ahead of you."

"Oh my. Urk!"

"Hey! The bag! Use the bag! Oh crap, do you know how hard it is to clean one of these things?"

Despite his best efforts, Hansen missed the barf bag again as his stomach executed a series of gymnastic maneuvers in sync with the motion of the helicopter. *How did I let Solomon talk me into this? "Join the service with me," he said. "Travel to far-off worlds and seek out new civilizations. Boldly go where no Centauri has gone before." Yeah. Nothing about dying in one of the most bizarre flying machines ever contrived by a sapient being on any of the three-hundred and sixty-two worlds of the Stellar Commonwealth.*

"Sorry," Hansen muttered as he tried to dry-swallow another dose of Dramamine. Closing his eyes didn't seem to help. The cockpit reeked with the brown scent of the worn leather seats, human sweat, and the harsh smell of machine oil. The noise and vibration from the engines made it impossible to use any form of meditation to calm himself and regain control of his system. By the time the chopper landed on the Med Flight circle in front of the Bay Area Medical Center, Hansen was reduced to the dry heaves.

The Medical Center was an L-shaped, two-story building with a red-brick façade and acres of glass. It was one of the most advanced trauma centers in the Midwest.

As soon as the chopper's side door opened, Hansen rolled out and fell to the ground. Turning to rest his back against one of the chopper's landing struts, he lay limply on the concrete apron until the rest of the medical team had disembarked.

"I'll be fine," he said to them in a weak voice. "Just give me a minute. And a towel."

Rolling over, he rested his forehead against the cool grit of the concrete and took several deep breaths. *I can do this. I can—*

"Urk!" Hansen arched his back as his stomach made one final protest.

"This will help," one of his corpsman said as she knelt next to him and pressed a cool, wet cloth to his forehead.

"Thanks," Hansen gasped. A few moments later, the spinning sensation behind his ears slowed down and he ventured to roll over onto his side, facing the entrance to the Bay Area Medical Center's Emergency Room.

Three men dressed in khaki Navy uniforms stood outside the doors, watching him. The tall, slender man in the middle wore sunglasses against the late afternoon sun, but Hansen still recognized him. The man's dark brown hair was gray at the temples, and his skin had the kind of tan produced by a lifetime of outdoor exposure. Even from a distance, Hansen could feel the weight of the man's gaze, implacable, judgmental; the sunglasses only heightened the effect.

Hansen wiped off his khaki blouse with a fresh towel from the orderly. Then he got to his feet. He wobbled with the first few steps, but the orderly steadied him with a firm grip on his elbow and he made it across the landing pad without incident.

"Commander Nuance," Hansen said, saluting the man in the center of the group.

"Commander Hansen," Nuance responded, returning the salute. "Looks like you had a rough flight."

"I'd rather not talk about it. What's Solomon's status? Is he still in the ER?"

"Yes, and I've got a man in with him now. The ER doctor said that he's in serious condition, so I thought it best to bring you here as quickly as possible. Hope you don't mind."

"Of course not. You did the right thing." *But I may kill you for this later…*

Hansen's next words were drowned out by the roar of the helicopter as it took off. His eyes stung for a moment as the wind from the chopper's blades sent a gust of grit flying off the concrete.

"Can we go inside?" Hansen asked after the noise subsided.

"Oh, yes, of course. That's why you're here, doc."

Hansen and his team followed Nuance into the building. The nurse at the reception desk rose to stop them as they marched by, but Nuance waved his badge at him and said, "Military Intelligence, we're here on official business."

"I don't think that man's very happy with us," Hansen said, looking back at the receptionist, who was now punching keys on his phone. "If he's calling Security—"

"I'll handle it, doc." Nuance led the group to an alcove in the ER. He pulled the alcove's curtains aside to let Hansen through, and then pulled them closed again.

Solomon lay on his back on a hospital bed. He was surrounded by medical equipment producing more chirps, gurgles, wheeps, and furtles than an evening concert by the denizens of a pond. A blonde woman wearing blue surgical scrubs stood to one side of him with her hand resting on his wrist. A similarly-dressed man on the other side of the bed faced the medical devices and appeared to be taking notes on a clipboard.

"Who are you, and what are you doing here!?" the woman demanded, stepping forward to confront Hansen.

"I'm Commander Hansen from Great Lakes Naval Base. I'm a specialist in trauma and Admiral Dutchman sent me to attend to Commander Solomon."

"That's not necessary. We have the situation well under control. Please return to the waiting room. I'll brief you on his condition as soon as I finish here."

"I'm sorry, doctor, but I must insist. This is a matter of national security."

"National security my ass! You've got no authority—"

"I'm afraid that we do." Nuance held up his badge as he joined the conversation. "Due to the sensitive nature of the material that Commander Solomon works with, it's essential that only Doctor Hansen and his team have access to the patient."

"Why?"

"Doctor…Simmons, isn't it?" Hansen read the name tag on the woman's lapel.

"Yes."

"Doctor Simmons, I understand that this is highly unusual, but we take national security very seriously. In the case of a senior officer requiring medical attention, it is important to take all precautions. If he becomes delirious, there's a chance that he might reveal something sensitive. Only people with the highest security clearance can be allowed near him to make sure that no unauthorized persons hear him if he starts talking."

"Yes, but—"

"I'm sorry, but I have to ask you to keep all of your staff away from him, and we'll need you to put him in a private room. I've brought four medical corpsmen from the base hospital to help me with him.

"Now then, please give me his chart and fill me in on his current status."

Simmons sighed. "The patient was in a car wreck. It was so bad that the paramedics had to cut him out of the car. They followed protocol and strapped him on a backboard before they loaded him into an ambulance. When he got here, we ran through a standard triage protocol with him, checking his vitals, and determining the nature and extent of his visible injuries.

"He was lucky that the airbags worked. He fractured the femur and tibia bones in his left leg, but fortunately, they were both clean, transverse breaks and we were able to stabilize them with external fixation. He needs them to be repaired as soon as possible, and I've scheduled him into surgery tomorrow morning. He's also got three cracked ribs and a number of bruises and minor lesions. His X-rays didn't indicate any other broken bones, though I've diagnosed a severe concussion. We were just going through some CAT scans of his head and spine to make sure we didn't miss any more subtle injuries."

"I see." Hansen stepped past Simmons to examine the set of X-rays displayed on the nearby computer monitor. He clicked through them, taking his time to examine each one in detail. He stopped at an X-ray of Solomon's skull, and then zoomed in to take a closer look at the region behind the ear.

"Doctor Simmons, can you please come here and look at this?" Hansen pointed to a faint dark line on the image.

"Of course." Simmons bent over the monitor and then exclaimed, "Damn! How did I miss that?"

As Hansen pointed to the back of Solomon's skull on the image, he held his hand over the temple, an area that he definitely did not want the human doctor to see. Even deep surgical alterations can't hide everything, and removing from the skull all traces of the boney nodes that support a Centauri's forehead antenna would have damaged the underlying nerves. *One look at those and tomorrow's surgery could change into a dissection, with a CIA xenologist playing a featured role.*

"It's easy to miss a hairline fracture in this location unless you're a trained neurologist. But it's worse than you would know, Doctor Simmons. Commander Solomon had rubella complicated by encephalitis when he was young. I need to take an EEG reading right away to ensure that the accident hasn't triggered another episode of encephalitis. He's also being treated for a heart condition known as left bundle-branch block, which should have shown up on his ECG. An accident such as this puts him at risk of sudden cardiac arrest."

"But, but we had no way to know that! He's not wearing a med-alert bracelet."

"Perhaps it came off during the accident. Now please leave me alone with my patient."

Before Simmons could protest further, Nuance took her by the elbow and walked her out of the alcove. The two men who had accompanied Nuance followed him out, escorting the orderly who had been helping Simmons with them.

As Nuance pulled the privacy curtain closed behind them, Hansen heard him say, "Doctor Simmons, please show me where you keep your files. All of the medical records concerning this patient are hereby classified confidential and are the property of the US Government. I need you to turn over all of Commander Solomon's charts and X-rays to Doctor Hansen immediately."

Once alone with Solomon, Hansen began a thorough examination. He tisked with concern as he reexamined the X-ray of the skull. "Just as I feared, my friend," he said quietly. "Anybody not familiar with our anatomy would think that this was an ordinary hairline fracture, something easy to treat. But it's not. I wish you were in one of our medical centers back home. There's a lot that I could do for you there. But extraction at this point would draw attention that we don't need, compromising our mission. So I'll do what I can for you here."

Hansen packed Solomon's head and neck with ice, then opened his bag and set out several tiny vials of medicine. *As long as I'm at it, I might as well give you your annual hormone injections. Can't have you reverting back to your natural female form in front of the humans. And we both agreed that it was for the best to maintain male genders during this assignment, though having any intimacy while we're both in that orientation creates other issues that these folk are still working through.*

He drew minute amounts of each of the medications into a syringe and then injected them into the access port of Solomon's IV unit. When he was done, Hansen sat down next to the bed, took Solomon's hand in his, and held it close to his chest.

So many years together. We've come so far. Too far for it to end like this.

Hansen closed his eyes, fighting back the tears.

7

The crumpled brown trash bag sitting in front of Admiral Dutchman was one of the most threatening things he'd seen in years.

Glaring at it, he tapped his fingers on the round conference table on which the bag sat. The soft drumming sound filled the silence. Several officers from Naval Intelligence sat around the table with him, also staring at the bag with obvious concern. It was the reason that the team's leader, Commander Nuance, had insisted that the admiral come up to Marinette right away to see in person what was going on, even though it was nearing midnight before Dutchman arrived onsite. The group had taken over Commander Solomon's office at Northwood for this purpose.

"Are you absolutely certain, Commander Nuance?" Dutchman asked.

"Yes, sir. We verified the document control numbers with the station log. These are from the Eschaton project."

"And you say that some pages are missing?"

"Yes, sir. Solomon's briefcase broke open during the crash. Papers were scattered all over the inside of the car and on the pavement. The State Patrol collected them and put them in this bag before we arrived at the scene. I had my men check to make sure that none were overlooked but this is all that could be found. It took us a while to sort through them but the longer manuscript was helpful. Unfortunately, that one's missing some pages, and it doesn't have any document control numbers."

"But it's legit?"

Nuance reached into the bag and took out the manuscript in question. He thumbed through it and said, "Yes. The details all check out and there's just too much detail to be ignored. What we have here are the confidential notes of a spy working at Northwood, and he's obtained access to the Eschaton documents."

"And your analysis of Commander Solomon's accident?"

"Is that it was no accident, sir. Doctor Hansen has confirmed that Solomon hadn't been drinking or using drugs. It was the middle of the day, with clear skies, dry roads, and perfect visibility. And there were no skid marks like you would see if he had hit the brakes. Solomon's driving record is spotless; there was no reason for him to crash. Interviews with the witnesses have proved inconclusive, but several people mentioned seeing a dark-colored minivan nearby. We're following up on that, but have found nothing substantial at this point. All the evidence points to him being forced off the road and that somebody then tried to grab the Eschaton documents in an effort to hide their espionage activities."

"Do you have any idea how Solomon came into possession of this document?"

"Yes, sir. The mail room at the shipyard logged a package of this size being delivered to him this morning. The return address was for a literary agency that's also located in Marinette."

"What a coincidence," Dutchman said, exchanging looks with the intelligence officers sitting around the table, who all nodded in agreement. In their world, "coincidences" just didn't happen.

"Commander, I want that literary agency investigated. Turn it upside down until you find out how they got their hands on this document. Confiscate any and all documents related to this one and bring them here along with anyone who's seen them. In particular, I want to talk to whoever it was who sent the package to Solomon. We need to get to the bottom of this, and quickly. Am I clear, commander?"

"Yes, sir."

"Then get busy."

As Dutchman made to rise from his seat, Nuance said, "Sir, there's one more thing you should know."

"What's that?"

"Sir, the spy appears to be an alien."

"Well, of course the spy's an alien! The only question is which country. Russia? China? Somewhere else?"

"Uh, sir, he doesn't appear to be that kind of alien."

"What do you mean?" Dutchman was visibly puzzled.

"If the text is legitimate, and there are several reasons to believe that it is, then the spy is from another world."

"Another world? As in outer space?"

"Yes, sir."

"Commander, perhaps it would be a good idea for you to have a chat with Doctor Hansen yourself. You've been under a lot of pressure lately..."

"Sir, I'm just relating what's in the document."

"Let me see that!"

Dutchman skimmed through the pages, pausing to read some of the text in more detail. As he did so, his frown deepened. Throwing the manuscript down on the table, he exclaimed, "This is awful!"

"Sir, yes, sir. It's some of the worst writing I've ever seen. The kind that makes you want to gouge your eyes out after reading the first paragraph."

"No, you, you..." Dutchman stopped himself; the days when a subordinate could be properly cussed out were long past. Taking a slow, deep breath, he said, "I meant the implications of this."

"Oh, I see, sir."

"I'm not sure that you do, not yet anyway. Aliens from outer space? Hogwash! That's just a ruse to distract us from the real spy. But if, as you claim, this is a legitimate document, then why would an agent send it to a literary agency for publishing? Wouldn't that be the last thing that they would want to happen?"

"Yes, sir, and it took a while to figure out what happened. While we were assembling the documents, we had the linguistics team go over them. They think that the cover letter used to submit the document to the agency was written by someone other than the person who wrote the manuscript."

"Are they sure?"

"Yes, sir. They said that the writing indicated the cover letter was written by someone with about a third-to-fifth grade education."

"And the manuscript itself?"

"Had the grammar of a second grader, at best, but the writer used technical terms requiring a college education. That fits the profile of a spy who might have been selected based on their technical training rather than their linguistic skills."

Nuance leaned forward as he continued, "Based on this analysis, we think that somebody might have sent the document to the agency without the spy's knowledge, perhaps a family member or a friend who became aware of the spy's activities and wanted to blow the whistle on them. There's also a strong likelihood that the spy is part of a cell. They usually comprise two spies and a controller. In which case, one of the spies might have turned on his comrades."

"If that's the case, why didn't they just send it directly to us or to the FBI?"

"We don't advertise our address to the general public, sir, and the local FBI field office only has one agent in residence. She has to cover three states including Chicago. If our squealer sent her a copy it would be months, perhaps years, before she even looked at it. The person who sent the document might have gotten antsy waiting and tried a different approach to draw attention to the problem."

"Makes sense, but none of it convinces me that we are dealing with beings from outer space. I'm going to need physical evidence before I even consider that possibility. When

I see an alien standing in front of me, with DNA testing proving that he's non-human, well, then you'll have my attention."

Dutchman stood. "Gentlemen, I don't have to tell you how serious this situation is. Our ballistic missile defense system is all that stands between us and nuclear Armageddon."

Holding up his hand, he began ticking off commands on his fingers.

"Nuance, have Homeland Security step up their screening of everybody passing through this region's transport hubs. I want one hundred percent verification of all travelers.

"Get a list of all employees and contractors working at Northwood.

"Pay a visit to that literary agency and confiscate all of their records. Bring in anybody who has seen or knows about this document.

"And bring up a company of marines from the Great Lakes Naval Station. I want them standing by in case we need more boots on the ground."

"Sir, yes, sir!" Nuance and the other officers stood to salute and then rushed from the room.

When they were gone, Dutchman took a seat behind Solomon's desk and templed his fingers as he considered what he'd just heard.

Catching a spy red-handed could get my career back on track. Might even be my ticket back to a sea command. But this alien thing? Could sink me if it's a hoax. But if it's real? The Pentagon at least. Maybe even the Joint Chiefs...

Could this day get any worse? Claire took a sip of coffee, singeing her tongue as she did so. Even a cup of Wilson's black velvet didn't seem to be enough to make it through what had become the meeting from hell. She always dreaded the agency's Tuesday morning status meetings. The cramped meeting room held a long, narrow table seating ten people, and it smelled like leftover meatloaf. Wheat-hued fabric covered walls decorated with inspirational posters urging heroic actions from the agency's overworked and underpaid staff. For an hour, Claire's boss, Hal Lutke rambled on about his latest vacation. After that, she languished through another hour listening to everybody's status reports, long-winded exercises in self-promotion that never seemed to change. *And now this.*

"Kudos to our star agent, Tina!" Lutke said, gesturing for Tina to stand. There was a brief ripple of applause as she did so. "It took a lot of work, but the presentation that you put together wowed them at the writers' convention last night. And to show just how much I appreciate you working over the weekend, I'm giving you a gift certificate to the Gray Gull bed and breakfast in Door County. Enjoy a long weekend on me. You deserve it!"

"Thanks, Hal!" Tina said with a grin, turning to take in the adulation of the other staff before she sat down.

What about me? Claire's cheeks turned red. *I wrote the damn thing for her! Don't I get a mention?*

"Oh, and Claire," Hal said, turning to face her. "I noticed that you took a pass on three of the manuscripts in the slush pile last week."

"Yes, sir, I did. They were resubmissions."

"Right. Well, I guess I forgot to mention that one of them was from my wife's nephew and that it was to be reconsidered?"

Claire froze with her cup halfway to her mouth. "I'll take another look at it, sir. It must have been an oversight on my part."

"Be sure you do. The kid's got raw talent and I'd like to see him get a—"

Whatever it was that Lutke wanted his nephew to get was lost in a sudden clamor of noise from outside the conference room. A moment later, the door opened and three men pushed their way into the room. The first was a tall man dressed in a khaki Navy uniform with an impressive patch of service ribbons on the left breast. Claire watched with interest as the man scanned the room, his gray eyes flicking from face to face as if he was evaluating each person's likelihood of causing trouble. The two men behind him wore black uniforms and helmets. Claire had seen enough Bond movies to know that the guns the men carried were machine pistols with enough firepower to level the entire conference room.

Claire felt a pulse of fear as she put her coffee down. *This can't be real. What in the hell is going on?*

"Please remain seated," the man in the khaki uniform said. "I'm Commander Nuance with Military Intelligence and we're here with warrants to search your offices."

"What's the meaning of this?" Lutke demanded.

Ignoring the man, Nuance looked around and asked, "Is Claire Miller present?"

Every eye in the room turned to look at her as Claire slid down as far as she could in her chair.

"That, that would be me," she said.

"Ma'am, I need you to come with me. Now."

"But, why?"

"That will be explained later. Now, are you coming quietly or not?"

Claire didn't have a chance to reply. Anything she might have said was lost in the commotion as the men in black grabbed her, lifted her from her chair, and frog-marched her out of the room.

"Hal?" Claire called as she was dragged away, but her boss just sat speechless. The last thing that she saw as she was taken from the room was Tina reaching across the table, grabbing Claire's cup of black velvet, and taking a sip.

"Which office is yours?" Nuance asked as his men pulled Claire into the center of the main office space. A half dozen more men in black were waiting there.

"That one," she said, pointing to a small cube in the corner of the room farthest from the windows.

"Take everything," Nuance said to his men. Turning back to Claire, he asked, "When mail comes in, who sees it and where is it kept?"

"We're a small agency and I'm the junior agent, so I'm the one who handles any incoming mail that looks like it contains a manuscript. Why?"

Nuance ignored her question. Leaving three men behind to retrieve everything from Claire's cubicle, he ordered her taken to a waiting car.

"Please, what's going on?" Claire asked as she was led away. Her arms hurt from the coarse gloves of the men gripping them and she banged her thigh against a desk, bruising it as she was pulled along.

As soon as they entered the long, narrow hallway outside her office, she dug her heels into the beige carpeting and wrenched an arm loose so that she could take out her cell phone.

"None of that!" one of the men said, face-planting her against the floral wallpaper as he twisted her arm up behind her back, forcing her to drop the phone. "Can't have you calling your accomplices to warn them."

"Ow, you're hurting me!" Claire cried.

The man pressed his forearm into the back of Claire's head with so much force that it pushed her face out of shape and brought tears to her eyes. "You ain't seen nothing yet, you traitor! Wait till I get you back to—"

"Enough of that!" Nuance said, putting a restraining hand on the man's shoulder. "Until she's been interrogated and we complete our investigation, she's just a person of interest. Though it does look pretty bad pulling out your cell like that, Miss Miller. You're not to have contact with anybody until the admiral approves it." Nuance picked up Claire's phone and put it in his pocket.

"But I have a client meeting this afternoon!" Claire whined. "I was just trying to call them to let them know that I'd be late."

"You're going to be more than late, sweetheart," Nuance's man said with a chuckle. Pulling Claire's elbows behind her, he pushed her toward the end of the hallway, down a flight of stairs, and then outside to a waiting vehicle.

Shouldn't this be black? Claire thought as the man shoved her into the back seat of a pink SUV, wondering if she'd been kidnapped by the cast of a Bugs Bunny cartoon. *In the movies they're always black.*

Nuance slid into the seat beside her and buckled her seat belt before they drove off.

"Thanks," she muttered. "Now can you please tell me what's going on? And where's my purse?"

"That will have to wait," Nuance replied.

"Look, how do I know that you are who you say you are?"

"You saw my badge."

"How do I know it's legit? And, well, what's with the pink getaway car, anyway?"

Nuance scowled. "Budget cuts. We didn't have enough vehicles to transport our people up here on short notice, so I had to borrow my wife's car."

"Your wife drives a pink SUV?"

"She sells cosmetics door-to-door." Nuance looked away, forestalling any further conversation.

The ride was brief. Claire was still trying to understand what was happening to her when the SUV pulled into the parking lot in front of Northwood's main office building. The building was a white, two-story, cinder-block construction with small windows. To the right, Claire could see two of the facility's five main assembly buildings, each five stories high and the size of a football field. They were both big enough to house one of the naval ships that Northwood specialized in constructing. A small patch of oak and pine trees shaded a thicket of sumac and blackberry bushes on the left side of the building.

"What are we doing here?" she asked as she was dragged from the car.

There was no answer. The men holding her did not wait for a command. Instead, they took her straight into the shipyard's main office building, where they locked her into a small office that had been stripped of everything, leaving just bare, off-white walls and a gray linoleum floor. There wasn't even a chair to sit on.

What's happening to me? Claire paced back and forth. *Who are these people and what do they want? I don't have money, and I haven't done anything.* Claire paused for a moment. *I wonder if I need a lawyer?*

Hours passed while Claire circled the room like a mouse in a squirrel cage, absent-mindedly rubbing her topaz broach as she walked. Lunch time came and went, and it was supper time before she heard footsteps in the outer hallway.

The door opened and one of Nuance's black-clad agents entered the room. She could see two soldiers dressed in camo out in the hallway. They had rifles, and they were pointing the guns at her.

"Come with me," the agent said, leading her out into the hallway. "No trouble, understand?"

"Yes, yes, I understand," she said. "What—"

"No talking!"

The heels of Claire's shoes clicked on the worn vinyl floor as she walked. *I should have left my sneakers on this morning. At least then I could have made a run for it.*

Looking at the soldiers accompanying her, she decided that trying to run might not be a good idea, even if she did get the chance.

There was a brief pause while the agent knocked at the door of an office. Then he ushered her into the room, saying, "Admiral, here's the woman from the literary agency that we picked up."

The first thing that Claire noticed when she entered the room was the warm, stale air. Like many of the older office buildings in Wisconsin, the Northwood facility had baseboard heat but no air conditioning. Despite the presence of wood wainscoting, the off-white walls and gray flooring gave the room a drab, tired feel that leached the energy from her like a long day at the gym, but without the rewarding sense of having accomplished anything.

Claire stopped when she recognized Commander Nuance, who had led the team that took her prisoner. He was standing to one side of a desk that was manned like a gun turret by an officer in a dress blue Navy uniform. For several moments, the officer just stared at her. His ice-blue eyes reminded her of her father when he was in one of his moods. Without thinking about it, she tried to step back, but she found her way blocked by the uniformed guards.

"Please sit," the man said, gesturing to an office chair in front of the desk. "I'm Admiral Dutchman, and I believe that you have already met Commander Nuance."

"Thank you," Claire said as she sat down. "Please, sir, can you tell me—"

Dutchman held up a hand, stopping her mid-sentence.

"Just wait," he said. "We have a few things that need to be cleared up and very little time to do so. Very little indeed."

"I don't understand."

"Of course not. You're just an innocent caught up in all of this, aren't you?"

"Well, yes, I am, whatever this is."

"Bullshit!" Dutchman slapped his hand down on a stack of manila folders on his desk. "I have top secret files here that were stolen from one of my staff just two days ago and they have your name all over them. But you know nothing about it, eh?"

"Secret files?" Claire said, horrified. "I...I've never seen anything like that. I'm just a junior agent. The agency doesn't handle that sort of thing."

"Is this your writing?" Dutchman asked, sliding a battered envelope across the desk and pointing to the return address label on it.

"Oh my God!" Claire recognized the envelope that she'd mailed to Commander Solomon on Saturday night. "Yes, it is. But there weren't any secrets in the manuscript, I swear it!"

"Do I look like an idiot?" Dutchman said with quiet earnestness as he leaned back in his chair. "We found over a dozen technical papers with the manuscript when your accomplice tried to kill Commander Solomon."

"Wha—somebody tried to kill Solomon? When?"

"Monday, as he was driving to his hotel."

"I was at work on Monday," Claire said.

"We know that. Doesn't mean you weren't involved."

"But I wasn't! I'm innocent, I swear it."

"If that's true, then you need to work with us. Tell us everything you know about this manuscript. I want to know who gave it to you, how they came by the information contained in it, and how many other people know about it."

"But I know nothing," Claire sobbed, putting her face in her hands. Dutchman's cold manner and relentless questioning brought back bad memories from her teen years when she could do nothing right, no matter how hard she tried to please her father. Without understanding what was going on, she couldn't help but feel that she was letting people down once again.

She could sense the officer's eyes on her as she struggled with old feelings of inadequacy, of being out of the loop and powerless. *This guy thinks I'm a loser.* She felt her mouth go dry as she looked up and met his stare. *And maybe he's right.*

Dutchman pulled a thick file from the stack, laid it on the desk, and said, "This is your file." His voice was soft now and Claire felt drawn in against her will. "Everything about you, who you are, who you know, everything is in here."

"How did you get that?" The room was hot, almost stifling, but Claire felt goosebumps on her arms.

"We're with Military Intelligence. It's what we do. I see that both of your parents are dead. Mother of cancer when you were twelve, and your father, well, that's a damn shame. Looks like he never amounted to much anyway." Dutchman paused, lanced her with his eyes. "Taking after him, are you?"

"No," Claire answered in a small voice as his words cut deep, lacerating an ancient wound.

"And a brother and sister. I see that you've tried to contact them several times and failed. As you have with everything else in life." The look in Dutchman's eyes was the same as the look on the face of the judge who had separated her from her family when she was a teenager, but Claire felt a sudden surge of hope.

"What?! You have Sam and Becca in there? Do you know where they are? Are they okay? Where are they? Please, tell me, I need to know."

Dutchman watched her reaction with hooded eyes. "Do you miss them?" he asked, catching her off guard.

"Why...yes. More than anything!" Claire was confused, her initial reaction tainted with a sudden feeling of suspicion. *Where is this going? Can this guy actually help me?* She caught a faint hint of Dutchman's astringent aftershave as she leaned forward, gripping the edge of her chair with sweaty palms, intent on what might come next.

After another pause, Dutchman continued, "You do know that you're in a lot of trouble, don't you, young lady?"

"No, I told you, I don't understand anything that's going on."

"This document that you sent to Solomon contains classified information about one of our country's ballistic missile defense systems. Please don't offend my intelligence by continuing to claim that you know nothing about it."

Dutchman's lips tightened into a thin line, although his eyes remained empty. Without warning, he lunged forward, slapped Jake's manuscript down on the desk, and screamed, "Cut the bullshit! This has your name on the return address and your fingerprints are all over its pages! Now I want to know where you got it, who you got it from, and when!"

"But, it just came in the mail on Saturday morning." Claire was terrified of the man but couldn't look away, held captive by the sheer force of his glare.

"How convenient," Dutchman said in a quiet voice as he sat down, cool and calm as if nothing had happened. "How very convenient for you." He smiled. "Ms. Miller, I can see that you care about your brother and sister very much. I'm in a position to help you find them again. All I need is for you to help me first. And you'd be doing your country a great service. Is that too much to ask?"

"No, of course not. Can you really help me find them?"

"The information you need is right here in this file."

"May I see it?"

"Yes, when this is all done, and so long as you cooperate with our investigation, then I'll see what I can do."

Claire felt sure that she was being played, but the chance to find Sam and Becca overruled her caution. *I need to make this right for them. I failed them after Mom died, and then when Dad did what he did. It's no wonder they never responded to my letters. But even if they want nothing to do with me, I still need to see them, to explain what happened. I need them to forgive me.*

Claire hugged herself and began to tremble. She felt Dutchman's gaze like sunburn on her skin, burning through to expose her deepest secrets as she withered before him. She closed her eyes for a moment so that she wouldn't have to see the glint of satisfaction in his eyes. When she did, she could smell her own sweat, rancid and cold as it soaked through her blouse.

"Now then, Ms. Miller, tell me everything you know about the author of this document," he said.

"All I have is his name and address. It's Jake Andersen. He's single and lives alone right here in town on Merryman Street. At least, I think he lives alone. That seemed to be what the cover letter said."

Dutchman sighed. "Ms. Miller, we already know that. We do have the cover letter, you know. I was hoping that you could provide us with more detail than that."

"I'm sorry, I can't. I haven't even met the man. We just got the manuscript last week and I haven't had a chance to reply to him yet. I don't even know if that's his real name or a pen name that he uses for publishing. I was waiting for Commander Solomon's evaluation of the manuscript before I accepted or rejected the book. Once we have a manuscript in hand, we seldom contact the author until a decision about publishing it has been made."

"Pity," Dutchman said. "I wanted to help you with your family problem. But perhaps there's still a possibility to do that. I'm going to have Commander Nuance release you for now. I want you to avoid all contact with this Andersen character until you hear from us again. I want to have a little chat with him myself, but if he goes into hiding, you might be able to help us lure him out. You'd be willing to do that for us, wouldn't you?"

The voice in Claire's head screamed *No!* But all that she could muster was a weak, "Yes, I guess I could do that. If you promise—"

"No promises. I said that I might help you if you proved to be of assistance. So far, you've given me nothing. But if you do manage to provide material aid during my investigation, then I might change my mind later. Is that clear?"

"Yes, sir."

"Very good." Dutchman leaned forward. "Don't let me down here, Claire. Your track record isn't very good, and it would be a shame if you failed to live up to your end of the bargain."

Speechless, Claire slid down in her chair, making herself as small as possible.

At a gesture from Dutchman, Nuance took her by the arm and led her from the room.

Before she was permitted to leave the building, Claire was processed like a criminal by two of Nuance's agents. They took photographs from all sides, along with fingerprints and retina scans, finishing up with a blood sample. Claire tried not to cry when one of the agents poked a needle into her arm to obtain the sample. She was sure that he went out of his way to make it hurt.

When Nuance's agents were done he returned Claire's cell phone and purse to her. She made a point of checking the contents of her purse in front of the agents. She counted her money one bill at a time and made sure that her credit cards, keys, and other personal items were all accounted for. It was a childish gesture, but it was all she could do to show her anger at her treatment.

"Done?" Nuance asked, raising an eyebrow as she snapped shut her clutch.

Claire just glared at the man. *Bastard!*

"Let's get you home then," he said in a neutral tone.

Claire saw that it was late evening as she was led from the building. She'd missed lunch and supper, and she felt mild nausea as a result of her hunger. The puncture wound on her arm where they'd drawn blood contributed to her discomfort. Claire pressed a piece of gauze down on her arm to try and stop the bleeding, but when Nuance shoved her into the back seat of his pink SUV, she lost the gauze. The ride back to her apartment was short, but by the time she got there, she had blood on her ivory blouse and all over her hands.

At least I didn't get any on my purse, she thought as Nuance escorted her into the building. A uniformed soldier was standing outside the door to her apartment, which was hanging open.

"Remember, you're to have no contact with Andersen without contacting me first," Nuance said as Claire cleaned herself up at the kitchen sink, running cold water into the stainless steel basin and then soaking her arm in it. "If he calls, keep him on the line as long as you can so that we can trace the call."

"Trace the call?" Claire looked back over her shoulder. "Are you monitoring my phone?"

"Of course we are. What did you expect?"

"I guess I don't know what to expect. I've never heard of anything like this happening before, at least not outside of a novel. What am I supposed to do?"

"Go back to your normal routine. But you're to return to your apartment every evening by seven p.m. for a debriefing on the day's events. Under no circumstances are you to leave town. Somebody is trying to recover that document and they'll stop at nothing to get it back. You might be in danger if you stray far from our protection."

"But what if I have to go someplace to meet with an author or to do some fact-checking for a book?"

"Does that happen often?"

"Well, yes, and I did have an appointment to meet an author today. I hope we don't lose him as a client because of all this.

He's kind of touchy and more than a little paranoid. It took me weeks to get him to agree to meet with me. And if I show up trailing a federal agent, I'll never see him again."

"That's the least of your problems. Who is it that you were supposed to meet and why do you need to leave town to do it?"

"His name's Bob Fredrick. He's a local author and Greenpeace activist who's working on a documentary about the environmental threats facing the Menominee River. I set up the meeting with him so that he could show me some of what he's writing about. I need to spend a day on the river with him to get that info."

"Is the Menominee the same river that flows through town?"

"Yes."

"How far upriver do you need to go?"

"He wants to meet upriver at Rubys Corner. I don't know if he plans to go up river or down from there."

"Okay, I'll send an agent along with you."

"Oh Christ, that's going to send him right over the edge. Didn't you hear what I said? He's with Greenpeace and he'll freak if one of your agents shows up. Besides, what if he doesn't want to meet with me now? I was supposed to meet him this afternoon. I bet he thinks I just blew him off. What should I say?"

"Be creative, but do not under any circumstances mention anything about our investigation."

"That's going to be a little difficult with one of your agents standing next to me, isn't it?"

"Let me know an hour before you leave and I'll make sure my agent is dressed for a day on the water. Tell your client that you've brought a cameraman with you."

Nuance checked his watch. "I have to go now. Make sure you follow your instructions, understood?"

"Yes, I understand."

"Very good."

Nuance left without another word, leaving Claire alone in her apartment. She paced from room to room, struggling to process everything that had just happened. When she entered her bedroom, she paused.

The soothing scent of lavender filled the room and she took a deep breath of it. A moment later, the calming effect disappeared when she realized what that meant. Somebody had opened the drawers in the dresser where she kept her sachet of lavender. Her cosmetics and hair brush were still on top of the dresser where she had left them that morning, and they did not look like they had been touched. She pulled the top dresser drawer open and examined its contents. At first, she saw nothing out of place, but then she noticed that the socks were on the wrong side of the panties. *They searched my apartment. While I was out, some complete strangers went through everything I own, even my most intimate apparel. Then they went to a lot of trouble to put everything back the way that it was.* Goosebumps formed on her arms as she thought about that.

Claire returned to the living room and then sat down on the couch, sliding a wad of paper towels under her arm so that she didn't bleed on its tan fabric. Without thought, she picked up the TV remote, and then put it back down. Leaning back with her eyes closed she wondered, *what the hell have I got myself into?*

9

While Claire was making the acquaintance of some of the nation's less personable intelligence officers, Jake was getting started on his evening routine before going to work.

A quick shower was followed by a breakfast burrito washed down with a Coke. Sprawled on his couch, Jake dialed in to the Northwood system and checked his email to see if there was anything that needed immediate handling. After scrolling through the routine system status messages he found a long list of tasks from his manager. There was also an email from his manager letting him know that a number of employees were working offsite while the hallways were being painted. Jake, however, was required to be onsite.

Jake scowled. "Crap! I could do everything from home if they'd loosen up a bit."

Grabbing his cell, he sent a quick text to Felipe. "Hey bro, have you heard about the hallways getting painted?"

Felipe's response came in less than a minute. "Yep, the place is empty, but I haven't seen any work being done. Everybody disappeared after lunch when the memo came out."

"I wonder why we didn't get advance notice?"

"Boss said it's tied in with the offsite meetings. Do you think they're laying people off?"

"Nobody told me, and UNIX admins are always told beforehand so we can revoke people's security clearances. And the company just landed a big contract with the Navy, so unlikely. Probably just sensitivity training or something like that."

"Makes sense, there's a few guys in the metalwork area that have made cracks about my being Mexican. I told them I'm from Brazil, but they don't get the difference. Anyway, I was sent offsite with the other consultants. We're in an office building down the street. Took a while to set up. I need to work late to catch up on things."

"Cool, I'm headed in after I catch up on a few chores. I'll let you know if I find out anything."

10

After leaving Claire's apartment, Nuance took a moment to review his plan for searching Jake Andersen's house that night. He couldn't think of anything that might have changed or altered the situation, so he drove back to the office building where Dutchman had established his headquarters.

Nuance's first stop was the room that housed his team's supplies. He checked out a Kevlar vest, night-vision goggles, and a night-black combat uniform. Changing quickly, he went to the building's small cafeteria, where he found a squad of marines and four of his agents waiting for him. They'd received their orders earlier in the day and were already geared up and ready to go.

Addressing his team, Nuance said, "We should have the place to ourselves for most of the night. Andersen's manager has confirmed that he works the night shift, and will make sure that he doesn't leave early. You've all been briefed on what we're looking for, but keep your eyes open for anything else suspicious. And stay vigilant. The spy has already tried to silence one person, and he might show up at any time with plans to do the same to Andersen. If that happens, remember that we want to take that individual alive at all costs. Use Tasers and rubber bullets if needed to take him down, but do not use lethal force. I repeat do NOT use lethal force. Restrain the subject at the first opportunity so that he has no chance to take poison or kill himself by any other means. It's okay if you break an arm or leg. Just keep him alive for interrogation. Questions?"

One of the agents raised a hand. "Sir, what if the spy shows up and he's not alone?"

"Same terms of engagement, Jenkins. Anybody with him is also a suspect and so also to be taken into custody no matter who they are. Anything else?

"No? Good. I'll go over the operational plan one more time, and then we'll head out. The marines are to set up a one-block perimeter around Andersen's house. The intelligence agents will follow me in. We'll do a quick sweep to make sure the place is empty, and then perform a detailed search. When that's done, we'll load up and clear out. Leave no trace of our presence. It might already be too late, but just in case, we don't want to alert anybody of our interest in this matter."

A few minutes later, Nuance and his team were on station at Jake's house. Even though it would be a few hours before Jake returned home, Nuance wanted a chance to search the residence before the suspect could destroy any evidence. Entry proved easier than he had expected. As with so many small towns in Wisconsin, due to the low crime rate, people in Marinette seldom locked their houses when away. He supposed it was also a pain in the ass to fumble for your keys at the front door when the temp hit thirty below in the winter. Nuance and his team entered the property without making a sound, flipping down the night-vision goggles strapped to their foreheads as they did so.

"Report," Nuance whispered into a throat mike.

"Nothing," his men responded as they each searched their assigned room.

"What's that smell?" somebody asked over the radio link.

"Wet dog," another agent answered.

"Anybody see a dog?" Nuance asked.

He received a chorus of noes in answer.

"Then don't worry about it," Nuance ordered, a decision that he would soon regret.

The team had just finished their sweep when one of the marines called Nuance over the radio to let him know that a male matching the suspect's description was approaching the house.

"Dammit!" Nuance swore. "His boss was supposed to wait until midnight to let him off work. Well, it doesn't matter now. Everyone take your position. As soon as he's through the front door we'll take him down."

Less than a minute later, a young man fumbled his way through the door carrying a laptop, a pizza box, and a stack of papers. With his arms full, he gave a half-hearted kick to close the door but failed. Leaving the door open, he edged forward until his shin bumped into the room's coffee table, then he bent to set down his burden.

"Now!" Nuance yelled, and his men pounced.

"Got him!" yelled one of the agents, followed by a loud shriek of surprise from their target.

Despite having the element of surprise, Nuance's agents found the man harder to restrain than they had expected. As they grabbed for the man's arms, he spun around, dropping his laptop and papers as he juggled the pizza box. The corner of the laptop landed square on one agent's foot, sending him hopping away. The pizza box flew open, striking another agent in the face and knocking aside his goggles. The agent howled in pain and then fell to his knees as steaming cheese and marinara sauce smeared in his eyes.

With one agent holding onto his elbow, the man tried to run out the door. The agent spun him back into the house just as another agent fired off a blast of pepper spray. Nuance watched in amazement as the first agent inadvertently maneuvered the man out of the way of the spray and took the blast in the face himself, going down with a cry. Rushing forward, the agent with the spray tripped over the fallen agents and so joined them on the floor in a tangle of boots and curses.

As Nuance and the agents who remained standing closed in on the man, a blur of brown fury streaked through the open door and launched itself into the fray.

"He's got a dog with—yikes!" yelled one of the agents as the dog collided with him.

"Federal agents! Surrender and put your hands in the air!" Nuance yelled as the dog sank his teeth into the remaining agent's shin. The man went down with a groan of pain and rolled into Nuance, taking his legs out from under him and landing him square on top of the pile of agents struggling on the floor.

The agent with the pepper spray discharged another blast, blinding most of the other people in the pile. Nuance and his agents cursed as they tried to wipe the burning fluid from their faces. While they did, the man who they were trying to catch fled into an adjoining room.

"After him!" Nuance yelled as he struggled to his feet in the dark. His night-vision goggles had been knocked off in the melee and the pepper spray was still making his eyes water. Without waiting for his men, Nuance lumbered after the man.

As he entered the room, Nuance fumbled around the door frame until he found the light switch. All it did was turn on a red lava lamp located next to a small, untidy bed, painting the room's off-white walls a bloody hue. The old oak floor creaked as the man Nuance was chasing emerged from under the bed. Nuance could see him chewing something.

"He's destroying evidence!" Nuance rushed forward, only to trip over a pile of dirty laundry on the floor. As he sprawled on the ground, Nuance saw the man grab a bottle from the nightstand and chug the amber contents in one impressive gulp.

A Jack Daniel's label was plain to see on the bottle, and as Nuance rose to his knees, the man stopped, looked at the bottle, and then looked wide-eyed at Nuance.

"Urp!" the man said, dropping the bottle and grabbing his tummy in distress.

"Freeze!" Nuance commanded, drawing a pistol and pointing it at the man's head.

Before he had a chance to put the man in cuffs, Nuance felt a searing pain in his butt as the dog, forgotten for a moment, struck from behind, biting deep into an area that was not adequately covered by Nuance's Kevlar vest or by his group medical insurance.

"Aiieeee!" Nuance jumped forward in pain, stumbling over the man as he did so. His gun went flying as he fell down again.

"Hey!" yelled the man as Nuance plopped on top of him.

"Grrrrr!" The dog snarled as it chewed further into the intruder's soft tissue.

"Get it off, get it off!" Nuance cried, hoping that one of his agents would come to his aid. But it wasn't one of Nuance's agents that rescued him.

"Stop it, Chaucer, you stop it right now!" Nuance's rescuer said, grabbing the dog by its collar. "Chaucer, I said let go! You let go right now or I'll tell Unca Jake!"

The dog released its grip on Nuance, giving the man a sullen glare as it was dragged away.

Nuance rolled over and looked up in astonishment. A small biped with a face like a tiger and clad in a violet onesie with a large picture of Saturn on the front confronted him.

"It's another perp!" shouted one of Nuance's agents as he staggered into the room. His eyes still blurry from the pepper spray, the agent pulled out his Taser and hit the little biped with a bolt, dropping it in its tracks. Another of the agents pushed past him with a blanket, which he threw over the dog just as it spun to attack. Moments later, the dog was subdued, too.

"Get all these perps out of here!" Nuance said. "We can come back tomorrow to finish searching the place."

Slipping a pair of handcuffs onto the man, the agents dragged him, the small biped, and the muffled hound out of the house and loaded them into a waiting SUV.

Nuance followed as best he could, limping as one of his men helped him along. Unable to sit due to the location of his injury, he was forced to lie on his side during the ride back to their base of operations. He hoped that he didn't bleed on the pink leather upholstery; getting his ass chewed by his wife would be much worse than by the hound.

As soon as the convoy arrived at their makeshift headquarters, their prisoners were hustled inside. While his team locked the prisoners up in separate rooms, Nuance took a few minutes to have the squad's medic patch up his lacerated cheeks.

The medical orderlies had taken over one of the windowless gray rooms just down the corridor from Admiral Dutchman's office.

"Laugh and I'll have you court-martialed," Nuance growled as the medic examined his wound.

"Wouldn't dream of it," the man said, trying to hide a smirk. "Now, I'm going to have to put some clamps in to close this up. Would you like a painkiller first?"

"No, I need a clear head to interrogate the prisoners. Just do your job and get it over with."

"Okay," the medic said, putting down a syringe of local anesthetic that he had prepared. He picked up a medical stapler and proceeded to snap a dozen metal clamps over Nuance's wounds, sealing them shut.

Nuance gritted his teeth as each staple dug into his skin, determined not to show weakness. When the medic was finished, Nuance looked back over his shoulder and examined the bulky bandage covering most of his right buttock.

"Does it have to be that big?"

"Yep. Need to protect the wound. Now lie still. I have to give you a shot of antibiotics and a tetanus booster. Just in case."

"In case of what?"

"Infection. Animal bites are bad for that."

"How will I know—" Nuance paused to wince as the medic stuck a long needle into his left butt cheek. "How will I know if it's infected?"

"Your ass will fall off. I'm done here, now get out. I have other patients waiting."

Pulling up his bloodied pants, Nuance limped out of the makeshift surgical suite and headed down the hall to where the prisoners were detained.

As he did so, he relaxed a bit. After two decades in naval intelligence, he was confident that he had experienced every facet of interrogation possible. None of it prepared him for what was waiting for him at the end of the hallway.

11

The man that Nuance and his agents had picked up during their raid spent several hours sitting in a room by himself. His head was spinning thanks to the bottle of Jack that he'd used to wash down the bag of hash that he'd kept hidden under his bed. The fire in his belly told him he'd made a serious mistake. *Why'd they call me Jake?* Felipe wondered.

"Is anybody there?" Felipe asked in a plaintive voice. There was no answer. *It's got to be the DEA. Or ICE. At least I got rid of the drugs before they caught me. I'd have been totally screwed if they'd found all that hash on me.*

Then he heard the click of footsteps approaching in the hallway that led to his room. They stopped outside his door and he heard two men talking.

"I want to see the man first," one voice said. "Is the room ready?"

"Yes, sir," another man answered. "We used the standard configuration for an interrogation room. There's a desk and chair for you, with the prisoner zip-tied to a chair facing the desk. Marinette doesn't invest much in office décor or furnishings, so there were no creature comforts to remove. In fact, the industrial gray paint and linoleum are perfect for creating the psychological effect that you want."

"Excellent."

Then the door opened and a tall man wearing a soiled black military uniform entered the room. Felipe noticed that the man had a large lump on one side of his butt, as if he'd stuffed a newspaper down his pants for padding.

The man stepped behind the desk and said, "Mr. Andersen, I'm Commander Nuance with Military Intelligence. I have some questions for you. Everything will go much better for you if you give complete and truthful answers. Do you understand?"

"Who did you say?" Felipe asked, and then he had an inspiration. *They think I'm Jake! If they're with ICE, then all I have to do is play along and I'll be outta here in a flash.*

"I said that my name is Commander Nuance. Are you having trouble understanding me?"

"Oh, uh, I understand. Yeah. Hi, Mr. Nuance," Felipe finished in a weak voice.

Nuance scowled, and then eased himself down into the chair on the other side of the desk. His sigh as he sat down made it clear that he appreciated Marinette's use of Navy funds intended for ship construction on well-padded office chairs instead.

Felipe looked around at the soft rustle of cloth and saw another agent standing behind his chair. When he looked back, Nuance was glaring at him. Felipe watched with surprise and mounting concern as yellow and blue polka dots appeared on Nuance's face, then paired off and began a slow, elegant waltz. *Must be the hash.* The yellow dots turned into daisies, twined their stems together, and started dancing in circles around the blue dots. They were singing in light falsettos as they pirouetted across the man's features. *Yep, it's the hash. I shouldn't have eaten the whole bag. There must have been enough in there to get a rock band high. Or maybe two.*

After a long silence, Nuance asked, "What's your name?"

"My...na...name?" Felipe mumbled, confused by the effects of the drugs that he'd swallowed.

"Are you Jake Andersen?"

Felipe struggled to understand the question. "Jake? Oh, yeah, I know h...him...oohhh." Felipe's voice trailed off with a soft groan. Nuance's words were coming at him like solid objects sliding across the desk. Some of the words broke apart en route, with their letters forming new and unexpected configurations. The letters in the word "Andersen" floated off the table and disappeared into orange-scented puffs of smoke.

"I'm, I..."

"You're Jake?" Nuance raised an eyebrow, looked at the man behind Felipe and then shrugged. The walls moved up and down with Nuance's shoulders as he did so.

"Is it okay if I call you Jake?" Nuance asked.

"That's cool," Felipe said, his head wobbling. He watched the shadows begin an elegant waltz across the wall behind Nuance, who failed to realize that Felipe was talking about something entirely different from the question he had posed.

"Jake, are you familiar with this document?" Nuance held up a copy of Jake's manuscript.

"Yeah, oh wow, man. Where'd you get..." Felipe stopped, fascinated by a fly that had made its way into the room and landed on the desk. It had a head at the end of each leg, and all the heads were singing a barbershop quartet tune. *That's weird. Quartets don't have six singers.*

"Never mind where we got it." Nuance leaned forward, wincing as the motion tightened the bandage on his butt. "You do know that you're in a lot of trouble, don't you?"

"Who, me?" Felipe started crossing and uncrossing his eyes, intrigued by the resulting double images.

"Yes, you! And you can quit the bullshit!" Nuance yelled, slapping the manuscript down on the desk. "I want a straight answer from you and I want it now!"

Startled back into a moment of clarity, Felipe stared at Nuance in alarm.

"Now then, do you know what is in this document?" Nuance demanded.

"Huh? Oh, yeah, I guess so."

"So you know about the Eschaton data in here?"

"Oh. Well, yeah."

"Who do you work for?"

"Huh? Oh, Northwood Shipbuilding. I'm in the IT sec...section." Felipe had trouble finishing his sentence as the drugs took hold again. *Gray. Why is everything in here gray? Funny,*

I never noticed how gray tastes like peppermint before. I wonder if the architects were stoned when they designed this place.

Nuance paused. Narrowing his eyes, he asked, "Are you an alien?"

"What?" Felipe was having trouble understanding Nuance's questions again. The words now appeared to be written on the sides of blimps that were drifting toward him through the air. He leaned forward and tried to catch one in his mouth. It tasted like bubble gum, which made him giggle.

"An alien. You know, not from around here."

"Uh, yeah, you got me." An immigrant from Brazil, Felipe lived in constant fear of immigration agents even though he was legal. With one last mighty effort before he lost all control of his faculties, he cried, "But I got a green card!"

"Not gonna help you where you're going," Nuance said, his voice grim. "Now then, where are you from?"

Felipe took a few moments to think about that. As his head bobbled about, he noticed a small window near the ceiling. A full moon glowed through the pane and the stars around it began to dance as Felipe tripped out.

Entranced, Felipe nodded his head toward the window and said, "Space..." His eyes began to roll in the opposite direction to his wobbling head. "The moon is so close...what a trip!" As he drifted away in his hallucination, he began to mumble nonsense. "Argle-bargle."

"What was that?" Nuance said.

"Argle-bargle."

"When did you get here?"

"Argle-bargle. Argle-bargle, argle-bargle, argle-bargle."

Nuance looked at the agent who was standing behind Felipe. "Can you make out what he's saying?"

"No, sir. Sounds like a foreign language to me, but it's not one I've ever heard before."

"Me either," Nuance said with a frown. "Well, I've got what I wanted. I need to question the other prisoners and then report to the admiral. Keep a close watch on this subject until the medic has time to get a blood sample. That should answer the question as to whether he is, in fact, an alien."

12

After finishing with the man he believed to be Jake Andersen, Nuance made his way into the next room, another depressing gray box like the one he'd just left. As soon as he entered the room, he had a sinking feeling. *Oh Christ, it's just a kid! We tasered a kid. And it's just a little girl. Damn! If she's been hurt, we'll all be court-martialed.*

Like the man in the other interrogation room, the child was zip-tied to a chair. Her violet onesie was dirty and torn in a couple of places. Nuance didn't need to see the stain on it to know that she had wet herself when she'd been tasered, as the smell of urine filled the room. A plastic, Halloween-style tiger mask sat on the desk, revealing a pale young girl with disheveled brown hair and eyes. Her eyes flashed more lightening than Nuance would have expected from a person of such a tender age.

Easing himself into the chair facing her, Nuance said, "I'm Commander Nuance of the US Navy." Keeping his voice firm but as gentle as he could manage, he asked, "What's your name?"

"I'm Daphne."

"Hi, Daphne. I bet this all seems confusing to you, but I need to know what you were doing in Jake Andersen's house tonight."

"I live next door," Daphne replied, pushing her lower lip forward. "I was watching Chaucer for Unca Jake while he was at work. I do that a lot, you know. He says I'm somebody who can be trusted."

"And Chaucer is…?"

"His dog."

"I see. And you said that Jake Andersen is your uncle?"

"Of course he is. Don't you know anything?" Daphne's eyes narrowed.

"Well, no, not everything. That's why I need to ask a lot of questions. Now, if you were watching Jake's dog—"

"Chaucer."

"Yes, Chaucer. If you were watching Chaucer, then why didn't you stay at home? And why were you up so late? It must have been well past your bedtime."

"It *was* past my bedtime, and I was in bed. My mom tucked me in and you can just ask her. She'll tell you."

"So why did you go to Jake's house if you were already in bed?"

"Chaucer woke me up. He was growling and then he jumped out the window. I thought Jake was in trouble, so I put on my tiger mask to look fierce and went after him, 'cause I'm supposed to watch him. That's what you do, you know. When you're responsible. Unca Jake says I'm the best and that's why he has me watch his dog."

"So you climbed out the window and followed the dog. What happened then?"

"Well, I saw the door of Jake's house was open, so I followed Chaucer inside. I heard a lot of shouting and barking. I thought maybe something had happened to Jake, so I followed the sound of Chaucer's barks. I'm not sure what happened then, but I think somebody hit me. It hurt a lot." Leaning forward against her restraints, Daphne demanded, "What were *you* doing there? Are you burglars?"

"No, we work for the US government."

"How do I know that?"

"Daphne, this will go quicker if you let me—"

"You're a bad person!" Daphne shouted. "The sheriff's going to put you in jail. You can't kidnap me and get away with it. You'll see!"

"Daphne, trust me, you haven't been kidnapped."

"Then why am I tied up?"

"It's part of our procedure."

"Sure, that's what they all say. You just wait. When Unca Jake hears about this he'll fix you. He'll fix you good."

"Daphne, how well do you know your Uncle Jake?"

"Better than anybody. And don't think cause he's not so big or fierce looking like some jock, he can't do something. He's got....he's got powers. He can do special stuff."

"Indeed?" Nuance tilted his head, intrigued. "What kind of stuff have you seen him do?"

"Serious stuff, like with computers and, and things. He's real smart, too, like Einstein but smarter," Daphne finished.

"I see. Tell me Daphne, how old are you and how long have you lived here?"

"All my life. I'm only eight years old, but I'm a good reader. For my age, anyway. Ms. Eliot says so."

"And who is she?"

"She's my teacher. And if I'm late for class tomorrow on account of you kidnapping me, there's going to be trouble. You're in for it if she catches you, and she always does. Even Timmy, and he gets away with just about everything. He brought a toad to class and she caught him. Boy, did he get it."

"I'm sure he did," Nuance muttered, deciding that there was no point in questioning the girl further. "Daphne, just as soon as we clear up a few more details, I'm sure that we can get you home. With any luck, we can do that before you have to go to school so nobody has to get into any trouble. How does that sound?"

"Well, if you're going to let me go that's okay. But you better be quick. Kidnapping's a serious thing and Jake's going to be angry when he finds out, even if you do let me go. You might want to start running now, while you still have a chance."

"I'll keep that in mind." Nuance stood and headed for the door. On his way out, he told the agent guarding the room that Daphne could be released from her restraints and allowed to clean herself up, but that she was to be kept in the room until the admiral approved her release.

Nuance paused in front of the next door down, then screwed up his courage and entered the room. To his relief, the dog was hogtied and muzzled to keep him from biting anybody.

"So your name's Chaucer, eh, boy?" Nuance used a soft, soothing tone as he knelt down next to the dog. "Well, I can't blame you for trying to protect your owner. I've got a collie at home myself, and she's a good dog. She'd do the same as you, if it came down to it." Nuance ran his hand along the dog's back, keeping his touch light and gentle.

With a sudden lunge, Chaucer head-butted him.

"Ow!"

Nuance cursed as he fell over, landing on his injured backside. *I should have let the medic put more padding on that.*

With the help of three of his agents, the dog was subdued again and Nuance was able to thoroughly inspect the animal. Finding nothing out of the ordinary about it, he hurried from the room followed by the other men. Nobody relaxed until the door was shut and latched.

"Keep an eye on this one," Nuance said. "I need to report to the admiral with what we've found. Most likely the girl and dog will be released later, but I want them kept under lock-and-key until then. Also, find a vet to do a blood test on the dog, ASAP. He looks clean, but I want him checked for rabies, just to be safe."

"Yes, sir," the agents said, returning to their station in front of the door.

With a sigh, Nuance turned and limped away.

13

Admiral Dutchman paused in his work to check his watch. It was after three a.m. and Nuance still hadn't reported in from the raid on the Andersen house. *I wonder if something went wrong? No, Nuance is a pro, I bet it went like clockwork. Besides, it was an empty house. What could go wrong?*

He closed the email from his superior at the Pentagon that he'd been reading and rubbed his face, the stubble of his beard harsh against the palms of his hands. Closing his laptop, he sat back and took a sip of cold coffee, rinsing the bitter brew around like caffeinated mouthwash.

The email made pointed reference to an apparent lack of progress with his investigation into the "Solomon Incident," as it was being called. The paucity of operational details in his daily status reports was also flagged. Dutchman scowled. He detested the constant meddling and micro-management by the buffoons at the Pentagon. *A bunch of sailors who've never set foot on a warship, at least not during a campaign. Always safe ashore when the cannons fire. Now they want in on my investigation.*

Sharing credit for busting an active spy cell was not something that Dutchman relished. But he was running out of time. He figured that he could hold off the brass for another week before they sent an inspector to review the situation. And if they found out that he'd asked Nuance to break into a civilian's home without a warrant from FISC, the Foreign Intelligence Surveillance Court, he'd be in the brig faster than a sailor on shore leave could dial Tinder. But anything he put in a warrant request to the FISC would be copied back to the Pentagon, and that would put him through the wringer, too. *A week. Nuance has to crack this in a week or my ass is grass.*

A knock on the door made him jump, spilling a few drops of his drink onto the gray metal desk.

"Come in," he called.

A moment later, Nuance limped into the room and came to attention.

Dutchman returned his salute and gestured to a chair in front of his desk. "At ease, commander, and have a seat."

"Thank you, sir, but if you don't mind, I'll remain standing." Nuance rubbed his backside as he spoke and Dutchman noticed the bulge at the back of Nuance's slacks. As the door closed behind Nuance, Dutchman caught a whiff of antiseptic mixed with stale urine.

"Commander, you seem to be in need of freshening up." Dutchman raised an eyebrow. "And is that pepper spray that I smell?"

"Yes, sir."

"May I assume, then, that the raid did not go as planned?"

"That would be correct, sir."

"What happened?"

"Sir, we made the initial entry as planned and were able to perform an initial sweep of the residence. But before we could go any further, multiple intruders appeared. There was a struggle, and some of my team were injured. All of the parties involved were successfully apprehended, though, and none of the team suffered any serious harm."

"Multiple intruders?"

"Yes, sir."

"Wasn't Andersen supposed to be held back at the office by his manager?"

"Yes, and he was. I just verified with Northwood that he is still on-site and unaware of our activities, even though one of the intruders tried to pass himself off as Andersen."

"Then who were the intruders? And why were they there? We don't have a leak, do we?"

"Sir, no, sir. I'm confident that we have no leaks. I believe that the intruders were there for the same reason we were, searching for evidence of the spy's activities at Northwood. Most likely with the intent to destroy anything they found and silence anybody who is aware of their activities."

"Makes sense. Are you done interrogating the people you picked up?"

"Yes, sir."

"And?"

"Sir, the man is giving us trouble. After several minutes of questioning, he admitted to being an alien and made specific references to traveling through space. But then he started speaking in a language that none of us could understand. I have a translator working on it, but so far she's baffled."

"So you still think that our spy's an alien, eh? Did you take a DNA sample for testing?"

"The medic is working on that now, and the sample should be on a fast jet to D.C. within the hour. The National Security Lab is waiting to process it. I was able to get it flagged for priority handling, so we should have the results within twelve hours, sir."

"That's excellent turnaround. Good job, Commander. I take it that the State Lab was not able to assist with the task?"

"Thank you, sir. No, they were not. They're working through a sixty-day backlog of samples from homicides and rapes. The best that they could promise was a five-day turn-around."

"Not surprising. It'll be interesting to see if your 'alien spy' theory pans out. What about the other ones you picked up?"

"Ah, yes, well…um, about that, sir. I have them waiting in the hallway. It seemed…prudent to have you see them for yourself." Nuance opened the office door and gestured for Daphne and Chaucer to be brought in. His agents complied, with one on each side of the chocolate Lab holding the dog on tight leashes. The dog was still muzzled, but the men leading him looked nervous.

Dutchman examined the girl. Despite her soiled onesie, tangled locks, and frail appearance, she managed a convincing glare in return. But that was nothing compared to the look he got from the dog standing next to her. He felt his short hairs curl in response to the animal's silent focus; it reminded him of marines preparing for a landing in hostile territory.

"Who's this, Commander?"

"This is one of the other intruders we picked up. Her name's Daphne, sir."

"Daphne? Is she an alien, too?"

"No, sir, she's a little girl."

"Then what the devil is she doing here?"

"The strike team picked her up by mistake during the raid. She was in the same house as the alien we captured, sir."

"Was she alone?"

"No, sir, she had a dog with her, the one standing next to her."

"Is it an alien?"

"No, sir, it's a chocolate Lab."

At a gesture from Nuance, the agents led Daphne and Chaucer out of the room, closing the door behind themselves as they went.

Dutchman glared at his subordinate. He could feel his cheeks flush with heat as he struggled to contain his rage. In a whisper, he asked, "Are you telling me that the hand-picked team of combat veterans we sent to apprehend a hostile alien spy brought back a little girl and her dog instead?"

"Sir, that would appear to be the case. Sir."

"Oh, I see. Now then, did I mumble when I gave my orders? Was I unclear in any way?"

"Sir, no—"

"PERHAPS I SHOULD HAVE SHOUTED!" Dutchman leapt to his feet, spittle flying from his lips. Leaning in so close that he drenched the wilting man's face with saliva, he continued, "What on God's green earth were they thinking? What did they use for brains, Play-Doh?"

"Sir, they—"

"How did this clusterfuck happen?"

"Well—"

"No, don't tell me! I don't even want to know! Just FIX THIS! Am I clear?"

"Sir, yes, sir."

"Dismissed!"

"Sir, yes, sir. Before I go, sir, there's the issue of the girl?"

"Send her home! But for Christ's sake, be discreet about it. Have the local sheriff do it, and give him some song-and-dance story to cover up what really happened. Her parents are going to be furious. The last thing we need right now is to draw attention to ourselves."

"Sir, yes, sir."

"Was there anything else, commander?"

"Actually, there is, sir. I was wondering if we have the warrants yet from FISC? We took quite a risk tonight entering Andersen's house and then apprehending the suspects. Any evidence we uncover might be tainted and thrown out of court if we don't have the paperwork nailed down."

"Commander, I believe I explained the situation prior to the raid. The warrants are in process and will be backdated to cover your activities."

"Understood, sir, but I'd feel a lot more comfortable if I had the actual paperwork in hand. Is there any way to speed up the court?"

"No. This is a delicate matter, and because of the implications regarding the nation's strategic defense, it's being processed on an eyes-only basis. Only the top brass at the Pentagon are in the loop, which is slowing things down. It will help them—" *and me* "—considerably if we can provide some hard evidence. That's got to be done quickly, though. I can't emphasize this enough—the clock's ticking. We have less than a week to find out who's behind the spies and to plug the leak at Northwood. Otherwise, the situation will escalate out of our hands. The last thing we need is a bunch of political hacks from the NSA taking over the investigation and turning it into a circus." *And getting credit for everything.*

"Yes, sir, I understand."

"By the way, commander, I've given more thought to how to play the Miller woman you picked up from the literary agency."

"Sir?"

"We don't have time to wait and see how deeply she might be involved in all of this. I want you to move her into a more active role. We need to put this character Andersen under a microscope. See if she can be useful in drawing him out. You have plenty of leverage over her—use it."

"Yes, sir. But after watching her fall apart when you questioned her yesterday, it's pretty clear that she's fragile. If I lean too hard on her, she might break."

"If she's involved with these spies, that'll be the least of her problems. Push hard. Am I clear?"

"Yes, sir."

"Good, now get that child back to her family. Dismissed."

"Yes, sir."

14

Hospital Corpsman Third Class Sanders reviewed his instructions from Nuance as he made his way down one of the long, sterile corridors of the Northwood office building. His combat boots beat softly on the linoleum as he walked. *Get a blood sample from the male suspect for DNA testing. Get a blood sample from a dog to test for rabies. Piece of cake.*

The corpsman was tired after pulling a double-shift. He had spent eight hours at the hospital working with Doc Hansen on the agent who had been injured in the car wreck. Then he took the night shift, patching up the injured agents when they returned from their raid. *Injured, my ass!* Sanders chuckled. *Pepper-sprayed themselves! Don't think they'll get Purple Hearts for that. And Jenkins—burned his face with pizza. Wow. Just, wow.*

As he approached a guarded door, Sanders checked the items on the small tray he was carrying, making sure he had everything he needed.

One of Nuance's black-clad agents waited at the door next to a soldier dressed in camo.

"Jenkins, I have orders to take some blood samples from your suspects," Sanders said. "I'd like to start with the man."

"He's in here." Jenkins opened the door and gestured toward Felipe.

"Is there a reason he's still tied to a chair?" Sanders laid out his kit on the desk facing Felipe.

"Yeah, he's totally whacked out. When we untied him earlier, he fell over. So we tied him back up. Seemed better than leaving him on the floor."

"That's not gonna matter when Dutchman gets through with him."

"You got that right, poor bastard. But he's got it coming. Poked his nose in where he shouldn't."

Sanders squatted down to get a good angle on Felipe's right arm. He swabbed it with an alcohol pad, then tied a rubber tube around the man's bicep. When he slid a needle into the vein in Felipe's elbow, Felipe's eyes opened, and he leaned close to the medic.

"Argle-bargle!!"

"What did he say?" Sanders nearly dropped the syringe in surprise.

"Got me!" The agent chuckled. "Even Nuance ain't heard that language before."

"Argle-bargle." Felipe's voice dropped to a whisper as if he was trying to impart something of cosmic importance to Sanders.

"Whatever you say, fella. Just hold still for a minute and it'll go a lot easier for both of us."

"Bargle! Bargle! Bargle!" Felipe managed to hop his chair backward. As he did, the needle slid out of his arm.

"Hey, grab him!" Sanders duck-walked after Felipe, brandishing the syringe as he waddled forward.

"Sure, I got 'im. Wait! Ow!"

Felipe twisted his chair just as Sanders lunged toward him with the needle, and the corpsman stuck Jenkins in the leg instead of Felipe.

"Sorry." Sanders pulled the needle out of the agent's leg and wiped it clean with an alcohol swab.

Jenkins put Felipe in an arm lock while Sanders stuck the hapless prisoner with the needle again.

"Argle?" A tear ran down Felipe's cheek, accompanying his plaintive, albeit inarticulate, speech.

"Done with this one." Sanders put the vial containing Felipe's blood in the rack on the tray. "Oh crap, I left the labels back in the treatment room."

"Want me to get them for you?"

Sanders grinned. "What, and have you miss the fun with our next patient? He did a real number on Nuance's backside. Not sure I want to tackle that dog without help."

"Well, it was worth a try."

Sanders waited outside the dog's room until Jenkins and another agent had entered and subdued the hound. When they were ready, he joined them inside the windowless, gray box.

"Which end do you need to work on?" Jenkins had won a coin toss and took the tail end of the dog in order to be as far from the beast's jaws as possible.

"Your end. I'll take the sample from his rear leg."

Sanders used an electric beard trimmer to shave off the hair above the knee joint of Chaucer's back leg. Then he gave it a quick squirt of alcohol to sterilize the area.

"You guys are doing a great job. Now comes the tricky part. Some animals go limp when the needle goes in, others go wild. Make sure you have a good hold on him while we do this."

"We?" Jenkins looked at Sanders with raised eyebrows.

"Yes, 'we.' I need you to put your hand under the knee joint so that he can't pull his leg back. Yes, that's right, just like that. Now then, put your thumb here, right over the vein, and squeeze down. Perfect. See how it's bulging up? Makes it easier for me to work."

Sanders slid the needle in quickly, popped a test tube onto the syringe, and was done drawing the blood sample in a moment. Chaucer didn't even twitch during the process, and lay still as the men relaxed their holds.

"Whew, glad that's done!" The words were barely out of Jenkin's mouth when Chaucer twisted and heaved, knocking all three men down. The sample tray went flying, and Sanders watched in amazement as Jenkins, who was notoriously clumsy, rolled across the floor and caught it mid-air.

"Nice reflexes!" Sanders said.

"Looks like your samples came out of the rack. Which way do they go?"

"I put the man's vial on the left. Put the dog's on the right."

Sanders watched closely while the agent did as instructed. Picking up the tray, he then returned to the team's makeshift clinic. The courier who was supposed to collect the samples hadn't arrived yet, so Sanders slumped into the room's sole chair.

The room was small, and like most of the other offices at Northwood, the floor and walls were a faded, industrial gray. There were no windows. The air was warm and stale from the baseboard heaters, and a couple of fluorescent ceiling fixtures bathed the room in sterile, blue-white light. Sanders blinked against the harsh illumination.

A gurney was pushed up against one wall, and a credenza by the back wall was covered with a jumble of medical supplies and boxes that had spilled over onto the floor.

Scooting his chair over to the credenza, Sanders cleared a small space for his sample tray and then prepared labels for the test tubes.

Wait a minute.

Sanders frowned, rubbed the grit out of his eyes and leaned forward to examine the tubes. *I told the agent to put the man's vial on the left. But did he use his left or mine? Crap! What if he switched them?*

For several minutes, he stared at the samples. *Well, I think I got more blood from the man than from the dog. Yeah, that makes sense. The tube with more blood in it has to be the man's sample.*

Affixing the labels to the tubes, Sanders packed them for shipment, then sat back and closed his eyes. The rap of the courier's knuckles on the door jolted him awake.

"Got a package for me?" a man asked from the doorway.

"Yeah, it's right here, ready to go."

Sanders handed the courier the package of samples, then signed the courier's log to document the transfer of evidence.

As soon as the man had left, Sanders sent a text to Nuance to let him know that the job was done.

15

Jake dragged his feet all the way home from work, so lost in his thoughts that he didn't notice the cool morning breeze off the lake ruffling his hair or the lemon-drop fragrance of early-blooming magnolias along the sidewalk. *What a night! I can't wait to get home and get some rest. At least it should be quiet for sleeping. Nice thing about living in a town like this. Nothing ever happens, though it might be nice if it did once in a while. Man! I'm too tired to even get some chow.*

It had been one of those nights when it seemed like every time he had been ready to leave work, his boss had found something else for him to do. Jake thought it was odd that the man had also stayed late, but the amount of work he wanted done explained the change in behavior. Jake was still in a fog when he shambled through his front door.

"Crap." Jake stopped and looked around. Books and magazines littered the floor along with several video game cartridges and DVDs that had spilled from an overturned box. The smell of stale pizza mixed with a sharp, peppery scent that he couldn't place. It stung his nose and made his eyes water. "Felipe, you slob, why do you always leave the place in such a mess?"

Jake set down his laptop bag, draped his dark gray hoodie over it, and then stooped to examine the mess on the floor. *That pizza's never coming out of the carpet.* With a sigh, he turned the coffee table right-side up and began straightening the room.

When he was done, he did a quick walk through the house looking for Chaucer. *Must still be at Daphne's. Otherwise, he'd have scarfed up the pizza the minute it hit the floor.*

Jake trotted over to his sister's house and knocked on the door. There was no answer, so he let himself in. *Must be at work. Daphne's probably at school.*

The door to Daphne's room was closed. Jake tapped on it with his fingernails. When there was no response, he cracked the door open and saw Daphne nose down in her bed, her pillowcase fluttering with each breath. There was no sign of Chaucer, so he eased the door shut and checked the rest of the house. He found Chaucer next to a water bowl and food tray in the laundry room with the door closed. It wasn't the first time he'd found his dog locked up and Jake wondered what the hound had done this time to earn a time out.

Chaucer jumped up and put his paws on Jake's chest as soon as Jake opened the door. Then, with a loud woof, he rushed from the room. Before he followed Chaucer out, Jake took a moment to jot a quick note to Daphne thanking her for watching the dog.

As soon as they were back in Jake's house, Chaucer raced from room-to-room, snarling as he poked his nose into every nook.

"What's got into you, boy?" Jake rubbed the dog's shoulder and chest to quiet him down.

Chaucer whined and looked around as if he was trying to communicate something important.

"I don't know what it is, boy, but it'll have to keep. I'm bushed and need to crash."

As he headed for his bedroom, Jake noticed Chaucer take up a position by the front door as if he was guarding it, but he was too tired to do more than shake his head over the dog's strange behavior.

It felt as though his head had just touched the pillow on his narrow bed when Jake woke to the chime of an incoming call on his cell phone. It was still morning, and the blackout shades on his windows were outlined with bright lines of sunlight. *Crap. Now what?*

"Hello?"

"Jake! We need to talk about your dog!"

"Oh, hi, Sarah. What's up?" It was his sister, and given Chaucer's status when he'd returned home, the call was not unexpected.

"Jake, Chaucer got out last night, and Daphne spent half the night looking for him."

"I'm sorry, I'll—"

"Sorry?! Jake, the sheriff brought her home. The sheriff! It was four a.m., and Daphne looked as if she'd been through a war zone. I had to give her a bath before I put her to bed, and she was so tired she was mumbling nonsense about spies and such. I had to call in to school and say she was sick. She was in no shape for class."

"Sarah, I'm really sorry Daphne—"

"Sorry? Jake, this has to stop. If you can't make that dog behave better, I won't let Daphne watch it for you while you're at work. Is that clear?"

"Yes, Sarah, and I'm sorry—"

"Sorry won't cut it. Jake, we moved closer to you so that you could help with Daphne while her dad's on deployment in the Middle East. Trying to hold down a job while raising a kid isn't easy. Daphne's a sweet kid, but sometimes it's all overwhelming. I need you to step up, Jake, not to cause more problems for me to deal with. Please, will you promise to work with Chaucer?"

"Yes, Sarah."

"Good. Now, I've got to get back to work before my boss catches me making a personal call. Daphne's at home, but I want you to keep Chaucer at your place today. She needs to get some rest. Okay?"

"Okay."

"Fine. Bye."

"Goodb—" Jake's sister hung up on him before he could finish.

As he set his phone down, he noticed Chaucer staring at him from the bedroom doorway.

"What?"

Chaucer chuffed in reply.

"Oh Jeez, Chaucer. Can't it wait just a bit?"

Chaucer whined, his front paws dancing a bit as he did so.

"All right, I'll take you out."

Chaucer barked and ran to wait by the front door with his tail wagging.

Jake got up and tried to put on a pair of jeans, only to find that he was still wearing the pants he'd had on when he came home from work.

"Well, that's not gonna work," he muttered, tossing the jeans aside. He rubbed his face hard, then headed out the back door.

"This way, boy," he called.

Chaucer raced across the house to catch up with Jake, knocking him to the ground as they both tried to exit the back door at the same time.

"Hey! Dammit, Chaucer, you behave!"

Chaucer ignored Jake and bolted around the house. Moments later he was back, running at full speed past Jake as he looped around the property again. The dog didn't stop until he'd made three circuits around the house. Then, he trotted over to the large oak in the middle of the yard and gave it a thorough watering.

"Are you done?" Jake sat down on the small wooden porch and rubbed his elbow where it had hit the ground. "Cause I'm gonna ground you if this behavior doesn't stop."

Chaucer stared at him, head tilted to the side as if he was giving serious consideration to the issue.

"Can we go in now?"

Chaucer wagged his tail and trotted up to the back door.

"Good, I need to get back to bed."

Less than half an hour later a telemarketer called, somehow bypassing the "do not call" setting on his cell. A short while after that, the rip of a chain saw jerked him back awake.

Peeking around the window shade, Jake saw his backyard neighbor hacking through the hard wood of an ash tree. Jake buried his head under his pillow and then pulled the blankets up over that, trying to keep the noise out.

At lunchtime, Jake got up to let Chaucer out into the back yard. While the dog went about his business, Jake got a couple of slices of white bread from the cupboard and some bologna from the ancient white fridge. Popping a Coke, he sat down at the round, Formica kitchen table. Sunlight lit the butter-yellow walls and weathered oak floors with a cheerful glow that didn't match Jake's state of mind.

He'd just let Chaucer back in when his phone chimed again. It was another telemarketer. Frustrated, he turned his cell off, then put it in the fridge for good measure. *Maybe now I can get some shut-eye. Not like I'm gonna miss any important calls, unless Sarah wants to rail on me again.*

16

Claire jerked awake at a loud knock on her door.

She was surprised to see that it was daytime. The clock radio on her kitchen counter showed eleven a.m. When had she fallen asleep? And on her couch? She rubbed the grit out of her eyes. The hairs lifted on her arms as she remembered how she'd felt the night before when she realized her apartment had been searched.

The knock came again.

Who is that? And how did they get into the building without being buzzed in?

Claire stood. She frowned when she saw the dried blood on her ivory blouse. *That's not coming out.*

She checked the deadbolt was in place. Through the door's peephole, she saw a tall man in a military uniform. Other than some scratches on his face, he looked ready for the parade ground. His khaki uniform had razor-sharp creases, and his black Oxford shoes glowed. Otherwise, the hallway was empty. She recognized Nuance, felt her pulse pick up when she did. *What's he want?* She was suddenly aware of the texture of the door, had never noticed the striations of color in the oak veneer.

"Who's there?" Claire bit her lip as she played for time.

"Commander Nuance. May I come in?"

"Why?"

"I need to speak with you."

"Can't you tell me from there?"

"Do you want your neighbors to know that you're in trouble?"

"No, no, of course not."

"Then shouting through the door doesn't seem like a good idea."

Claire's fingers trembled as she unlocked the door. "I thought you were sending one of your agents to babysit me today." She stopped the door with her shoulder when it was part-way open, ready to push it shut again.

"My men had a long night of it, so I gave them the day off to rest. Besides, I thought it would give me a chance to make up for yesterday. I didn't mean for you to miss lunch and dinner. That's not how we operate. But there was a mix-up with the assignments, and it was overlooked. I'm sorry about that. So I thought I'd take today's assignment as an opportunity to make amends by taking you to lunch."

"That's nice of you, commander." *But what do you really want?*

"Where would you like to go?"

"I brown-bag it most of the time, so there's no place in particular that I can think of."

"Oh, well, I just got here a couple of days ago and haven't had time to check out any of the local diners, so I don't have a clue myself."

Claire sighed. "Well, I've got yogurt and apples in the fridge, if you'd care to join me."

"Best offer I've had today!" Nuance pushed past her.

"Make yourself at home," Claire said with a hint of sarcasm. She caught a strong smell of disinfectant mixed with something peppery as he walked past, and then she noticed her own aroma. *OMG, I slept in my clothes and smell like a gym sock!*

Nuance settled onto a bar stool at her kitchen counter with a groan.

"Hurt yourself?" Claire asked hopefully, gesturing toward a lump in the back of Nuance's slacks that she suspected was too big to be a wallet, at least for a serviceman.

"You could say that."

"How'd it happen?"

"Not important."

Claire stepped behind the kitchen counter to set out lunch. She found its physical bulk comforting, as if she had put up a shield between herself and Nuance. The stainless steel pans hanging from the ceiling rack over the counter contributed to the sense of fortification, even though she knew it was a false sense of security, no better than a child's snow fort. The glow from a fluorescent cloud light on the ceiling reflected off the almond countertop and the stainless steel appliances with a cool, diffuse light.

Claire hoped that Nuance didn't notice the tattered pictures of her brother and sister pinned to the door of her fridge. A calendar from the Sierra Club was its only other decoration. She fished two tubs of plain Greek yogurt out and wedged them on the counter next to her aloe plant. It had outgrown its green-and-white ceramic pot and was threatening to take over the entire countertop.

She thought about Nuance bypassing her apartment building's security system, and her hands twitched. She dropped the silverware onto the floor, where it rattled like alarm bells. Taking a breath, she tried to calm herself as she took out clean spoons. Sharing a meal with him was like...*like having lunch with my father. And I couldn't even get that right.*

She felt his eyes on her as she slid a paring knife out of its wooden storage block.

"You okay?" Nuance raised an eyebrow.

"Yeah, just an old memory. Nothing you'd be interested in."

"You'd be surprised. I have an interest in everything about you right now."

"Oh, yeah? Well, you're the first man I've had say that in my apartment."

"I didn't mean it that way."

"I know. Just trying to lighten things up a bit." *And to change the subject. Having you pry into my life is creepy. There's things you don't need to know. That nobody needs to know.*

"I see. So, have you heard from Jake Andersen yet?" Nuance didn't alter his expression, and his tone remained innocent.

"No, and I wouldn't expect to for some time. Most authors understand that when they submit a manuscript to an agency, it's a case of 'don't call us, we'll call you.'"

"I see." He glanced down. A corner of his mouth twitched like he was suppressing a smile. *He's up to something!*

Claire set a couple of Granny Smith apples on the counter, the green of the apples a stark contrast to the almond-colored countertop. "Need your apple sliced?"

"No, thanks."

Claire sliced her own apple, pausing halfway through as she tried to work out what was going on. Glancing up, she caught Nuance staring at the blade, which was pointed right at his heart. Her mouth dry, she laid the knife down and popped a slice of apple into her mouth.

"Good choice." Nuance put his hands back on the counter. Claire hadn't noticed them disappear.

She bit down on the apple slice, and the tart juice hit her tongue like a shot of adrenaline.

"Ms. Miller, have you given any thought to your discussion with the admiral yesterday?"

"No, when I got home I was too tired to think about anything. None of this makes any sense to me. I have no idea what you want from me, or why."

"That's what I thought. You seemed pretty dazed when I dropped you off last night. To recap, we're investigating a security breach at Northwood, and Mr. Andersen is a person of interest in the case. You're in a unique position to help us because of your professional contact with him."

"But I thought I wasn't supposed to contact him without permission? Besides, I don't even know him!" Claire set down the slice of apple she'd been about to eat.

"That's something that needs to change. I want you to contact Andersen and find out everything you can about him."

"How?" Claire felt her stomach flip. She had a bad feeling about the direction the conversation was moving in.

"Ask him to lunch, flirt with him, do whatever it takes to get him to open up. Then find out where he got the information contained in the manuscript. Did he have any help? If so, from who."

"What? You want me to do all of your snooping for you? What if he's dangerous?"

"Based on his personnel file from Northwood, he doesn't seem like the dangerous type. You won't be in any real danger."

"But your admiral said that somebody tried to kill Commander Solomon!"

"Yes, but we don't think it was Andersen."

"But the other guy—"

"Is no concern of yours. He's been dealt with. What we need now is information. Will you assist us? Or do I call the admiral and let him know that the file on your siblings won't be needed?" Nuance held her in his gray-eyed gaze like a snake watching for its venom to take effect, his face absent any trace of pity.

"So that's how it is," Claire said in a quiet voice, one hand on her throat.

"Yes, that's how it is."

"Look, I want to help as much as anybody, but I won't...I won't be your whore. Even if it means going to jail."

"Would you do it for a chance to see your brother and sister again?"

Claire stared at Nuance, her hands clenched on the edge of the counter as her knees buckled. "You, you're a ..."

"Bastard is the word you're looking for, right?"

Claire sighed, fighting back tears. "When do you want me to do it?"

"Tomorrow. Arrange lunch with Andersen or something like that. Find some pretext for discussing the manuscript. That should draw him out. And be nice to him. You're not bad looking, and he's shy. Use that."

Claire looked down at her yogurt. The pure white cream mocked how foul she felt inside, as if some obscene oil had been splashed over her soul. She fingered her broach but found no comfort there. *I'm such a loser.*

"You're doing the right thing, Ms. Miller," Nuance said softly.

"It doesn't feel that way."

Nuance stood, his food untouched. "If you'll excuse me, I need to head back to the office now."

Got what you wanted, eh? Claire followed him to the door, her arms folded over her stomach, fighting a growing sense of nausea.

Nuance paused in the doorway. "By the way, I had a chat with your boss this morning. He won't be expecting you back for a couple of days."

"What? But my work...my clients!"

"Someone from my team will bring your computer and files over this afternoon. It will be easier for us to monitor your progress if you work from home."

"And if I need to meet with a client?"

"Do so. We'll stay in the background and shouldn't be noticed. But make sure that Andersen is your main focus. I want you to start on him as soon as I leave. Try not to waste valuable time on other people."

Nuance closed the door behind him as he left.

With her back pressed to the door, Claire slid to the floor and put her face in her hands. As a feeling of helplessness washed over her, she began to cry.

17

After Nuance left her apartment, Claire sat for an unknown time at the kitchen counter watching her half-eaten apple turn brown. She dabbed a spoon into her tub of yogurt a couple of times, but never raised it to her lips. Loneliness pressed in on her as she ran her thumb over her broach. *I wish I had somebody I could talk to about this. I wish Mom was still here. She'd know what to do.* The chime of her doorbell pulled her from her reverie, but she was still unfocused when she pressed the intercom button.

"Miss Miller?"

Claire didn't recognize the woman's voice, so she hesitated before replying, "Yes?"

"We have a delivery for you."

"A delivery? I don't think I ordered anything. Perhaps there's been a mistake?"

"Oh no, there's no mistake. We have a special delivery of some office equipment for you. There's a laptop, a printer, a Rolodex, and a number of other items, including a pair of white sneakers. In size eight. There's also a lot of paper, looks like manuscripts of some sort."

Claire's eyes widened as she realized that she was speaking with one of Nuance's agents. Her last shred of hope that it was all a terrible dream faded as she buzzed the agent in.

Besides the woman who spoke over the intercom, Nuance had sent three men to transplant Claire's office to her apartment. She was surprised to see that they were all dressed in dark brown khaki shorts and shirts with matching caps, and looked just like UPS drivers. The effect was spoiled a bit by a pistol that the woman supervising the operation had strapped in a holster under her armpit.

Lacking a desk, Claire had the agents set up the PC and printer on her kitchen counter. They put everything else on the floor next to her coffee table, except for a large manila folder. That they placed on the center of the table with military precision. The folder was unmarked, but Claire was not surprised to find it contained a copy of Jake's manuscript as well as the few scraps of paper she had related to it. A yellow Post-it Note stuck inside the folder had Jake's name, address, and phone number written on it in large capital letters. The phone number was underlined.

The agents finished in minutes and then left without speaking, except for the woman leading the team. She paused on the way out, looked at Claire, and said, "You know what to do. I suggest you get busy." Then she also left.

Claire sat on her couch and picked up her cell. As soon as she logged on a reminder appeared, prompting her to call Jake. His number was displayed in large characters.

She dropped the phone, jerking her hand away as if it was a toad with a full bladder.

"Think of everything, don't you?" she muttered.

Claire tried to think of what to say, how best to approach a conversation with Jake without giving him false hope regarding the publication of his book. *"Hi, I'm Claire from the Masters Agency. I'd like to meet with you to talk about your book. It sucks, but your work as a spy has generated a lot of interest."*

No, that's not going to fly. How about, "Hi, I'm Claire. Let's do lunch and talk about your book and why the government wants to lock you away forever."

That approach didn't appeal to her either. *Maybe I should just wing it. Introduce myself and then see where it leads.*

Claire picked up her phone and dialed Jake's number before she had time to change her mind.

The phone rang once and then went right to voicemail. "This is Jake, you know what to do."

Claire floundered for a moment. She had mentally prepared a greeting but was unprepared for leaving a full message.

"Uh, hi. Um, this is Claire. I'm calling about your manuscript. You know, the one you sent to me? I'm with the Masters Literary Agency. Could you, well, when you get this message, maybe give me a call? Thanks!"

A moment after Claire hung up, her phone dinged. Before Claire had a chance to respond, a woman with a soft southern accent said, "Miss Miller, you forgot to leave your phone number for Mr. Andersen."

"Who is this?" Claire remembered Nuance saying something about monitoring her calls, but this was over the top.

"That's unimportant, ma'am. Now, I believe that the commander gave you clear instructions on how to proceed. Would you like a quick refresher on what you're supposed to do?"

"The commander? Nuance?"

"Yes, ma'am."

"Oh. Well, I thought I was supposed to call Jake."

"And?"

"Maybe have lunch with him?"

"There's no 'maybe' about it, sweetheart. You're to set up a meeting and do whatever it takes to gain his confidence. Flirt, giggle, show some skin—hell, sleep with the man if you have to, but you need to do more than just leave a voicemail saying 'hi.' Am I clear?"

"Yes, I get it."

"Very good. Now try again."

The line went dead, but before Claire could put the phone down, it dialed Jake's number without her having clicked on the contact. Stunned, Claire stared at her phone, unable to move. When the call went through to voicemail, she was unable to speak and hung up in a panic. The phone autodialed Jake again.

How are they doing that? After the third autodial, Claire gathered her wits and tried to leave a coherent message for Jake. She remembered to give him her phone number and also mentioned getting together for coffee. It was the best she could do, and she felt a wash of relief when the autodialing stopped.

After briefly looking through the things that Nuance's people had brought over from her office, Claire decided to shower and change into fresh clothes.

The water was refreshing, and she turned the temperature up to scalding hot. She lathered herself in lavender bath gel and then stood under the spray for several minutes, baptizing herself in the scent.

While Claire dried her hair in front of the mirror, she wondered how she could feel clean on the outside yet so dirty on the inside. *I can't do this. I won't! They can't make me.* Then she sighed. *Reality? I'm such a loser, they can make me do anything they want. I'll just roll over and take it, like I always have.*

After dressing, Claire brewed some green tea in her favorite mug and settled on her couch with the box of papers that had been left by Nuance's team.

As she emptied the box onto the coffee table, she discovered that the papers had been collated and bound together with black binder clips. And they were in alphabetical order. *We should offer these people a job at the office. We might finally get organized.* Picking through the bundle, she pulled out the manuscript from Bob Fredrick, an environmental author she'd been working with.

After skimming through her notes, she gave him a call. He picked up right away.

"Hi, Bob? It's Claire."

"Hi, Claire. I'm glad to hear from you—I was worried something might have happened when you didn't show up for our meeting yesterday."

"I'm sorry, Bob. It's totally my fault. I decided to work from home for a few days and forgot that the reminder for our meeting was on my office PC, not my cell. By the time I got set up in my apartment and saw it, it was too late."

"I understand, but why didn't you call? Are you sure nothing's wrong?"

Claire frowned at his suspicious tone of voice.

"Bob, I'm sorry, I meant to, but my boss Skyped me just as I was about to dial. Have you ever had to listen in to a three-hour status meeting? I missed supper, and I didn't want to call afterward and disturb your evening. I'm sorry, I really am." *And I'm going to burn in hell for lying to you.*

"That's okay. Are you still interested in my project? They aren't canceling my book about the environmental threats facing the Menominee River, are they?"

"Oh, no, don't worry about that. Your book is at the top of my list. That's why I'm calling—to try and set up another meeting with you so we can go over some of the details you want to add to the manuscript. If that's okay with you?"

"Oh, well, of course it is! I'm free tomorrow morning, if that works for you?"

"Yes, that should be fine. Oh, and Bob?"

"Yes?"

"There is one other thing."

"What's that?"

Claire closed her eyes, pinching the bridge of her nose as suspicion returned to his voice. *Time to sell my soul. Like anybody would buy it. Futz.*

"I'd like to bring a photographer along. One of my colleagues is working with a guy doing a photo spread for one of those coffee-table books on the national parks. Unfortunately, they got their wires crossed and he showed up this week instead of next, so he's kind of at odd ends and not happy about it. If we can throw something worthwhile at him, it'll work for everybody. You get some pro shots of the river, and we entertain a client. What do you say?"

"Well, I guess. You're sure he's legit, right? 'Cause three years ago I was on a Greenpeace boat working on a whale rescue mission and the Feds tried to sneak an agent aboard. Things got pretty ugly."

"You don't have to worry about that, Bob. I wouldn't even know what a Fed looks like." *Except that they have a gaze like a snake and a soul to match. No, I've no idea what federal agents look like.*

"I'll take your word for that, Claire. We've been working on this project together for months now, and I know I can trust you."

"Thanks, Bob, that means a lot coming from you." *I just wish it was true.*

"So, can you meet me at Rubys Corner at around seven tomorrow morning as we'd originally planned?"

"Absolutely. It's a date."

"Super! See you then."

Claire's phone dinged as soon as she hung up. She felt her stomach lurch like she was on a roller coaster when the female agent who had called earlier spoke.

"Miss Miller, your appointment tomorrow morning is a concern. You need to be available to meet with Andersen at the first opportunity. Do I need to remind you that time is critical?"

"No, that won't be necessary. But Jake isn't answering his phone. If he does call me back—"

"Don't wait for him to call, Miss Miller. Show some initiative."

"Okay. But if I leave a dozen messages on his voicemail, well, won't he get suspicious?"

"That's a valid point. But it doesn't let you off the hook."

"I understand. If necessary, I can reschedule my meeting with Fredrick. Otherwise, is there any reason to put it off? I thought I could still work my regular job."

"No, you don't have to sidetrack everything. Just keep focused on your priorities. Clear?"

"Yes."

The woman on the other end hung up without saying goodbye.

Claire's hand shook as she set her cell down on the coffee table. She hugged a throw pillow to her chest and buried her face in it.

18

Late afternoon found Nuance catching up on his paperwork in the office provided to him by Northwood. Like Dutchman's, it had oak wainscoting, eggshell walls, and a floor that was the same color as the hulls of the destroyers that Northwood built.

One of the milder curse words in Nuance's vocabulary slipped out as he read a recently arrived email. It contained the preliminary results of Felipe's DNA test, and they spelled trouble with a capital T. As he read it, he realized that he'd been hoping for something else, that his alien spy theory would be proven wrong. *Dutchman's going to go off his chain when he sees this.*

After forwarding the email to his boss, Nuance sat back in his chair and thought about the implications of what it contained. Not even the flickering of the overhead fluorescent light in the office was enough to distract him.

There was a well-established approach to neutralizing a conventional spy ring, and he had more than enough people on site to handle such a situation. But aliens? There were no protocols for that, and everything he did would be viewed under a microscope for decades to come. And with Dutchman in command...*the man lacks subtlety. And patience. Great in a head-to-head conflict, but he's not cut out for this kind of mission.*

"God help us," Nuance muttered, rubbing his face with his hands.

He closed the laptop and made his way to Dutchman's office, which was located right next to his own. Other than an executive-grade swivel chair that the admiral had finagled for himself, the rooms were identical.

After a perfunctory knock on the door, Nuance entered the office, taking a seat while Dutchman finished reading his email.

"Commander, this is excellent news, although I must admit, it's still just a little hard to believe. We have a genuine alien on our hands, with DNA evidence to prove it! Do you know what this means?"

"I think so, sir. There's likely a starship parked somewhere overhead with technology so advanced that our best weapons will look like bows and arrows to them. They might not take it well if we do something dire to their people, even if they are spies."

"Not at all! If they were really that far ahead of us, they wouldn't need to use spies, they'd just drop troops and take over. No, what I'm talking about is opportunity. For you, and for me."

"Sir?" Nuance shifted in his chair. *When did getting a promotion become more important than protecting our country?*

"Listen, commander, this is the opportunity of a lifetime. The president herself will want in on it, and I'll be the person that she calls for information. Of course, I'll bring you along with me. You'll play a key role helping me apprehend the spies, and when I make it to the Joint Chiefs of Staff, I'll make sure that you're suitably rewarded. Hell! Handle this right and my— er, our names will be in the history books."

"Sir, we haven't actually cracked the spy ring yet. We just have the one person in custody."

"And that's a problem. If we sit on this much longer, the Pentagon will swoop in and we'll be sidelined. I estimate that we've got less than a week before that happens. You need to act fast. What progress have you made so far?"

"The evidence obtained from Andersen's house has been analyzed, but we found no trace of espionage activity, sir."

"What about the alien you have in custody?"

"Still haven't managed to get anything intelligible from him, sir."

"Well, what have you done? Don't tell me that you just went home for a long nap after raiding Andersen's place?"

"No, sir. I met with the Miller woman earlier today." *And the poor girl hasn't got a clue what's going on.*

"And? How did it go?"

"As planned, sir. She'll make contact with Andersen tomorrow."

"Willingly?"

"Not at all."

"Excellent."

"Sir?"

"You have a concern, commander?"

Nuance took a moment to choose his words, being careful to hide his thoughts from his face. "Yes, sir. She's fragile and likely to break."

"All the better. It will be more convincing when she betrays you to Andersen. When he realizes that you're investigating him, he'll panic. Do your agents know what to do when that happens?"

"Yes, sir. After we bring him in, we'll put him in a room with the other suspect. Then we'll give them a chance to escape. When they do, my men will wound one and let the other get away so we can follow him back to their base of operations."

"And you're still certain that there are more spies? Why wouldn't the aliens send just one operative?"

"Sir, experience in many theatres of operations has shown that the most effective way to infiltrate an organization is with a three-person cell. One does the dirty work, while another acts as a communication mule for the cell leader. If the active spy gets caught, then the cell leader terminates the intermediary, thereby preventing anybody from finding out who was behind the operation. If our aliens are more advanced than we are, then they'll have learned the same thing.

"Plus, there's the attempt on Solomon's life to consider as well as the effort someone put in to retrieving the manuscript. Clear indications that somebody is trying to seal the operation before we can catch those involved."

Dutchman leaned back in his chair and rubbed his temples. "I just got off the line with the Pentagon. If it wasn't for the DNA, we'd both be counting seal pups in the coldest Arctic station the Navy possesses. If we let the aliens slip through our fingers..."

"That won't happen, sir. Was there any difficulty with the other arrangements?" Nuance leaned forward, unable to hide his interest.

"Not at all, commander. The General Staff have a laser focus on this situation and they have made the full resources of our military available. Once you pinpoint the alien base, a squadron of fighter jets will seal the airspace above it while our marines storm their compound. An extra brigade of heavy infantry will be here by morning to reinforce your team for the assault."

"Thank you, sir."

"That will be all then, commander."

"Yes, sir." Nuance hesitated, gathered his courage, and then asked, "Sir? There's one more thing I need to clarify."

"And that is?"

"The status of the Miller woman and the child when all this is over."

"I thought that I had been clear on that subject."

"Yes, sir, you were. But she's not an alien or a spy, nor is the child. Your orders...well, they're American citizens." *And we're sworn to protect them, aren't we?*

"The FISC in D.C. has issued a federal warrant authorizing our action."

"So, the paperwork came through?"

"No, but I have a verbal on that. You can proceed."

Nuance stared at his superior. *He still hasn't gotten the warrants. We're acting without authorization, and it's my neck in the noose if we get caught. Damn!* "I see, sir. But surely there's an alternative to what you have planned?"

"Commander, you know what's at stake as well as I do. It's not enough to plug the leak. It has to be closed. Permanently.

"The child's story can be dismissed as just that, and a disinformation team will be set up to handle that task. It'll help that she's a service brat. Those kids are always outsiders. Moving to a new home every time their parent is reassigned, they never have time to make friends. It should be easy to paint her as a kook, maybe even delusional, and get her ostracized. After that, no one will ever believe a word she says."

"Sir, that's—"

"Necessary."

Like hell it is! Nuance struggled to remain expressionless, clamping his teeth together so that he wouldn't speak out loud.

Dutchman continued, "The woman is the real problem. The only way to make sure that she doesn't talk is to lock her up with the spies. I don't like it any more than you do, but we've got no choice in the matter. Will you have a problem carrying out that order?"

"No, sir. I know my duty." *But I wonder if that's the same thing as what you're asking me to do.*

"Very good. You have your orders, I suggest you get busy."

"Yes, sir."

19

When Jake left the Northwood office building on Friday morning, the sunrise reflecting off the lake made him squint. The light was so bright that it washed all the color from the sky. There was a faint smell of diesel and car exhaust from the morning traffic, along with a vibration in the sidewalk every time a loaded semi-truck grumbled past.

Most of this was lost on Jake as he walked, his body on autopilot while his mind churned. He hadn't seen Felipe for two days and he was worried. When he got home, Felipe was still missing. The last time he had seen his friend was Wednesday morning, when Felipe was heading out for work as Jake returned home.

They usually spent their evenings gaming in the living room, but Felipe hadn't shown on Wednesday evening, or on Thursday evening either. Even more concerning, Felipe hadn't responded to any texts or emails. Jake had even resorted to an actual phone call, but there had been no answer.

After dropping his backpack by the front door, Jake checked every room in the house. The living room was the same as he'd left it the night before; the game controller was untouched, and the TV was still on the same channel he'd been watching before turning it off.

The white sink and shower stall in the bathroom were dry, and there was no sign that anybody had showered or brushed their teeth in there for days beside Jake himself.

Felipe's bedroom was in the same state of disorder as it had been since last Tuesday.

There were even leftover enchiladas in the fridge from Monday night, something that Felipe would have scavenged long since.

Jake flipped through a stack of mail on the corner of the kitchen table. None of the letters addressed to Felipe had been touched, including a letter from his sister. *Something's wrong.*

While trying to decide what to do, Jake fetched Chaucer from Daphne's house. When he did, he was glad to see that things were back to normal there; Daphne had gone to school, and Chaucer was waiting for Jake by the front door.

Returning home, Jake emptied his backpack on the kitchen table and booted his laptop. While it was starting up, he ate a quick breakfast of Fruit Loops and orange juice.

Pulling the laptop close, he opened up a secure connection to the Northwood network and logged in. A quick check of the system access logs showed that Felipe had not logged onto the system after leaving work on Tuesday. Jake paused for a moment; what he had in mind could get him fired, but he needed to know if Felipe was okay. Using his root access as a system administrator, he opened a back door to the Northwood email server. It only took him a few minutes to verify that Felipe had not sent or received any emails since Tuesday either. *In for a dime, in for a dollar. If I get caught doing this, I'll lose more than just my job.* Jake scanned the emails for Northwood's Human Resources department, and then for the company's management team. There was no mention of Felipe or of Felipe's absence from the company. Everything looked normal.

Jake logged off, then got up and began to pace around the house. Chaucer followed him, helpfully knocking over any stacks of books and CDs that might get in the way.

After a few minutes, Jake started sending texts to the various gamers that he and Felipe had met online. He heard back from all of them within the hour. Nobody had heard from Felipe, and nobody had seen his avatar active on any of the online game sites. *Something's happened to him. I hope he's not in the hospital, or something.*

Jake returned to the kitchen, popped open a Coke, and stared at his cell phone. *I need to call the cops. But first...*

Jake went into Felipe's room and rummaged through all the places where his friend typically hid his stash. There wasn't much there, just a baggie on the floor with a few crumbs of hash brownie left in it, an empty bourbon bottle, and a few stubs of marijuana joints.

He rinsed out the bourbon bottle and put it in the recycling, then he flushed the rest of the items down the toilet, followed by a hefty dose of bowl cleaner. *That should do it.*

Then Jake called the emergency number for law enforcement.

"9-1-1, what's your emergency?" The voice of the woman who answered was calm, mature, and professional.

"Hi, uh, my name's Jake Andersen, and I want to report a missing person."

"When did this happen?"

"Wednesday morning."

"And who is missing?"

"My roommate, Felipe Oliveira."

"Did you see what happened? Was he kidnapped, or taken by force?"

"No. I don't know."

"Do you know of any reason why he might disappear on his own? Does he often go off by himself?"

"No, he only leaves the house to go to work or to pick up groceries and beer. He's never disappeared like this before."

"Did he leave a note or any indication of where he might have gone?"

"No. He's just gone."

"And what is your relationship with Felipe?"

Jake frowned, puzzled by the question. "Uh, I've known him since high school. We've lived together since then."

"I see. Is it possible that he's left you for another lover?"

"Another what?"

"Lover. Is it possible that he's just dumped you and moved on to somebody else without leaving a note?"

"No! We're not like that!"

"There's no need to get upset, Mr. Andersen. These conversations are confidential. Nobody's going to out you."

"But I'm not gay!"

"Of course not. My husband says the same thing, but we haven't been intimate for years, and he goes bowling with his best friend three times a week. Like I don't know that the bowling alley closed years ago!"

"Ma'am, I really don't need to know this—"

"Oh, it's okay. I've got my own thing going on."

"That's nice. Ma'am, about my friend…"

"Oh, yes. Sorry about that. Your 'friend' has left you." Jake could hear the air quotes around the word friend and ground his teeth in annoyance. "Now, before we get the sheriff involved, I was wondering if you've tried anything to bring him back?"

"Well, I called around and checked with all of our friends. Nobody's seen him."

"Oh, no, that's not what I meant. Have you tried any of those little things that can make a relationship special? I was watching Dr. Phil the other day, and there was a man on there who had just the best advice about how to rekindle your connection with somebody special."

"Ma'am, I don't think—"

"Don't knock it till you've tried it, Mr. Andersen. Light a few candles, put on some soft jazz, and dab a touch of lilac water behind your ears. It can work wonders."

"Ma'am?"

"Yes, Mr. Andersen. Is there anything else?"

"Yes, ma'am. I'd like to speak directly with the sheriff and file a missing person report."

"Well! I suppose, if you don't want my help, then just go right ahead and make a fool of yourself. But you can't make him come back if he doesn't want to. I'm just saying."

"Yes, ma'am. Thank you. Now, the sheriff?"

"Putting you through to the non-emergency number."

"Thanks."

"Have a nice day, Mr. Andersen. I hope you can patch things up with that special someone."

Jake waited on hold for ten minutes before a man from the sheriff's office finally picked up the line.

"Deputy Sweeney. Is this Mr. Andersen?"

"Yes, hi. How did you know who I was?"

"It's in the file that emergency services sent to us regarding to your call."

"Oh, that's pretty efficient."

"Also, I sit right next to Dolores, who took your call. It's a small operation here, you understand. Marinette isn't one of those big-city crime magnets. Just the occasional drunk driver, a cow wandering the streets, or somebody who's lost their keys. Don't get many lovers' spats, at least not between folks like you. Not that there's anything wrong with your personal orientation, mind, I'm as open-minded as the next fellow, and you gotta admit that some of those football players are ripped, but—"

"Officer?" Jake closed his eyes, pinching the bridge of his nose in frustration.

"Oh, yes. What was it you wanted?"

"My roommate has been missing for two days. Nobody's seen him at work, and none of our friends have heard from him. I'm worried that something bad's happened to him."

"Oh, I see. Well, we can check the surrounding hospitals for you, and put up notices. Can you give me a description of— excuse me a moment, I've got another call coming in and need to put you on hold."

Based on the rattling clunk that he heard, Jake concluded that being put on hold involved the deputy setting his handset down on the desk while speaking on another phone. The voices were muffled, so Jake had a hard time making out what was being said, but it seemed that a man was giving directions to the deputy, whose responses consisted of "yes" and "no."

After a minute, the deputy picked up the line again. "Mr. Andersen?"

"I'm here."

"Good, thanks for waiting. Mr. Andersen, can you provide me with a description of your roommate?"

Jake complied, relieved to be making some progress at last.

"Thanks, Mr. Andersen. Now then, we'll get right on this and will make inquiries on your behalf. Be patient. These things often sort themselves out after a few days. Your friend might discover that the grass isn't greener after all, if you know what I mean."

"I'm not sure that I do."

"Well, hang in there. We'll be in touch when we learn something."

After the deputy hung up, Jake looked down at his dog and shook his head. "Chaucer, I've got a bad feeling about this. But I'm stumped. If the cops can't help me, what can I do?"

Chaucer chuffed agreement and laid his head in Jake's lap. Jake sighed. Unlike Chaucer, he did not believe that most of life's problems could be solved by a good scratch behind the ears.

———————

In the Sherriff's office, Sweeny pulled off his headset and swiveled to look at the man sitting next to him.

"Satisfied?"

"Yes, thank you, deputy."

"This better be worth it, commander. Can't say we appreciate acting like a bunch of dumb-ass buffoons, just so you can spin out some cobwebs to fool an alleged spy. If the Sherriff hadn't gotten confirmation direct from your superior, we wouldn't have gone along with it."

Nuance rose and shook the deputy's hand. "I understand, and your cooperation in this matter is greatly appreciated. If he calls again, continue to string him along." Then he left.

Claire rose early on Friday morning to get ready for her meeting with Bob Fredrick.

She skipped her shower; after a day on the river, she expected she'd need to freshen up anyway. A quick check of the weather app on her cell showed clear skies and seasonal temps, so she dressed in jeans, a yellow cotton shirt, and a gray hoodie. She tucked her hair into a blue ball cap, slipped on her sneakers, and headed out.

When she got to her dented, faded-green Civic in the parking lot, she found a man kneeling next to the front tire on the driver's side of the car.

"Hey! What are you doing to my car?" Claire paused, ready to turn and run if the man was a carjacker.

The man looked up at her, then rose. He was tall, blonde, and she would have called him skinny except for a bit of pudge around the middle that fell short of a muffin-top yet still made his flannel shirt droop over his blue jeans. His large nose was matched with feet and hands that looked more like balloons on matchsticks than real human appendages.

"Good morning, Miss Miller. I'm Agent Jenkins." The man flashed a badge and smiled, showing a line of teeth in such disarray that Claire wondered if he had ever visited a dentist. "I believe Commander Nuance told you that I'd be joining you on your little excursion today."

"How do I know you're legit? You're not in uniform. And what were you doing to my car?"

"Of course I'm not in uniform. What did you expect? Kinda hard to go undercover in dress khakis." Hefting two large, black, camera bags, he said, "Mind if we stow these?"

"After you tell me what you were up to."

"Oh, well, a couple of your tires looked low. I got some Fix-a-flat out of my pickup and figured I'd patch them up before we go. The other three are done, I was just about to get the last one in front."

"Is that it, in the can?"

"Yep. This stuff's cool! You fasten this end of the tube from the can to your tire, then pull this tab—"

Pfffbt!

Claire stared, aghast, as Jenkins accidentally released the entire contents of the can, spraying brown, sticky goo across the hood and windshield of her car.

"What the heck do you think you're doing?!"

"Oops, sorry about that. These things can be a little tricky. Don't worry, it'll wash right off."

"I don't have time to wash my car. I need to be in Rubys Corner to meet with Bob Fredrick in half an hour."

"No problem, I'll wipe it off. Just take a minute."

Jenkins scrubbed the windshield for several minutes using an oily rag he produced from the floor of his pickup, but only managed to make the mess worse.

"Well, the windshield wipers should take care of the rest."

Claire shook her head, then unlocked the car, opening the trunk for Jenkins to stow his equipment.

"Looks like a lot of gear. Do you know how to use it, or is it just a prop?"

Jenkins unzipped one of the bags and took out a film camera that looked like it might have been new sometime before the First World War. "I've had this Hasselblad since I was a kid. Bought it used with money from cutting grass. Taken pictures in places you'd never dare enter. That's what got me into this line of work. The intel group saw some of the pictures from war zones that I published and recruited me to do the same for God and Country. Been at it ever since. Now, tell me about this guy we're meeting."

"His name's Bob Fredrick. He's a local author and Greenpeace activist working on a documentary about the environmental threats to the Menominee River. I set up the meeting with him so that he could show me what he's writing about. I need to spend the day on the river with him to get that info."

"Is the Menominee the same river that flows through town here?"

"Yes. Bob wants to meet upriver at a place called Rubys Corner, about halfway to Pemene Falls. I don't know if he plans to go up river or down from there. And you better have your story straight. He's with Greenpeace and will freak if he finds out you're a federal agent."

"Don't worry, discretion is my middle name!"

Claire doubted that, but she let the subject drop.

Once they were on the road, Claire found it difficult to see through the windshield of the car and had to drive with her head hanging out the window like a puppy on its first car ride.

"You seem pretty good at that. Do it often?" Jenkins asked.

Claire frowned. "I wouldn't have to if you hadn't goobered my windshield. But yeah, I have to do this sometimes in the winter."

"Why?"

"I get frost on the inside of the windows. Don't you get that in your pickup?"

"No, and it shouldn't happen." Jenkins switched on the car's heater without asking, turned it up to full, and leaned forward to sniff the dash.

"What in the world are you doing?"

"Checking for an antifreeze leak. And you've got one. That's why your windshield frosts over in the winter."

"How do you know that from smelling the dashboard?"

"Not the dash. The air from the vent. And it smells sweet, like maple syrup. A sure sign that you got a water leak in your heater core. You should get that fixed."

"Really? Just based on the smell, I should take my car into the shop?"

"Yep."

"And who's going to pay for that? You people know so much about me, you must know that I make diddly-squat at my job. After rent and groceries, there's not much left for other things. As long as the car starts, I leave it alone."

"Ma'am, that's not a good idea."

"Not like I have much choice. And if you're going to pretend to be one of my clients, then you should call me by my name."

"Sounds good, Claire."

"What about you? What do people call you?"

"Jenkins, just Jenkins will do."

"Fine."

Claire stopped briefly at a gas station to scrub off her windshield. Ten minutes later, she pulled into a gravel parking lot in front of an old two-story house with white clapboard siding and a steep, peaked roof, which had been converted into a tavern. The sign over the door identified it as Herb's Bait, Burgers, and Brews, the place where she was supposed to meet with Frederick. A short set of concrete steps led to a screen door; around the side, the parking lot extended down to a dilapidated wooden pier on the river.

When she stepped into Herb's, Claire's first thought was that it might be hard to tell the difference between what Herb sold for fish bait and what he put on your plate for breakfast. A large, U-shaped bar filled one end of the dimly lit room; a bait counter stood next to the door, and a half-dozen dark, Formica tables, some level, filled the rest of the space. The walls were covered with wood paneling that appeared to Claire to be in an advanced stage of decomposition. She wrinkled her nose at the sour smell of spilled beer. At least, she hoped it was beer; she was afraid to look down at the floor. Her sneakers squeaked in protest at each step as they made contact with the evil surface.

"Sweet!" Jenkins exclaimed, flopping down into a chair as he eased his camera bag to the floor. "I love these old places. They have the best chow!"

"I don't know, I'm not that hungry at the moment." Claire wished that she could leave with her appetite, which had bolted for the door at the first whiff of Herb's noxious atmosphere. She sat next to Jenkins and ran a finger across the table. It was sticky, and she made a face as she wiped her hand on her jeans. "In fact, I might skip breakfast."

"Your loss. Nothing like a good, home-cooked meal to put some meat on your bones."

"And E. coli in your gut. No thanks."

"Nonsense. When was the last time you heard about somebody getting sick at a mom-and-pop place like this?"

"Well—"

"Never! But those chain restaurants? Every week you hear about another case of food poisoning at one of them."

"Yes, but—"

"It's true," Jenkins smirked as he pulled a menu from the condiment rack on the table, pausing to shake a blob of ketchup off before opening it. "Course, there's two theories as to why that is."

"And they are?"

"One is that they buy their ingredients locally and use them up daily, so they're always fresh. No time to grow nasties."

"And the other?"

Jenkins ran his thumb over the table and squinted at it. "No germ could survive in this much grease."

Claire glared at the man. "I suppose you think that's funny?"

"Nope. That's why I use these." Jenkins pulled a pack of Pepto tablets out of a pocket and passed it across to Claire. "Help yourself. I dosed up before we left."

Claire's client entered the bar at that moment, and she waved him over to their table, rising to shake his hand. "Good morning, Bob. Thanks again for being flexible. I'm sorry about missing our meeting the other day."

Bob Fredrick was a short, fireplug of a man, with thinning brown hair, wire-rim glasses, and a weathered complexion from years of outdoor living. He was dressed in a light green camp shirt, dark green shorts, and hiking boots.

Jenkins rose to introduce himself. Claire was relieved that Bob accepted Jenkins' story without any obvious concern.

The bar's owner appeared as the group settled around the table. Herb was an overweight man with thinning gray hair, thick glasses, and a pronounced limp.

"What can I get you folks?" he asked, pencil poised over an order tablet.

Jenkins ordered first. "I'll have the Fisherman's Folly, eggs scrambled, bacon instead of sausage, wheat toast, and a pot of hot coffee."

"And you, ma'am?"

"Just coffee, thanks." Claire reasoned that if the coffee was hot enough, no germs could survive in it.

"You'll change your mind in a minute, Claire," Bob said as he placed his own order. "I've eaten here a number of times and the food's great."

"Thanks!" Herb said with a smile. "I'll let the little woman know. Wife cooks it all herself, don't trust no short-order cooks to handle anything as important as breakfast."

When Herb returned with their food, Jenkins inquired how he got his limp.

"'Nam. Damnedest thing you ever heard of."

"How so?" Jenkins paused with a forkful of eggs mid-air.

"I was with a heavy infantry unit, and we got dropped on Hamburger Hill."

"Heard about that one, damned shame. So, shrapnel?"

"Worse."

"Really? Bayonet?"

"Even worse than that!"

"Geez, that must have been something. What was it?"

"I tore my knee out when I jumped out of the chopper. Saved my life, though. I fell down and rolled into a ditch. The men who landed on their feet were mowed down like tall grass. Lost some good friends that day."

"Sorry to hear that. I was shooting film during Desert Shield and took some shrapnel in my shoulder. Actually worked out for me."

"How's that?" Bob frowned, joining the conversation.

"Cut some nerves, now my hand is steady no matter what else is going on."

Claire sipped her coffee and wondered if anything she'd just heard was true.

Herb chuckled. "Heh, that's something all right! Hey, look at this." He peeled back his shirt sleeve, revealing a scar that ran from his wrist to his elbow. "I got a bayonet right here in the forearm. That was during my second tour."

Jenkins looked impressed. "Cool! Look at this." He peeled back his shirt. "It's from a fifty-caliber sniper round, went right through the upper rib cage. An inch higher and to the right and it would have taken my arm right off."

"No way!"

"Yep! Happened in Columbia."

Bob leaned forward. "What were you doing there?"

"Shooting some pics of endangered spider monkeys."

"And they shot at you for that?"

"Nope, found out later that I was in the middle of a cocaine field when I took the shots. Certain folks got kinda upset about that. Didn't realize they had men up in the trees watching for law enforcement or reporters. Lost a Nikon I'd had since I was a kid."

Claire opened her mouth to speak, hoping to bring the conversation back to Fredrick's book.

Before she could say anything, though, Herb said, "Man, that must've hurt. Check this out, I took a round through the thigh. Got lucky and it missed the bone. Hurt like the devil, but the medic just taped it over and we kept right on shooting."

Jenkins' eyes opened wide. "That's awesome! Did I show you the shrapnel wound I got in Baghdad?

"No."

"Got hit right in the ass. I think the medic was high when he sewed me up, as the scar looks like a smiley face!"

"No way!"

"It's a fact! Take a look…"

"Hey, that's enough!" Claire closed her eyes as Jenkins pulled down his pants, bending over to show everybody his scar. "I don't need to see this. And we're in a restaurant, you know."

"You're right, young lady," Herb said. "But he's right, it does look like a smiley face. That's something you don't see every day!"

"I wish I'd never seen it at all. Jenkins, please pull up your pants." Claire made a moue of her face as she held her hand over her eyes.

"Oh, sorry, forgot there was a lady present." Jenkins grinned as he buckled his belt.

After breakfast, Bob led Claire and Jenkins down to the river, where a small aluminum fishing boat was tied to the dock. As soon as everybody had put on a life vest and taken a seat, he cast off, turning the little boat to the right so that it ran with the current. The low hum of the boat's electric trolling motor was lost amidst the rushing sound of the rippling water.

As he steered the boat, Bob said, "Before we talk about the Menominee River itself, you should know something about the Menominee people. They settled this region over ten thousand years ago, and they've been here ever since.

"Think about that—the Menominee maintained this pristine wilderness and lived in harmony with nature thousands of years before the first pyramid was built. So when I talk about conservation, it's because I know it can be done. Has been done. The example's all around us."

Bob turned the boat to the right before continuing. "We can only go downriver about three miles before we hit the

Chappee Rapids. It's a thrill to shoot the whitewater, but that's not why I brought you here."

He swept his arm in a wide arc. "Look at that. Notice anything?"

"It's beautiful," Claire said. "I see some paper birch and maples mixed in with some jack pines on a rocky shoreline, but not much else. Why? What am I missing?"

"Not a thing!" Bob grinned. "And that's my point. Other than the occasional place like Herb's, there're no houses, resorts, marinas, factories, or mines. You're looking at a natural shoreline, free from development, one of the last remaining undeveloped shorelines in the state, till you get to the dams, anyway.

"Wisconsin is a land cut and shaped by water," Bob continued, "and the Menominee is the last of the state's great waterways to remain undeveloped. Thanks to some farsighted people, the shoreline was set aside as a natural area many years ago. You'll find herons and egrets roosting on the islands and wading through the shallows, and the Menominee still harvest wild rice from the backwaters.

"Look there!" he exclaimed, pointing to a bald eagle as it swooped down and plucked a fish from the river.

"And all this is at risk. If the plans are approved for Back Forty's sulfide mine in the upper peninsula, it will vomit sulfuric acid right into the Menominee. Within a few years, the river will be as dead as the Ohio."

"I didn't know the Ohio was polluted?" Claire said, watching the eagle soar off with its prize.

"Badly. It's the most polluted waterway in America. Back in 2013, over twenty-four million pounds of industrial pollution were discharged into the Ohio—more than double what pours into the entire Mississippi River."

Jenkins grunted and shook his head. "That's a damn shame. Hey, I've got an idea! I'm headed back to D.C. after I finish up here. I could swing by the Ohio and snap some shots of the hot spots, then send them up to you for your book."

"Jenkins, that would be very much appreciated. Photos have power, and some good pics would help drive home my message. But honestly, I don't have the money to pay you. Claire, do you think a publisher would spring for that?"

Before Claire could answer, Jenkins said, "Don't worry about the money, Bob. I'll do it gratis. Just give me credit for the images, and make sure they're copyrighted."

Claire stared at Jenkins, puzzled by the man's clearly genuine interest.

Their tour continued for a couple of hours before Bob returned to the launch ramp.

"There's one more thing I want to show you, but we can't see it from the boat."

"We can't?" Claire was puzzled.

"Nope, we'll need to take a car."

"Can I ride in yours?" Jenkins asked as he stowed his cameras. "Claire's is a death trap."

"Not a problem!"

An hour later, Claire found herself standing on the 26th Street bridge crossing the Menominee River in downtown Marinette. To her right, she could see Boom and Stephenson islands, and then the Bridge Street bridge. *How did they ever come up with a name like that?* The bridge blocked her view of the mouth of the river where it emptied into Lake Michigan.

Bob led the way out onto the bridge. Stopping about halfway across, he pointed out over the river to a two-story industrial building located at the juncture between the far shoreline and a low dam that straddled the river. "That's the generating plant for one of five dams on the Menominee."

Puzzled, Claire said, "Okay, but I've seen this every day for two years, Bob. There's nothing special here."

"Oh, but there is, Claire. Look at where the dam meets the shoreline. Do you see the opening in the building on the waterline?"

"Yes."

"That's a fish lift, and it's one of the most important environmental improvements made to the river in the past twenty years."

"A fish lift? You mean, like an elevator?"

"Yes, indeed. And there's one just like it on the next bridge down. You see, sturgeon are too big to make it up a conventional fish ladder, so they haven't been able to swim upstream and spawn since the dams were built. The whole ecosystem based on the sturgeon collapsed. But these lifts boost the sturgeon up past the dam, opening up fifteen miles of river to them. It took years to accomplish and cost over a million dollars, most of it from private donors. But it was worth it. It's only been a couple of years since the lifts were installed, but the sturgeon population's already recovering."

"That's way cool!" Jenkins exclaimed, snapping a picture of the lift. "But if we can see it from here, it must be pretty big."

"It is. An adult sturgeon can exceed seven feet in length, and the lift tank has to be big enough to hold several at a time."

"So, where's the problem?"

"If the mine goes through, the river will be so polluted that the fish won't live long enough to spawn. And all of this will have been for nothing."

"That's a shame." Claire stared at the river. She imagined the flow of life up and down the waterway, how fragile it was, and how little it took for somebody to compromise it. "Bob, your book...I knew it was important, but I never really understood how much. People need to know about this. They need to feel it, just the way you shared it with us."

"I'm glad I was able to show you, Claire. You too, Jenkins."

Jenkins stood silent for a moment, shading his eyes with his hand. "Bob, I was moved by what I saw today. I've got some good shots, too. I'll get them to you as soon as I get back to my room."

Claire watched as Jenkins took his leave and walked away. Caught up in the drama of Fredrick's story, she'd forgotten that Jenkins was one of Nuance's agents. She wondered if he'd follow through on his promise to send his pictures to Fredrick. The man was a goofball, but he felt sincere, and she hoped that he would stick to his word.

21

"You two should be more discreet."

Hansen jerked awake. "Commander Nuance—"

"If the admiral saw you holding hands he'd court-martial you both for conduct unbecoming."

Hansen dropped Solomon's hand and rose to face Nuance, who was standing in the doorway of Solomon's hospital room. Solomon's bed lay between them, with an array of monitors to the left near the head of the bed. The taupe walls and floor looked weary, as if they'd seen too much grief, even though the medical center was only a few years old. A flat-screen TV played light classical music from its perch on the wall facing the bed.

"Just checking his pulse."

"Of course you were. Personally, I don't care, as long as it doesn't interfere with any of my operations."

"Then you'll..."

"Say nothing?" Nuance fixed Hansen in place with his eyes.

Hansen found that he couldn't look away. He shivered at their color, a gray colder than the depths of outer space.

"Yes. Please."

Nuance remained standing in the doorway, prompting Hansen to ask, "What, uh, what brings you over to the hospital? Solomon's still in a coma, and there's been no change in his condition."

"I was hoping to find somebody to change the dressing where I got bit by a dog. It started bleeding through and stained my slacks. If I get any blood on the upholstery of my wife's car, I'm toast. Unfortunately, my team's medic is still sacked out."

"Oh. Would you like me to—"

"No. Stay with your patient, doctor. I'll find a nurse to do the job."

"I could page someone for you?"

"Sure, if you don't mind. By the way, I need to speak with Commander Solomon urgently. Please notify me as soon as he wakes."

"I'm awake now." Solomon opened his eyes, meeting Nuance's gaze with his own. "Have been for a few minutes. Is there a reason you're here? Somebody poke a stick under your rock, made you crawl out?"

Hansen felt his mouth go dry. He recognized that tone of voice and didn't need to see his partner's eyes to know the sable threat there. Nuance and Solomon had disliked each other for years. *This could get out of hand fast!* "Jim, settle down, you've been in a car wreck and you're still doped to the gills. You shouldn't say anything until your mind's clear."

Neither of the other two men seemed willing to give up on their staring contest. Desperate, Hansen shook Solomon's shoulder, then placed his hand on his cheek, pulling the man's head to the side and breaking the stand-off. "Jim, I need to check you for concussion, now lie still."

Solomon twisted away, looking back at Nuance. "I just want to know what you meant by that comment. I don't take kindly to threats."

"It was no threat, Solomon. I've got more important things to deal with than a couple of little boys afraid to come out of their closet."

"What makes you think—"

"Can it, Solomon." Nuance folded his arms. "Like I said, I've got more important matters to worry about. And so do you."

"What do you mean?"

"Such as finding the spy that tried to kill you."

"Kill me? Spy? Nuance, what are you talking about?"

Nuance studied Solomon in silence for an uncomfortably long period. His poker face gave away nothing, but Hansen was certain that he was conducting an internal debate.

"Doctor Hansen, it would be best if you left the room. I need to debrief Commander Solomon and then bring him up to speed on our current investigation."

"Why do I need to leave? I have clearance for everything that our team handles."

"Not for this. It's eyes only. Sorry."

"Hansen stays." Solomon's tone brooked no argument.

After a long pause, Nuance sighed and said, "Very well, then, commander. Admiral Dutchman has opened a full investigation into the circumstances surrounding your accident. Based on documents that were found in your possession at the time, I doubt you'll be surprised to learn that the Joint Chiefs are getting daily briefings on our progress. I'm running point and I'll need your full cooperation. Let's start with the car wreck. What's the last thing you remember?"

"Hitting a light pole."

"And before that? Did you see who ran you off the road? Make of car? License number? Can you give me a description of the driver?"

"Sorry, I'm not following what you're talking about. What's all this about being run off the road?"

"Weren't you forced off the road?"

"No. Pretty sure not."

Nuance paused, blinked a few times as he considered Solomon's statement. "Then how did you manage to crash your car on a clear road in the middle of a bright and sunny day?"

Now it was Solomon's turn to hesitate. "I got distracted as I entered the intersection."

"Distracted? Did somebody hit you in the eyes with a laser pointer or something?"

"No. It's actually kind of embarrassing. I'd rather not say, unless—"

"It's necessary. I need to know."

"Lunch wasn't, er, sitting well. I went out for burgers with a couple of the guys from Northwood, and maybe I ate something I shouldn't have."

"Jim!" Hansen interrupted the discussion, furious at his partner. "You didn't have onions for lunch again?! You know what that does to your system!" *Our Centauri metabolism reacts to those kinds of vegetables like a lactose-intolerant human reacts to cream. It's a wonder the idiot didn't end up with violent diarrhea and projectile vomiting, although that would explain why he was distracted from driving. Not that we can tell Nuance that...*

"Guilty as charged. Sorry."

Nuance waved Hansen to silence as he resumed his questioning. "Commander, are you telling me that you crashed because of a stomach ache?"

"Yes. Well, yes and no. My stomach hurt, but I only looked down for a moment. When I looked up, I was at the intersection. Couldn't remember which way to turn. I checked the car's nav unit and I guess I was going a lot faster than I thought. When I looked up again it was too late to do anything but pray."

"Commander, if you're trying to cover for an accomplice..."

"What accomplice? What in the hell are you talking about?"

"Commander, top-secret documents regarding the Eschaton missile defense system were found in your car after the incident, including detailed notes written by a spy working at Northwood. Care to explain?"

"A spy? What notes from a spy?"

"Oh, come on! There were over three hundred pages in the spy's diary!"

"Wait a second. Are you talking about the book manu-script?"

"Yes. The one slipped to you by the Miller woman from the local literary agency."

"But, but that was just somebody's book. She wanted me to fact-check it. It did mention the Eschaton system, which was inappropriate, but it didn't give away any key details. I think it was just mislabeled and should have been categorized as fiction instead of non-fiction."

"But we found a number of internal documents about the Eschaton in the manuscript. The docs even had control numbers. There's no doubt as to their authenticity."

"Of course they were authentic. That's why I'm working up at Northwood, reviewing documents like those. When I headed back to my hotel after lunch, I secured them in my briefcase with...oh my God! I put the book manuscript in my briefcase with the Eschaton documents. Tell me, Commander Nuance, what was the state—"

"Scattered all over the road. Your briefcase was smashed open during the accident and its contents went everywhere. The State Patrol put the papers in a garbage bag for us, but they were all mixed together. It took most of the night for a team of seven agents to organize it into something that made sense."

Hansen shifted uneasily as Solomon and Nuance exchanged meaningful looks.

"Nuance, I think I should look at what your team put together. It sounds like they mixed up the documents. I could help straighten it out."

"That would be inappropriate, given the circumstances."

"Suit yourself, but you're wasting your time and everybody else's. There's no plot and no spy."

Nuance rubbed his chin before continuing, "Commander, your story is plausible and it fits the evidence. If it wasn't for one other thing, I'd close the investigation right now."

"What other thing is that?"

"We have an alien spy in custody."

"An alien spy? As in a Russian?"

"No, as in Star Trek."

Hansen found that he couldn't breathe. *They're on to us!* He felt Solomon go still under his hand. It took all of his discipline not to look down at his partner.

"That's preposterous," Solomon said.

"You'd think so, but we have DNA evidence. There's no doubt about it, the subject's non-human."

"And you've questioned him?"

"Tried to, but can't decipher his language. Not yet, anyway, but we will. Some of the Pentagon's best brains are working on it right now."

"There must be a mistake. Everybody knows that there's no such thing as aliens. You might as well say that the boogeyman broke in to steal our secrets. Is there any other physical evidence?"

"No, but we hope to find some soon."

"With Dutchman running things? He couldn't find a spy if one was standing right under his nose."

Hansen surreptitiously jabbed his partner, aghast at the comment.

Nuance frowned. "You're not wrong about the admiral, but I've got the situation under control."

"That's about as likely as the existence of alien spies."

"Oh, they're here, all right, and I have confidence that we'll flush them out soon. Events are moving forward in a satisfactory manner."

"Up to your old tricks again, eh? Who are you blackmailing this time?"

"Turning a spy isn't blackmail."

"Call it what you like, it's a dirty business. Wait a sec, you said Dutchman was in charge?"

"Yes."

"And I bet he's asked you to play fast and loose with regs, hasn't he?"

"He's promised the paperwork by the end of the week."

"And you believed him?"

"He's my commanding officer. I might not like how he runs things, but I have my orders. And he might even be right this time."

"I've heard that line about Dutchman before. I suppose he's already singled out his next victim? And you're just fine with it, aren't you?"

"I don't have to like it. That's the business we're in. If you were on the operational side of things instead of sitting behind a desk all day, you'd know that."

"That's enough!" Hansen said, trying to break up the argument. "This bickering is pointless. Commander Nuance, my patient needs rest. Unless you have urgent business remaining with him, I need you to leave."

"Sure, I'm done here."

Nuance stalked from the room, leaving Solomon and Hansen staring at each other.

"He knows," Hansen whispered. "I'm sure of it."

"No, he doesn't."

"But—"

"Shush! He thinks that he knows something, but he's way off base."

"I don't like it. We should get off this world while we still can. I can have our shuttle here from its hiding spot in Nevada in ten minutes."

"No, that would be a mistake. Running away would grab Nuance's attention, and that's the last thing we want to happen. Be patient. He's distracted by other events and he'll forget all about us in a few hours."

"I hope you're right," Hansen sighed, running a finger along Solomon's cheek. "This could go badly for us."

"It won't. Trust me." Solomon smiled as he rubbed Hansen's forearm, then reached down to gently squeeze his partner's crotch. "Though it would be nice to get away for a while and just be ourselves. I must admit to a preference for being female rather than male."

Hansen swatted Solomon's hand aside. "Behave yourself. And don't get your hopes up. I just gave you your shots, so you're stuck as a male for another year."

Solomon sighed. "What's the point in being omnisexual beings if we have to stick to the same gender for years on end?"

"In case you've forgotten, it's part of the job. We agreed to this when we signed up."

"Yeah, but I can dream, can't I?"

22

After speaking with Solomon, Nuance returned to his office at Northwood, closed the door, and sat brooding. The faint hum of the blue-white fluorescent overhead light failed to mask the distant bang of rivets being hammered into steel or the thrum of forklifts from the busy shipyard, but he was so wrapped in his thoughts that he didn't notice.

Solomon can't be right about the document; he must still be loopy from his concussion. But he didn't sound like he was out of it. No, he was clear-headed all right.

Nuance took out his copy of the manuscript and spread it across his desk. He pulled out the sections that had document control numbers on them and set them to one side. Then he worked his way through the remaining parts of the manuscript where the Eschaton system was mentioned. His team had highlighted them in yellow, making it easy for him to find what he was looking for.

He'd read those sections several times already, but always with the controlled documents in place. To his dismay, he found, as Solomon had suggested, that the text held together without them.

Could Solomon have been right about this? Nuance pinched the bridge of his nose.

Taking out his cell, he dialed the electronics expert on his staff.

"Ensign Johnson here. What can I do for you, commander?" The woman who answered the phone had a soft, southern accent.

"Ensign, have you finished analyzing the server logs from the Northwood systems?"

"Yes, sir."

"Were you able to verify access to the Eschaton documents?"

"No, sir. I checked all of them, and all the files have appropriate time stamps for access and changes. None of those correlate with Andersen's presence on the system."

"He's a UNIX admin, could he have overridden the time stamps on the files to cover his tracks?"

"Yes, sir. He had root access to the system and could have done that."

"That's unfortunate, but expected. Were you able to determine anything at all?"

"Yes, sir. The company's staff members have been cooperative, and they were able to give me approximate creation dates for all the files. Those dates match the dates on the system. From that, we were able to correlate when certain pieces of information were stored on the system with when they first appeared in the manuscript. There is a relationship there, but it isn't strong enough to hold up in court."

"And the content of those files? Leaving aside the documents with control numbers, what can you tell me about the rest of the files?"

"Well, the remaining files aren't flagged confidential. They aren't for public disclosure either, but there isn't any secret information in them."

"Thank you, ensign. That will be all." Nuance hung up and then looked at one of the highlighted sections of text again.

I can't prove that Andersen took any confidential information, not with Solomon's testimony that the controlled documents were not part of Andersen's manuscript. And whatever else I might think of the man, Solomon's never lied to me, and he has a clean record. Other than his kinky personal life. Could Andersen have used that to coerce Solomon's assistance? It's possible, but then why would Andersen run Solomon off the road?

No, the pieces don't fit together. But that leaves me with a shaky case. If it wasn't for the DNA evidence, Solomon's testimony would be enough to close the case. Andersen would be fired, of course, for misappropriating corporate assets, but he wouldn't be facing a short and unpleasant life in one of Roswell's examination rooms. And it would be my ass in the grinder, not Dutchman's. He's made sure of that.

Nuance got up and began pacing the room. This wasn't the first time he'd had evidence prove unreliable during an investigation, and his mind went back to his training. Stick to the facts, verify, and then verify again.

Verify again. With sudden resolution, Nuance locked up his office, told his team's administrative assistant that he needed to run out for a bit on a personal errand, and then left Northwood.

He hopped into his pink SUV, made his way to Highway 41, and headed out of town. When he reached a gas station at the edge of the city, he pulled in and topped off with gas. Opening the glove compartment, he took out a cell phone sealed in a plastic bag and wandered away from the car. *Never know when you might need a burner phone. Never leave home without one!* A small stand of maples next to the gas station suited his purpose; as soon as he was out of sight, he put on a pair of latex gloves and unsealed the cell.

Dialing a number from memory, he let the phone ring once then hung up. A few minutes later, the cell vibrated, alerting him to an incoming call.

Nuance answered, speaking immediately, without bothering with the usual pleasantries involved in answering a phone. "Thanks for calling back, Al. I have a situation here and need assistance."

"What's up, Fred? Did Dutchman finally lose his marbles?" The voice of the man at the other end of the line was distorted by the encryption software they were using.

"No, at least, not yet. I need some tests rerun. Discretely. Remember what we ran into a couple of years back in Yokohama?"

"Yep. The Yakuza bribed a courier to switch the urine samples from our suspects and we arrested the wrong men. By the time we caught on to what had happened, the perps had skipped town. We never did catch them."

"Well, the situation here is about the same. We've run into some complications, and given the sensitive nature of this case, I need to be sure—real sure—that the test results are reliable."

"Which lab are they at?"

"Homeland's DNA center."

"Not a problem. I have multiple contacts there and can get the job done under the radar. Will the lab know which samples to process?"

"Yes, but it's best if they don't."

"What do you mean?"

"They have two blood samples that I sent to them on Wednesday for DNA profiling. I'd like both samples re-run, but with full profiles. And I'd like the tests run in a double-blind fashion so that the techs don't know why the tests are being performed or what we're looking for."

"Interesting. Why?"

"Like I said, some of the other evidence here might be less reliable than I thought. I need to be sure about the DNA. The test results need to be airtight."

"Got it. It'll take longer to set up that kind of testing without drawing attention to our actions, but I should have the results for you by Monday. Do you need them sent through a secure channel?"

"Yep. No sense getting Dutchman worked up if the initial results are confirmed."

"And if they're not?"

"Then I've got one hell of a problem."

Nuance ended the call and then pried the phone apart. He pulled the SIM card and memory chip out and chopped them to pieces with a Leatherman knife he kept in his pocket.

Returning to the gas station, he went to the men's room. As soon as he was sure that he was alone, he went from stall-to-stall, distributing the shredded phone chips between the toilets and flushing them away. He put the empty shell of the phone in the trash. Without any fingerprints or digital memory, it was untraceable.

Back at his car, Nuance sat still for several minutes. *Going over Dutchman's head like this could get me court-martialed. But if Solomon's right, then I'm the one who'll get blamed when this goes off the rails.* On that pleasant thought, Nuance returned to his office.

23

Ding!

Claire lifted her head from her pillow and looked at the cell phone on her nightstand. It was six in the morning, and she didn't recall setting the alarm. *Not that I'd need one for a Saturday. The neighbors are usually at it about now.*

Ding, ding!

Before Claire could pick up the phone, she heard a woman's voice say, "Time to get up, Miss Miller. You have a busy day ahead of you."

"What the…?" Claire's stomach flip-flopped as she stared at the phone. She recognized the soft southern accent.

"Miss Miller? Please don't pretend that you can't hear me, or that you're still asleep. It's time to get up."

Claire swallowed, then picked the phone up. "This is Claire. What do you want now?"

"Miss Miller, you need to freshen up and get dressed. Put on something nice. You're meeting Andersen for lunch today, and you'll want to make a good first impression."

"But, but he hasn't called me back!"

"That's something we're well aware of. You'll have to be more aggressive in your approach now. Time is short, so it's critical that you to make direct contact with him today. Get dressed and go to his house."

"What if he's not there?"

"Then I'll let you know where he is, child. Either way, you need to take the initiative and make contact."

"But I don't know him, I haven't even spoken with him. I'm not sure—"

"Miss Miller, do you need assistance motivating yourself? We can send somebody over to help with that if you'd like."

"No, that won't be necessary."

"Very good. Now get busy." The line went dead with a click.

Claire went through her regular Saturday morning routine in a daze, pausing only to look in the mirror after her shower, surprised to see no outward signs of how much she'd changed over the past few days. Except for her eyes, where she thought she saw darkness rising in their jade depths. *I can do this. For Becca and Sam. I have to.*

When she was done straightening and cleaning her apartment, Claire tried calling Jake again. There was still no answer, and she hung up without leaving a message.

A moment later, her phone chimed, and the woman with the southern accent said, "Miss Miller? Why didn't you leave a message for Andersen? Are you sure you know what to do?"

Claire's mouth twitched in a brief hint of a smile. "Actually, I was about to leave for his house per your instructions, so there wasn't any point in leaving a message. But as long as you're on the phone, would you mind giving me his address? I could look it up myself, but you said that time is critical."

There was a pause, and Claire imagined that she could hear the other woman grinding her teeth. However, her brief moment of pleasure at sticking it to the agent was immediately replaced by a wave of guilt. *This is petty! I'm not going to let them pull me down to their level.*

At that point, the woman came back online and gave her step-by-step directions to Jake's house. It was only five blocks away, but the agent detailed every step, including how long each leg of the "journey" should take. Then she made Claire repeat the instructions back to her before hanging up.

Serves me right for being snarky. Claire tucked her copy of Jake's manuscript under her arm, then paused at the front door to check herself in the mirror. It was late May and the weather app on her phone showed the temp was in the fifties, so she added a dark gray hoodie to her blue jeans, sneakers, and ivory blouse. Then she adjusted her topaz broach. *Dad was so angry at the expense, but Mom had insisted, identical broaches for Becca and me. She wanted us to feel special. I wonder if Becca still wears hers?*

Claire left the apartment before her thoughts spiraled any further down that path.

As she stepped outside, she took a deep breath of the chill breeze off the lake, then smiled up at the morning sun. *Things will work out. Today will be a better day than yesterday. How could it get worse?*

Claire stopped at Wilson's before going to Jake's house. Taking a seat in a quiet corner, she sipped her coffee as she skimmed through Jake's manuscript.

"This is awful," she muttered after a few minutes, stopping to pinch the bridge of her nose as she contemplated the text in front of her. Taking a sip from her cup, she went back to work, determined to scan the entire manuscript before meeting with Jake. *I owe him that much, at the very least, before I betray him to Nuance.*

It took her three hours to finish the book, stopping partway through to buy a cinnamon roll to fortify herself for the task. She also needed time to think about the manuscript in front of her. The page numbers were written by hand, and there were a number of missing pages. Oddly, their absence had no impact on the flow of the narrative. Other sections of the text were blacked out, redacted in such a way as to make even the context of what had been removed unclear. Those areas did affect the flow of the text.

When she was done with the book, Claire leaned back with a sigh. *Huh. Not a bad story and I do like the characters. But the grammar! Ish!! This guy needs to go back to fourth grade for some remedial English lessons.*

Claire checked her watch and saw that it was nearing lunchtime. *Guess I can't put this off any longer.* Rising, she left the coffee shop and made her way to Merryman Street. When she reached Jake's house, she stopped on the sidewalk to look the place over.

"He's sleeping. You need to come back later."

Claire turned to see who had spoken and found herself facing a small girl with a large, brown dog at her side.

"Oh, hello. Do you know Jake Andersen, the man who lives here?"

"Of course I know Unca Jake. We live next door."

"Oh, I see. Well, my name's Claire, and I need to speak to your uncle."

"Why?"

Claire pursed her lips. *Time to lie. Heaven help me.* "As I said, my name's Claire, and I work for the Marinette Masters Literary Agency here in town. I'm here to speak with your uncle about a book that he sent to us."

"Really?! Wow, that's great! I knew it would work!"

"What?"

"Oh, I shouldn't have said anything. So, you're a real agent?"

Claire smiled. "Yes, why?"

"Ms. Eliot, that's my teacher, says agents are real important."

"That's very kind of her. Please tell her that I think teachers have the most important job in the world."

"I will. And my name's Daphne."

"Pleased to meet you, Daphne." Claire shook the girl's hand, sensing that she expected the formality. Then she crouched down in front of the dog. "Who's your friend?"

"That's Chaucer, but he's not my dog. He's Unca Jake's. But I watch him while Unca Jake's at work, which is most days, cause he works nights."

"Hi, Chaucer." Claire presented her palm for the dog to sniff, then gently massaged his jowls with both hands. Chaucer barked once, opened his jaw, and dangled his tongue out in a doggie grin as he eggbeatered his tail.

"He likes you," Daphne said with obvious approval.

"Well, I like him, too." Claire gave Chaucer a quick hug, then stood up. "Daphne, I really need to see your uncle. Do you think he'd mind if I knocked on his door?"

"Well, I don't know. I guess it would be okay."

"Thanks!"

Claire paused on the front porch for a moment to think about what she was going to say. Before she could knock, however, she heard a loud alarm go off inside.

The jangling of the alarm was followed by a young man's voice shouting, "Dang it! I turned this thing off! I know I did!" This was in turn followed by the muffled thump of something small yet substantial being thrown against a wall.

Claire wondered if the alarm had been set off by one of Nuance's agents, as they seemed to have complete control over everything electronic. The timing of it going off was certainly suspicious.

She took a deep breath and knocked on the door.

"Now what?!" The tone of the voice from coming from inside the house was not promising.

A moment later, the door was jerked open with an angry squeak, and Claire found herself facing a handsome young man, his curly brown hair flattened against one side of his head in a comically exaggerated case of bedhead.

Whatever the man had expected to find on his doorstep, Claire could tell that she wasn't it. He stood there with his mouth open, rubbing his eyes.

They stared at each other in silence until Daphne said, "Hi Unca Jake! This is Miss Claire. She's a real agent. And she's here about your book!"

"My book?" Jake asked warily, taking a half step backwards. "You don't have a restraining order, do you?"

"What?" Claire was confused. "Why would I have one of those?"

"Just checking," Jake said, still poised for flight.

Claire had heard anecdotes about eccentric authors, but she had never encountered one herself. All of her clients had been ordinary people, with their only peculiarity being a passion for sharing their work with a world that was as fickle in its taste for literature as a cat choosing its breakfast. Her first impression of Jake was that she'd finally found one.

"You are Jake Andersen, right?"

"Yes, guilty as charged."

"I'm Claire Miller, and I work for the Marinette Masters Literary Agency."

Jake's mouth formed an "Oh!" without actually saying it, as his eyes went wide and his brows reached up as if to straighten his hair.

"I hope I'm not disturbing you. Is this a good time to chat about your book?"

Jake seemed unable to answer. Before the silence could grow awkward, Daphne tugged at his T-shirt and said, "You should invite her in, Unca Jake. It's safe. Chaucer likes her."

Jake looked back into his house and clearly had doubts about inviting anybody inside not equipped with hazmat gear. Then he looked down at the worn T-shirt and shorts that he had worn to bed.

"Uh, I'm not really dressed for company, and the house is a mess."

"That's okay," Claire said with a twitch of an eyebrow. "I wouldn't like somebody to drop in unexpected either." *Like Nuance.* "It's about lunchtime. How about if we go someplace and grab a bite? We can chat over the meal, and I can expense the cost."

"You want to buy me lunch?"

"Yes, if you're up for it?"

"Well, yeah! Just give me a minute to change, and I'll be right out."

Jake bolted out of sight. Claire wasn't sure if she should follow him or wait outside, but after peeking through the half-open door, she decided that outside was the better option.

A bump in the back of her knee surprised her, knocking her off balance for a second. She looked down just as Chaucer pushed his nose into her leg again.

Stooping down, she scratched the dog behind his ears and said, "Now then Chaucer, I can't go inside. He didn't invite me."

Chaucer whined and gave her a push with his forehead.

"No, I really can't. It wouldn't be polite."

The dog whined again, then looked up at her, his eyes dripping chocolate sadness.

"Now, that's just not fair," she said, taking his ears in her hands and massaging them. "You shouldn't be giving me that look. Oh no, I'm not going to do it. Un-uh."

Claire was about to give in to Chaucer's determined efforts to get her to enter the house when Jake reappeared, dressed in a clean black T-shirt and jeans.

"Thanks for waiting. I just needed to text my sister to let her know that Daphne's coming with us for lunch. I'm ready to go now."

"Where would you like to go?"

"Someplace I can get a good burger, I guess. How about you?"

"Can Chaucer join us?" Daphne asked.

"Gosh, Daphne, I'm not sure Ms. Miller—"

"Claire."

"If Claire would be comfortable with that. This is a business lunch—"

"I'm fine with it, and I don't think Chaucer would forgive me if we left him out."

"Okay, but most places don't let dogs in. Felipe and I usually go to Ethel's, which is just around the corner. It's in between my house and Northwood, where I work, so I stop there pretty often for chow, anyway. As long as we sit outside, they're fine with the dog being there."

"Sounds good. Lead on!" Claire followed Jake down the sidewalk. Her thoughts in such turmoil that she hardly noticed Chaucer trotting along beside her or Daphne walking between Jake and herself, holding both their hands.

24

As the group made their way to Ethel's, Claire felt her inner conflict grow. These were good people. Jake was so artless that she doubted he even knew how to spell the word subterfuge, and Daphne, well, Daphne was adorable. *And Becca was about the same age when they took her away. How can I betray her again?*

Claire zipped up her hoodie as the sun slipped behind a cloud. The lake breeze carried the mossy scent of the lake inland to mix with the aromas of the lilacs and cedar trees dotting the neighborhood, but the chill wind also gave her goosebumps. Her reverie was interrupted by Daphne.

"Miss Claire, what's it like being an agent?"

Claire was surprised by Daphne's question. "It's a lot like any other job, but I do a lot of reading, and I like that."

"But it's special, right? I mean, you could publish any book. If you wanted to."

"I wish it was that easy. We're just the go-betweens connecting authors with publishing houses."

"That's still special." Daphne stubbornly refused to let go of her point.

"Thank you, Daphne." Claire screwed up her courage and asked, "Jake, would you mind if I asked a few questions about your book?"

"Of course! I mean, I'd be happy to answer them. You really liked it, then?"

"It has potential." *But then, so did the Titanic.* "Tell me, where did you get the idea for the story?"

Jake glanced down before answering. "Oh, well, I was looking through some company propaganda at work and saw a press release about the latest destroyer Northwood's building for the Navy. It mentioned the anti-missile system on the ship, but I didn't think much of it at the time."

"No?" Claire had the distinct impression that Jake was fibbing, though she couldn't see why.

"No, it's not really my field of interest. I'm a UNIX admin, so the nuts and bolts of computers are more my thing. Anyway, I was playing Attack on Zargon after work and noticed how much the missiles in the game looked like the ones in the pamphlet about the Eschaton system. I've always wanted one of my books to be made into a video game, so I thought it might be cool to learn a bit more about the system and see if I could work it into my next book. One thing led to another, and the story just wrote itself."

"I see. Did you get permission from Northwood to use the information that you found?"

"Permission? I guess I didn't think I'd need it. The info was all public domain. Well, most of it was. But I didn't put anything that was actually confidential in the book."

"Jake, this could be a real problem—"

Chaucer suddenly began barking, interrupting Claire. He bolted after a squirrel, trampling a bed of purple periwinkles as he chased it up a tree. Then he rushed back, lumbering into her knee with his shoulder hard enough to make her stumble into Jake.

Jake caught her by the elbow as they both said, "Sorry!"

They stood like that for a moment, before Jake released Claire's arm with a startled look on his face. Claire smiled, while he blushed. "Not a problem," she murmured.

"It's just...I mean...Chaucer..."

"It's okay." Claire patted Jake's arm, causing his blush to spread to his ears. She reached down and scratched Chaucer's head. "He's just a playful puppy. There's nothing wrong with that."

Before Claire could ask Jake more about his book, they arrived at the diner he had suggested.

Ethel's Diner was located in a two-story building made of worn, buff-colored fieldstone, on the corner of Main Street and Shore Drive. It was just three blocks from Jake's house and across the street from Marinette's middle school. The aroma of char-grilled meat beckoned them inside, but it was a popular spot, and the only table available for a party of three was outside, which Chaucer's presence would have necessitated anyway.

Jake and Claire sat facing the street with Daphne on Jake's left-hand side. As she sat down, Claire surreptitiously wiped her finger across the wrought iron table. It was clean and dry. Even more promising, the menus were free from condiment splatters. Spotless tableware nestled in thick red linen napkins. Claire smiled. *Quite the upgrade from Herb's Bait, Burgers, and Brews.*

The conversation lapsed while they read their menus. Ethel's was dog-friendly, and when the waitress brought them glasses of water, she also brought a bowl of water for Chaucer. After a big, noisy drink, he flopped down with his head on Daphne's feet.

Claire took advantage of the silence while they read their menus to think about what she should do next. Now that she was actually in the situation, Nuance's instructions to 'Learn all you can about him' seemed pretty vague. After scanning Jake's book, she was sure that it was an innocuous, albeit poorly written, sci-fi story, projecting current theory into a plausible scenario to achieve the suspension of disbelief necessary for such a work to succeed. What was she supposed to find out?

When the waitress returned to take their orders, Jake chose a burger with fries and a Coke, and Claire asked for a salad with a grilled chicken breast. Daphne got the mac & cheese off the kid's menu and also asked for a Coke, but Jake insisted that she have milk instead.

After ordering, they sat in silence. The food came quickly, though, preventing the silence from becoming too awkward.

Claire drizzled some raspberry vinaigrette over her salad, then scooped a crouton and a nugget of soft feta cheese onto a forkful of crisp greens. The crunch of the crouton heralded an explosion of flavor in her mouth, as the tangy dressing and cheese blended with the mild lettuce.

"This is great!" Claire sliced a bit of grilled chicken breast off the piece on top of her salad. As she swallowed, she felt Chaucer's cold, wet nose poke against her knee. Without looking down, she cut off another piece of chicken. Then, while Jake was busy with his burger, she slipped it under the table to the dog.

Daphne grinned at her, and Claire winked back.

Between mouthfuls, Claire tried to draw Jake out some more about where he got the ideas for his book. Occasionally, she'd look up from her salad and catch him staring at her. When she did, he looked away and busied himself with his own meal, and he might have pulled off an air of nonchalance if he hadn't run his finger through the ketchup on his plate instead of his French fries.

Claire couldn't suppress her smile as he stared at the offending finger and blushed. She realized that Jake was too shy to make conversation and that her questions were mostly getting yes or no answers. After slipping another bite of chicken to Chaucer, she decided to change the subject in the hope of getting him to open up.

"Jake, you mentioned that you work nights. Who watches Chaucer while you work?"

"Oh, Daphne does. At least, she used to. My sister, Sarah, put a stop to that after last week's drama."

"Why? What happened?"

Daphne's eyes widened, but with a mouthful of cheesy noodles, she was unable to speak. Before she could swallow, Jake leaned forward and said, "Last week she got in hot water for sneaking out after bedtime. The story I heard is that

Chaucer got loose and she spent all night looking for him, not getting home till almost five a.m. My sister gave me a good tongue-lashing over the whole business."

Daphne glared at Jake for a moment and then swallowed. "It wasn't my fault. Or Chaucer's. And it wasn't fair of Mom to ground me for two days! That isn't what happened at all, anyway."

"Oh, dear!" Claire raised her eyebrows. "What did happen?"

Daphne put her spoon down and leaned forward. Speaking in a hushed tone, as if she were trying to keep a secret, she said, "It was those burglars. Chaucer and I caught 'em sneaking around Unca Jake's, but they kidnapped me. Us really, cause they took Chaucer, too. Then they took us to their hideout, and a bad man asked me lots of questions that didn't make sense. But I told him to let me go, or the sheriff would get him for kidnapping. Cause that's a crime, you know."

Daphne took a sip of milk and continued, "Anyway, he took me to see an even badder man—"

"Daphne, 'badder' isn't a real word," Jake said. "And why didn't you tell me about this before?"

"I was grounded, remember? Anyway, the second man was real bad. And he was real mean, too. Even the bad man who kidnapped me was scart of him."

"Did he hurt you?" Claire felt her face flush with anger as she glanced at Jake, who had stopped eating, a look of concern on his face.

"No, but I thought he might. He looked like he wanted to. But that didn't worry me, cause Chaucer was there."

"What scared you, then?"

Daphne screwed up her face and tilted her head to the side. "It was the way he looked at me. Timmy brought a snake to school once, and he got away with it, cause he gets away with everything. But nobody would touch it. The way it looked at you gave me goosebumps. The bad man had the same look."

"We should tell this to the police right away," Claire said to Jake.

"Damn straight we will!" Jake turned back to Daphne and asked, "Did you get the names of these men? Can you describe them?"

"One of them told me his name, the one who asked all the questions. But it was a funny name and I'm not sure I remember it right. But I'd know him anywhere. He was dressed all in black, like a ninja, and he was tall, taller than you, Unca Jake. And he smelled funny.

"Oh, and he had trouble sitting down, on account of he had a big bandage on his butt."

Claire's hand went to her throat as she felt the air squeeze out of her chest. "Daphne, did the man have gray eyes?"

"Yes, ma'am. I forgot about that."

"And his name…"

"Like I said, it was a funny-sounding name. Like a cow, you know? 'Moo-once,' or something like that."

"Nuance?" Claire asked softly, barely able to breathe.

"Yeah! That's it. How'd you know?"

Brows furrowed, Jake turned to Claire. "Yes, how did you know that?"

"I've met him." Claire felt like a boat that had slipped its mooring, her thoughts thrashing like splintered oars while everything around her floated away.

"Met him? When?" Jake's anger focused on Claire as she raised a napkin over her mouth as if to hide.

"He took me…we had lunch…he wanted to know something."

"What?"

"About you."

"Me?" Jake sat back, surprised.

"Yes." Claire's voice sank to a whisper as she mentally curled in upon herself. "I'm sorry."

Jake stared at her for a moment or two, then asked, "What did this Nuance character want to know about me?"

"He thinks you're a spy. I'm supposed to…" Claire couldn't finish. She pressed her napkin to her lips as if to block any more words from escaping her mouth.

"A spy? Me?! Who is this guy?"

"He's a naval officer."

"Where can I find him? And what about the other guy, the one with the empty eyes?"

"That's Admiral Dutchman. And no, you don't want to find him."

"Why not?"

Claire swallowed. "What Daphne said. It's worse than that. He's…" Claire closed her eyes, trying to keep from trembling at the memory of her encounter with Dutchman.

"You're scared." Jake's voice was soft and sympathetic. "What did they do to you?"

Claire couldn't answer, just shook her head and looked away.

"Did they threaten you?"

Shaking, Claire nodded yes.

"Bastards!" Jake jumped to his feet, knocking his chair over backward. "Where are they?"

"They have offices in Northwood's main building."

"You're kidding! That's where I work. Why haven't I seen them?"

"I don't know. But there's more than just the two of them. They have at least a dozen marines with them."

"But that's not possible."

"Unca Jake, she's right," Daphne spoke up, drawing Jake's attention back to his niece. "They're bad people. Just ask Felipe. He saw them too."

"Felipe? But he's been missing since Wednesday night when you went—oh my God! Daphne, when these men kidnapped you, did they take Felipe too?"

"I don't know for sure, Unca Jake, but they might have. He was fight'n with them when I got there. Chaucer tried to help, but then I got zapped and fell down. I didn't see Felipe after that."

Jake rounded on Claire. "And you knew about this?"

"Yes, some of it, I'm sorry."

"And my book? Was asking about that just a pretext to spy on me?"

"Jake, I didn't want to. I'm—"

"Done here! Daphne, go home and take Chaucer with you! I'm going to pay a visit to this Nuance character. If he's holding Felipe, I'll…well, I'll figure that out when I get there. But there's gonna be trouble!" Jake slapped some money down on the table to cover his and Daphne's meals and then stalked away.

Claire watched him go, wanting desperately to say something to bring him back, but sadness and guilt had her by the throat. Her mouth worked, but no sound came out. *What have I*

done? I knew this was wrong. Why didn't I stand up to Nuance? I'm
such a loser. Now I'll never see Becca and Sam again.

Claire's bitter thoughts were interrupted by a gentle touch
on her arm. Daphne was standing next to her, holding out a
napkin. Claire reached up and found that her cheeks were wet.
She took the napkin, and Daphne gave her a hug.

"It'll be okay, Miss Claire. It's not your fault."

"That's kind of you to say, Daphne, but it is. It's all my
fault."

"Actually, it isn't. I guess I have a confession to make."

"How's that?" Distracted by her own misery, Claire responded without paying much attention to what the child was
saying.

"See, Unca Jake tries so hard. And he's really, really good.
But he can't get a break. He's written a couple of other books,
but nobody would publish them. And that made him sad. So I
decided to help."

"Help? How?"

"It was me. I sent his book to you."

"What?"

"I found where Chaucer had buried it in the back yard. He
does that to most of the stuff Unca Jake writes. So I asked my
teacher how to publish it, and she told me what to do."

"She told you?" Daphne's story pulled Claire out of her
self-pity as she began to sense what had happened.

"Ms. Eliot said to send it to an agent. And that if I said it
was non-fiction then it would have a better chance, cause non-
fiction is important."

"And so you sent it to me?" Claire's eyebrows rose as
Daphne gained her full attention.

"Yes, ma'am. I'm sorry. I shouldn't have lied about the book, being non-fiction and all."

"That's okay, Daphne." Claire gave the girl a hug. "You've done nothing wrong. People do far worse to get themselves published, trust me."

Claire hugged Daphne again, and this time Chaucer joined in, shoving his nose into Claire's armpit and making snuffling noises.

"We should go." Claire released Daphne from the hug as she stood up. "I'll walk you home. Then I need to think about what to do next."

Daphne held Claire's hand as they left the diner. After they'd walked half a block, she pulled her to a stop and asked, "Miss Claire?"

"Yes?"

"Is Unca Jake in trouble?"

"Yes, I'm afraid he is. Very much so."

"It's that mean Moo-once character, isn't it?"

"Him, and the other one."

"Can you help him?"

"I will if I can, Daphne. I will if I can."

25

The Northwood office where Jake worked was only four blocks from Ethel's Diner, and he made the trip in less than ten minutes. Oblivious to the blued perfection of the sky, the hum of traffic on Main Street, or the ozone smell of passing cars, Jake walked heads-down, eyes focused on a point well beyond the sidewalk ahead of him. By the time he arrived, he'd worked himself into a frenzy, furious at Claire's betrayal and determined to find out what had happened to Felipe. And he was angry with himself, too. *I thought she liked me. I'm such a jerk. As if a cute girl like that would look at a dork like me.*

Carding in through the employees' entrance, Jake went straight to his boss's office. The door was open, and Jake was about to barge in without knocking when he had a thought.

Jake diverted to his small, gray-walled cubicle and logged onto the company's network. *They think they're smart, eh? Let's see them hide from a UNIX admin.* It took longer than he expected to find what he was looking for on the system. In the end, he listed the IP addresses for every piece of electronics in the building, including devices that weren't on the Northwood network. Then he subtracted all the known pieces of equipment. *Got 'em! Man, these guys are good. No wonder I never spotted them before.*

Jake engaged a sniffer, a device that monitors every bite of data flowing from a system, and attached it to one of the unknown IP addresses. The raw data capture looked binary. *Most likely a video stream.* So he piped it to a media app, sat back, and watched…himself.

Jake stared in disbelief at the video of his cube. It showed the back of his head. He lifted his right hand, and his hand moved on the screen. He turned to see if he could spot the camera just as a tall man dressed in a khaki uniform appeared at the entrance to his cube.

"Looking for something, Mr. Andersen?"

Jake sat back in his chair, too surprised to say anything.

"Please step away from your keyboard, Mr. Andersen, and don't do anything foolish."

"Who are you?" Jake remained seated. The fury that had evaporated when he saw himself on camera quickly returned.

"Commander Nuance, Military Intelligence." Nuance gestured, and two men dressed in black uniforms stepped forward. "Bring him."

As Nuance walked away, Jake found himself seized and wrestled into an armlock before he even realized he was in a fight. His efforts to free himself only caused the men holding him to twist harder, making him cry out in pain.

The men didn't speak, just frog-marched Jake out of his cube and down several hallways until they reached an unoccupied office. Nuance was waiting at the door.

"Prep him," Nuance said.

The agents forced Jake into the room, a dreary gray space like the one he'd just left, then zip-tied him to a chair. After making sure he was secured, they left.

Jake looked around. The room was empty except for a gray, steel desk, and the chair that he was sitting on. The gray-green walls had no pictures or windows, and together with the gray linoleum floor, created the effect of being trapped in a very dull box, a sensation accentuated by the room's stuffy, warm air. *It was a trap. And I walked right into it.*

26

Jake shifted in his chair, trying without success to relieve the pressure from the zip-ties that pinned him in place and pinched off the circulation in his arms and legs. The only sound in the room was his own heartbeat, fast at first, then slower. As with most of the Northwood offices, the air was a bit stale and smelled of welded steel. As time passed, his unease grew. *What the heck is going on? Who are these people? How can they come into my place of work and just grab me from my desk?*

Voices outside his door caught his attention. He tried to make out what was being said, but the conversation was brief.

Then the door behind him opened. Jake twisted round to see three men enter the room, two in black uniforms and a third in military camo.

"Hey, what's going on?" Jake demanded.

There was no answer. The black-clad agents grabbed him. One held his body, while the other pinned down his right arm.

"Hey, stop it!"

The man in camo wiped the inside of Jake's elbow with an alcohol swab, held up a syringe and said, "Hold still, and this will go easier for you. I just need a blood sample."

"Like hell!" Jake tried to wrench himself free of the men who were holding him but had no success. They were experienced with troublesome prisoners and gave him no opportunity to evade the needle.

They were done in a minute. The man in camo labeled the vial of Jake's blood, then all three men left the room.

A piece of gauze taped over Jake's puncture wound developed a red spot as blood seeped into it. Jake muttered to himself, summoning all the invective that a creative writer could muster, which was quite a bit given the circumstances.

The soft click of the door opening brought his head around. Nuance entered the room carrying a thick folder. After he sat down at the desk, he leafed through the papers in the folder, then looked up.

Jake felt his anger slip away, replaced by fear. Nuance's stare was like a sheet of ice closing over a lake, killing everything in its path.

When Nuance spoke, his voice was even colder than his eyes. "Please confirm for me that you are Jake Andersen, employed by Northwood Shipbuilding as a UNIX administrator."

"Yeah, that's me. Why? What's this all about? Am I under arrest?"

"That will be determined at a later time. For now, you're being held for questioning in a matter concerning national security."

"Held for questioning? Hey, I want a lawyer!"

Nuance sat back in his chair, steepled his fingers, and regarded Jake in silence for a moment. "Your wants, Mr. Andersen, are immaterial to this investigation."

"No way! I know my rights!"

"Mr. Andersen, the FISC court has issued a warrant for your arrest for espionage. Under the terms of the Patriot Act, I'm authorized to hold and question you for as long as required and in whatever manner I deem necessary to protect the interests of this country. Suitable legal representation will be provided for you when I am done. If there's anything left to represent."

Jake stared, appalled.

"Now then, Mr. Andersen, will you cooperate?"

"Yes," Jake whispered. "What do you want?"

Nuance glanced down at his folder, a hint of a satisfied smile on his face. "First smart thing you've done in weeks, Mr. Andersen," he murmured. "Now then, tell me about your operation here. What was your objective? Who are your fellow agents? Where is your base?"

"Base? Agents? I don't understand."

"Please don't insult my intelligence by pretending innocence. We already have one of your partners in custody, and we've found out some interesting facts about him. Very interesting, indeed. I think that you know what I'm talking about.

How long did you think you could hide and pass yourself off as one of us?"

"Hide? I'm not hiding anything!"

"Then tell me the truth! Why are you here?"

"Because you arrested me!"

Nuance's expression didn't change, but Jake somehow felt like he'd just said the wrong thing.

"Look, Andersen, we already know what you were up to. We found your book with all the Eschaton data. Top secret stuff. That alone will put you and your friends away for a lifetime. But there's also the other aspect of all this. Who you represent, and what they plan to do with our missile defense secrets. Well, we actually have a good idea about that, too. All I need from you is confirmation of what we already know. Give me that, and things will go easier for you and your team."

"My book?"

"Yes. That little diary you wrote with all of our defense secrets in it."

"That? How did you get it?"

"Honestly, it nearly slipped past us. Your team's mistake was trying to kill one of our agents to get it back. Your little scheme backfired when the police arrived before you could retrieve the documents."

"Kill? Scheme? Wait a sec, I didn't try to kill anybody!"

"Doesn't matter whether it was you or one of your team. You're involved, and that makes you an accessory. The only difference is that your friend will fry, while you just get a lifetime vacation in a cement cell."

"My friend?"

"Friend, teammate, partner. Call him what you like, we have him. He tried to pass himself off as you, but we figured the truth out pretty quick."

"Who are you talking about?"

"Fellow could pass for Latino, if we didn't know that he was from much, much further away. Like you. Now then, let's go back to the missile secrets you stole."

"But I didn't steal anything! Well, okay, I did use some stuff that I found on the company network, but it was public domain, anyway!"

"Do you expect me to swallow that baloney?"

"No, I mean, yes. I mean…it's the truth. The book's just a story I made up. It's pure fiction. You've got to believe me!"

"Why?"

Jake's mouth worked, but no words came out.

"Look, Jake, this is not just about you. Your partner, Felipe, is in serious trouble for assaulting our agents. Add espionage to the mix, and he'll never see the light of day again. Not that he'll last long on a dissection table in our Roswell facility, anyway. Maybe you're willing to sacrifice him, but what about Claire?"

"Dissection? What are you talking about? And Claire's working for you. Why should—"

"That, my friend, won't fly. We know that you passed the documents to her. She's in this up to her pretty little eyebrows, and if you care for her at all, you'll cooperate. Otherwise, she'll end up on the table with your buddy. And I understand that the doctors don't plan to use anesthetics. They have no idea what would work on somebody like you, anyway."

"You're crazy!"

"Jake, you and your friends can be spared all—well, most—of the nastiness. I have broad leeway in your disposition. Help me, and I can help your friends."

"But I don't know anything!"

Nuance slammed his palm on the table. The whip-crack noise made Jake jerk back in his chair. "Dammit, Andersen, I'm trying to help you! Do you know what they'll do to you? To an alien?"

"But I'm not an alien!"

"Your partner is. Why wouldn't you be too?"

"But he's legal, he's got all the right documentation."

"Of course he does. I'd expect nothing less from an advanced civilization. But you can't hide your DNA. We know where he's from, and in a very short while we'll know the same about you. Now tell me, who was Claire supposed to pass the document to?"

"I don't know, I didn't send it to her in the first place."

"Then who did?"

Jake opened his mouth to say that Daphne had sent the book to Claire, but he realized just in time what that meant. *I can't get her involved in this. Whatever this is.*

"That's what I thought. Look, Andersen, time's running out for you. Tell me the names of the other people in your spy cell and we won't have to explore other forms of interrogation."

"Other?" The saliva in Jake's mouth was like a thick rope from fear. "You mean, like waterboarding?"

"Waterboarding is for amateurs. We use techniques that won't kill you, but will make you wish that we had." Nuance smiled as he leaned forward, the effect that of an alligator sidling up to its prey. "Things that aren't covered by your health insurance or dental plan."

"Look, I really don't know anything! How many times do I have to say that? I can't tell you something that I don't know!"

Nuance stood, putting the papers away in the folder. "I'm sorry you're taking that attitude, Andersen. I'm going to give you a little time to think things over before we move on to the next phase of our discussion. I don't like to do this sort of thing, you know, but I'll do whatever it takes to bring in your fellow spies."

Jake slumped in his chair after Nuance left. His shirt clung to his chest, cold with sweat. *I need to keep Daphne out of this. And how'd a girl like Claire get involved with these people? What did they do to her?*

27

Admiral Dutchman raised his eyes as Nuance entered his office. "Take a seat."

There was a soft squeak of leather as Nuance lowered himself carefully into a chair.

Dutchman gestured to his laptop screen and said, "I watched the interrogation. Care to explain why you went so easy on him?"

"Yes, sir. The suspect maintains his innocence, and the evidence linking him to the security breach is not as strong as we initially thought. Worse, we've found nothing after repeated searches of his home, his office, and his electronic devices. If he's got anything to hide, it has to be at a different location, one that we have yet to identify."

"I've seen your note on that subject, commander, but it changes nothing. Have you forgotten the DNA evidence? That's not easy to fake. But switching around some page numbers in a document? How dumb do they think we are, to fall for a ruse like that? No, I believe that your original analysis of the situation remains solid. We will proceed on that basis."

"Yes, sir."

"Which brings us back to your handling of Mr. Andersen."

Dutchman stared at Nuance, letting the silence stretch to drive up the tension in the room. Nuance returned his stare without altering his expression. *Nuance is a tough cookie. It would be fun to try and break him. But this is no time for games.*

Closing his laptop, Dutchman leaned back and steepled his hands. "I will remind you, commander, that time is short. We need results, or this investigation will be taken out of our hands." *And I'll lose all the credit for it.* "How do you plan to break the current impasse?"

"Sir, I plan to implement the staged escape that we discussed. Based on the psych profile of the woman, I expect her to attempt to free Andersen within the next twenty-four hours."

"Twenty-four hours is a long time, commander. Find a way to speed things up."

"Yes, sir, if you think that's necessary. But the psych officer is convinced that the woman will crack within that period and will attempt a rescue without any prompting from us. If we interfere and push her, it might produce less satisfactory results."

"The psych officer is a timid, pencil-pushing desk jockey and I'm disappointed, commander, that you would pander to such tripe! Have you forgotten the nature of the intrusion and the deadline we're facing?

"No, sir. I'm well aware of the criticality of our investigation."

"Well, then?"

"I'll have my team prod her into action this afternoon."

"And?"

"I've already had the team prep for the second phase of the interrogation. After we re-capture the subjects, we'll use enhanced techniques to break them and induce regression."

"How far are you prepared to go?"

"As far as I need to, sir. We have two prisoners, so we can afford to lose one of them. If the staged escape leads us to additional spies, we'll have even more to work with. That gives us some leeway in our methods. We'll combine sensory stimuli with physical stressors to induce pain, fear, and uncertainty in the prisoners. The psych officer—" Nuance paused to look at Dutchman. Seeing no reaction, he continued. "The psych officer thinks that they'll both break with minimal effort. Neither has any history of athletic or military training, nor have either of them participated in any studies that might have helped to build the mental discipline required to withstand such techniques."

Dutchman frowned. "Commander, you're talking about these subjects as if they were just a couple of city boys fresh out of college. Are you forgetting what we're dealing with here? Any training they've had would have been performed long before they were inserted into the Northwood facility. And we have no idea what kind of mental disciplines an alien civilization might have developed to prepare their spies for just this scenario. We've already seen how well they can mimic human physiology. If it hadn't been for the DNA test, we'd never have suspected a damn thing. Make no assumptions about any training they might, or might not, have had."

"Understood, sir. Our lack of knowledge about the subjects has inclined me to adopt a cautious approach. They've been examined for suicide implants, and we didn't find any, but if they are more advanced than we are, then we might not recognize something organic in nature."

"Didn't you say a minute ago that you had a 'spare tire,' so to speak?"

"Yes, sir. I catch your drift."

"Very well, then. Now walk me through the escape you have planned."

"Yes, sir. I believe that the Miller woman's guilt will, with a little push from us, induce her to confront me and demand to know Andersen's status."

"Demand?" Dutchman raised an eyebrow. "What makes you think a little mouse like that will have the backbone to 'demand' anything?"

"She's repressing a lot of anger fueled by guilt over the breakup of her family. When she finally cracks, a different persona will emerge, one obsessed with easing her guilt. We've already tangled Andersen's situation up with her family's tragedy in her mind. She can't do anything about her family, but she'll believe that she can help Andersen, which by transference should drive her to act on his behalf."

"What makes you so sure of that?"

"We observed their interactions when they met and then again over lunch. Their body language showed a mutual attraction. They kept leaning in as they spoke, and they demonstrated a heightened level of animation when speaking. The thermal imagers also indicated some heat build-up in their genital regions. They're into each other, although they don't realize it yet."

"Okay, so the woman will pay you a visit. What then?"

"We put her in with Andersen and the other alien, and then give them a chance to escape."

"That seems a little thin. Won't she suspect something?"

"I'll act reluctant to allow her to see him, and then give in grudgingly. I'm pretty sure I can sell the scenario to her."

"What about the other two? Skilled agents won't fall for such a ruse."

"We'll put them in a room where they can, with a little initiative, gain access to the building's systems. Tech-savvy characters like those two shouldn't need any other opportunity to escape."

"But what if they decide not to?"

"They know what's in store for them if they don't escape. Besides, their cover is blown, so they have no reason to stay. They'll bolt at the first opportunity."

"And then?"

"We'll wound one and recapture him, letting the other man go. We also haul the Miller woman back in. Alone, and with clear evidence that we mean him harm, the escaped alien is certain to seek a safe haven. We'll follow him to the group's secret base and then send in the marines."

"Very well, commander. Make it so."

After Nuance had left, Dutchman opened his laptop and reread the latest email from the Joint Chiefs. *Want a status update, eh? Concerned about my lack of progress and insufficient detail in my reports? By tomorrow morning I'll be untouchable. Unless Nuance screws up. But, that'll be on him, not me.*

Claire felt betrayed by the sapphire sky and the scent of fresh-cut grass as she walked Daphne home from Ethel's Diner. *No day this bad should look this good.* Daphne's hand was warm in hers, and she felt awkward, receiving more comfort from the child's touch than she gave back. The inversion of roles emphasized her feeling of teetering on a balance ball, not knowing which way she might fall.

If Jake confronts Nuance, he'll end up in jail. Claire didn't want that to happen, but she had no idea how to prevent it.

When they reached Daphne's home, Claire waited on the sidewalk until the girl was safely inside. Chaucer paused to push his nose against her palm, gave it a good licking, and then followed Daphne into the house, looking back several times as he did so. Watching Daphne walk away was like watching a ship sail away in a movie. Each step seemed to take longer as time seemed to stretch, an unbearable feeling of tension forming in Claire's breast.

Claire walked back to her apartment in a daze, people and places floating past her, just out of touch, out of reach, like photos gyring in a breeze. When she got inside, she sat at the kitchen counter, mind blank, forehead on her hands, staring at the faded picture of her sister on the fridge.

Half an hour passed while she sat frozen, detached from the world. Her cell rang, but she didn't answer it. It rang again several more times, then switched itself to maximum volume.

Claire shifted to look at it, curious at this thing that had intruded on her emptiness, forcing her to pay attention to it. She finally picked it up.

"Miss Miller, we need to talk." The woman's soft, southern accent was familiar, and Claire felt like she should know it somehow, but she was having trouble focusing her thoughts.

"Miss Miller?"

Claire stared at the phone, unable to speak.

"Look, Miss Miller, I know you can hear me. Now listen up! Your performance over lunch was abysmal. It was so bad in fact that I'd describe it as a complete failure. You do under-stand what will happen if you fail your assignment, right?"

"Failure…" The word slithered around Claire's mind several times before it slipped out.

"Yes, complete failure. And if I had my way, you'd never see your brother or sister again. Not after that wretched effort."

"Never?"

"Never. But Commander Nuance said to give you one more chance. Even though you screwed up. Do you understand what I'm saying?"

"Understand?" Claire looked back at the pictures on her fridge. Suddenly the room came into focus as she felt a pulse of heat deep inside. Her eyes felt dry and hot. *He'll stop at nothing to get what he wants.* She took a deep, shuddering breath and then said, "Oh yes, I understand."

"That's better. Now let me make this perfectly clear for you. You're out of time. You need to find something useful about Andersen today, or we'll make sure you never see your siblings again. And you know we can do that."

"What if I can't find anything? I'm not even sure there's anything to find—"

"That would be unfortunate for you."

The line suddenly went dead, leaving Claire to stare at her phone as her stomach roiled with urgency and hopelessness, twisting itself into a tight little ball right dead center where she needed to breathe. *Failed again.*

Claire sat motionless for what seemed like hours, staring at the pictures on her fridge while her mind hamstered in tight little circles, unable to stop yet unable to move forward either. *Failure* echoed over and over in her head like tiny footsteps tapping a relentless rhythm to her distress.

She thought that her head might split open from the building pressure of thoughts that she couldn't escape. Pressing her palms to her eyes as if to hold it all in, she was distracted by a scent. Her right hand smelled of dog where Chaucer had licked it. It was the smallest of things, but the smell pulled her back, drew her attention away from the cyclone racking her brain.

I forgot to wash my hands.

Claire rose and made her way to the bathroom, where she stared into the mirror as she scrubbed Chaucer's saliva from her hands. She washed them once, and then she washed them again and again. Not to get rid of the smell, which was gone after the first scrub; rather, the warm water and the lavender scent of the soap was like a ritual, a baptismal cleansing that laved her soul in oil. She breathed deep of the lavender, drew it in, let it carry her where it would.

The face in the mirror changed to that of an older woman. *Mom. What do I do now?*

And Claire remembered. Advice from long ago, from when she had gone rafting with her mother. The water was running fast around them, and she could see whitewater ahead, dominated by a whirlpool that was already pulling them in. *The way out of a vortex is through it.*

Claire stopped washing her hands and picked up a towel to dry them, holding it up to her face as she did so that she could still enjoy the scent.

I can't help Becca and Sam. I can't even help myself. But Daphne, and Jake?

The way out of a vortex is through it.

Claire tossed the towel aside and strode to the kitchen counter. Grabbing her purse, she picked up her cell from where she'd dropped it on the floor earlier.

She didn't bother to lock the door on her way out. *Burglars are the least of my worries. Besides, Nuance's people are watching my place like hawks. Who needs home security when you've got Homeland Security?!*

Ten minutes later, she marched through the front door of the Northwood office, buttonholed the marine who was stationed just inside, and asked to see Nuance.

The soldier spoke into his headset, nodded when he received an answer, and then gestured for Claire to follow him.

Nuance was seated at his desk when she entered his office. Other than a desk and chair, the only other furniture in the room was only a single, uncomfortable-looking chair. Nuance didn't invite her to sit, and Claire wasn't in the mood for social niceties anyway.

Leaning on the back of the unoccupied chair, she said, "Commander, Jake Andersen was coming to see you this afternoon. Can you please tell—"

"Be quiet." Nuance leaned forward as he interrupted her, lancing her with his gaze. "Miss Miller, you're supposed to be out gathering information about Mr. Andersen, speaking with his neighbors, his friends, or even that sweet little niece of his. Going through his house. Checking what books he's read. Not storming into my office."

Claire tried to match Nuance's gaze but felt her will crumbling. She bit her lower lip in hesitation, then said, "I'd be surprised if your people hadn't already examined all of those things, and done so more thoroughly than I ever could. And that's not what you originally asked me to do, anyway."

"Oh, so you remember after all, do you?"

"Yes, and I've done everything—"

"You've done nothing!" Nuance shouted, standing to lean over his desk. Claire took an involuntary step back, intimidated by Nuance's physical outburst. "You put off meeting him for days. Then, when you finally did get a chance to speak with him the first thing out of your mouth was a confession that you were spying on him! How did you expect that to play out? What have you been using for brains, Jell-O?"

"No, it wasn't like that."

"Oh, please. Cut the crap. I have a video of the whole disaster. It couldn't have been worse if the frigging Titanic had hit your table."

"The Titanic?" Claire was momentarily confused by Nuance's mixed metaphor.

"You know what I mean." His voice dropped to a soft, disturbingly normal tone. "Now tell me, how do you plan to fix this?"

"Fix it? Look, I think you've made a terrible mistake. I just don't believe that Jake is a spy."

"Really? After one botched lunch date, you think you know all about the man."

"He's not the type!"

"And who is 'the type'?"

Claire stared at Nuance, then whispered, "You are."

Nuance sighed theatrically. "Miss Miller, you are so naïve it hurts my brain to talk to you. Spies, real spies, don't walk around with signs on their foreheads announcing their chosen profession. They are trained to blend in, to pass themselves off as ordinary people. They look like you, like the people all around you and that you work with every day. And they can look like Mr. Andersen."

"But I don't get that feeling from him."

"And what kind of feeling does he give you?"

Claire blushed. "He's a nice guy. That's all."

"We'll soon find out."

"What do you mean?" Nuance's tone conveyed a hint of anticipation blended with understated malice that made the hairs on Claire's arms stand on end.

"I mean that as a result of your failure to obtain useful information from Mr. Andersen, I'll be speaking with him myself."

"You've arrested him, then? He's here?"

"Yes, and yes. Not that it's any concern of yours. I'm done with you."

"But the woman on the phone said I'd get another chance!"

"Did she? What did you have in mind?"

"Let me speak with Jake! I'm certain that I can get to the bottom of this whole mess."

"Why would he trust you? You just betrayed him, and I kinda think you're the last person he wants to see right now."

"I need to try."

Nuance sat back down, steepled his fingers, and looked steadily at her for a few moments. "Well, I can't see where it would do any harm. But I don't expect much, given your past performance. You've got half an hour."

Nuance tapped a message on his cell. A minute later, one of his agents and a marine in camo appeared to escort Claire from the room.

They took her down several hallways, stopping at a door near one of the building's emergency exits.

"Wait here," the agent said, pushing her inside then closing the door behind her.

Claire looked around; the room looked the same as the others she'd seen in the building, except that it was empty, with not even a desk or chair to sit on. There were no windows, just a locked closet door in one of the dingy walls. She'd barely had time to survey the room when the main door opened, and Jake was shoved in.

"What are you doing here?" he asked, his face flushed with anger.

Claire swallowed. "I'm here to help you."

"Haven't you done enough of that already? And what exactly do you think you can do to help, anyway?"

Claire felt her face flush as she looked away. Then, on a sudden impulse, she stepped forward and laid her hand on Jake's arm. "I don't know. But I can't—"

Claire was interrupted by the door opening again. Two agents frog-marched a man into the room, then slammed the door on the way out.

Jake and Claire both stared at the newcomer.

"Hi!" Felipe said, then slumped against the wall, sliding to sit on the floor.

29

After Jake stormed off to confront Nuance, Daphne worried about him all afternoon. Her concern mounted when he didn't show up for supper. Jake usually joined her family on Saturday nights for dinner, and her mom waited for him for an hour before she gave up and served the food. Daphne guessed what had happened, and she figured it was her own fault for telling Jake about Felipe's arrest. But she couldn't tell her mom. That would cause more trouble.

They'd barely sat down at the worn oak dinner table when her mom's cell rang. "Go ahead and finish, Daphne, this might be a while."

Daphne picked at her deep-fried perch, slathering each bite of the sweet fish in tangy tartar sauce. Some of her broccoli also managed to get a dab of the sauce, masking its bitter flavor.

Her mom was still on the phone when Daphne finished, so she washed up and then headed out the door. "Mom, I'm taking Chaucer out for a bit."

"Go ahead, dear."

Daphne felt a growing pressure inside, like a balloon filling with guilt. She felt it pushing her to do something to help Jake. But what? Daphne needed to think about how she could fix the problem she'd caused, so she headed to her favorite spot to do so, a sandbar on the southeast edge of town. Her mom didn't like her to stray that far from home, some thirteen blocks, but Chaucer was with her. Besides, nothing bad ever happened in Marinette. That's what her uncle always said. But now Jake himself was in trouble.

Hopping on her bike, Daphne peddled along the sidewalk with Chaucer trotting alongside her until she reached Red Arrow Park at the entrance to the sandbar. Dropping her bike at the entrance, she cut through the park. As she did, she brushed her fingers across the cold, rough surface of a four-foot high granite boulder that stood there. It was a memorial to the 32nd Armored Division that gave the park its name. Every time she passed it, she thought about her father. She hadn't seen him since his unit had been sent to the Middle East, over a year ago. Sometimes she cried when she thought that someday there might be a boulder for him.

Daphne skirted the shallow lagoon that ran down the center of the sandbar. As she did, the faint, rotten-egg smell of the stagnant water gave way to the spicy-sweet resin of the jack pines that ran next to the lagoon with some white birches. Halfway along the narrow, fawn-colored beach that separated the trees from the lake, she spotted a sign warning of nesting plovers. A couple of the tawny little birds scooted across a sand dune like tan bowling balls, making soft *pee-werp* calls as they fled her presence. Nearby, some white and gray gulls cast long shadows on the darkling sand. They ignored her as they squabbled over a luckless crayfish, their greedy "mine, mine, mine" calls muted in the evening air.

Daphne skirted the plover nesting area and kept going until she reached the tip of the sandbar. Once there, she kicked off her sneakers and sat down, scrunching her toes in the sand. The coarse grit tickled her feet, but for a change, she didn't enjoy it.

For a time, she just sat looking out at the water. The last rays of the sunset highlighted the tips of the waves with ruby sparkles as the lake settled down in the evening hush. A flight of cormorants skimmed over the water, silent and dark against the indigo sky as they returned to their roost. Daphne shivered as the rising offshore breeze leached the warmth from her legs. She pulled her navy hoodie a little tighter against the chill and frowned.

"Unca Jake should've been home by suppertime, Chaucer. And perch is his favorite." Daphne paused as she used her tongue to work loose a bit of the sweet fish that was stuck in her teeth.

The dog looked up from where he lay next to her and whined.

"He always comes over for Saturday dinner. Now, Mom's worried, cause he didn't show." Daphne leaned close to Chaucer and waved her finger in front of his nose for emphasis. "I bet that mean Commander Moo-once has got him. I wish I hadn't told Unca Jake about him. He's gone off to rescue Felipe and he hasn't come back."

Chaucer whined, then barked twice. Daphne scratched his ears. He gave a little kick of contentment, then settled down with his head on her lap, looking up at her, his soft brown eyes glowing with canine adoration.

"The problem is, we don't know anything for sure. Mom said we shouldn't worry, he's a big boy, and whatever he's up to, he can take care of himself. But what if he's the one needs rescuing?"

Daphne hugged her knees to her chest as she gave the matter some thought.

"Chaucer, we got to do something."

Brushing the sand off her feet, she put on her sneakers and stood up. Chaucer came to attention, tail wagging with a dog's natural intuition that something was up. Picking up her bike on the way out of the park, Daphne headed home. She explained the situation to Chaucer on the way.

"We got to find out what happened to Unca Jake. But we can't get Mom upset again. So here's what we'll do. After she's in bed tonight, we'll sneak down to the shipyard. That's where the bad guys are holed up."

Chaucer chuffed agreement.

"Yep, we'll have to be quiet. And maybe disguise ourselves. Just in case we get spotted. You can't be too careful, you know?"

Daphne checked Jake's house before going home. It was silent and dark, confirming her fear that something had happened to him.

When she did arrive home she found her mom sitting at the kitchen table. Yellow light from the ceiling fixture gave a honey glow to the table's worn oak and picked out auburn highlights in her mom's long, chestnut hair. The room's only window opened a dark rectangle against the floral wallpaper where faded roses hinted at better days long past.

Her mother was hunched over her cell. Untouched, her plate of perch, broccoli, and mashed potatoes had grown cold on the table next to her. She didn't look up when Daphne entered the room.

Daphne watched her for a minute. "Mom?"

"Oh, hi, Daphne. I'm sorry, I didn't see you come in."

"Mom, is everything okay?"

Her mom brushed a tear from her cheek and then rose to give the girl a fierce hug. "Yes, dear, things will be okay."

"It's Dad, isn't it?"

"Yes, dear. I'm sorry, but his tour's been extended. It'll be another six months before he can come home."

"It'll be okay, Mom. Dad's real good at soldiering." Daphne could feel her mother's ribs through her brown fleece pullover as she squeezed her tight. The pullover had been snug when they first moved to Marinette, but now it hung loose and sack-like. Her mom had lost a lot of weight over the past year, but when Daphne asked about it, she'd just said that she was dieting.

Her mother looked around and seemed surprised to find that it was already dark. "Daphne, honey, it's getting late. Where have you been?"

"I was just down by the park, Mom."

"I wish you wouldn't go down there after dark. It's not safe."

"It's okay, Mom, I had Chaucer with me."

Her mom scowled down at the dog. "He can be more trouble than help."

"But he's fierce, Mom. If there was trouble, he'd do something. 'Member that skunk that got into Unca Jake's back yard? Chaucer sure gave him a piece of his mind!"

Her mom smiled. "Actually, dear, Chaucer got the worst of that engagement. Jake made him sleep on his back porch for three days until the smell died down."

"But Mom, he chased the skunk off! That's real heroic stuff. 'Specially cause he suffered in a good cause."

"Oh, he suffered all right. So did everybody who came near him afterward."

Daphne's mom gave her another hug. "Now then, it's time for good little girls to take a bath and head for bed."

"Can Chaucer stay in my room tonight?"

Her mom sighed. "I suppose. It looks like Jake's out late, and we can't just leave the poor thing alone in his house. But no shenanigans! I don't need another visit from the sheriff!"

"Yes, ma'am! Thanks!"

The bathroom had a white tub and fixtures. Light blue tiles covered the wall around the tub, matched by pale lavender floral wallpaper and a gold-flecked blue linoleum floor. Chaucer curled up next to the bathroom door while Daphne filled the tub with hot water.

While she was taking her bath, Daphne squeezed some of her mom's lilac-scented cream rinse onto her hair, thinking that the scent would help her to sneak through the flowering bushes scattered around the shipyard.

When done, she put down fresh food and water for Chaucer, making sure to give him extra chow. "Now, you eat all of this," she whispered. "You need to keep your strength up if we're going to help Unca Jake later."

Daphne lay in her bed for what seemed like hours, waiting for her mom to go to sleep. She could smell fresh-cut grass on the light breeze rippling the curtains of the window over her bed. Her patchwork quilt was pulled up tight to her neck so that when her mom came in she wouldn't notice that she was fully dressed.

But her mom didn't come in, not for some time. Daphne could hear the soft click of her mother's shoes as she paced the kitchen. The sound stopped and Daphne heard the clink of the tea kettle as her mom poured hot water into a teacup. Then the pacing started again. That made Daphne sad. She knew that her mom was lonely, that she missed her dad, and that she was worried sick about him. Daphne couldn't do anything about that, but she figured that she could help her uncle. And maybe that would help her mom be happy again.

Finally, the pacing stopped and her mom came in to give her a goodnight kiss.

It was a long time after that before Daphne heard the soft, regular breathing that let her know that her mom had fallen asleep.

"Shhh!" As Daphne slipped out of bed, she shushed the dog before he had time to bark. "Chaucer, you be quiet, okay?"

Daphne pulled on her hoodie and sneakers, then slipped out the window, followed by the dog.

"We need disguises, Chaucer. Got any ideas?"

Chaucer wagged his tail, but seemed to come up short otherwise.

"Maybe we can find something at Unca Jake's."

Daphne slipped into Jake's house through the back door. She made her way through the small kitchen, bumping into the dining room table in the process. Jake had left the blinds drawn over his bedroom windows, so she turned on the light, confident that she wouldn't be spotted.

Aside from a rumpled bed, the room had a small lamp sitting on a wooden nightstand and a cheap, laminate dresser that was missing a knob from one of its drawers. Posters of various death metal groups and supermodels covered two of the walls. Hundreds of sheets of paper had been stapled over the wall next to the closest. The closet stood open, its bifold doors pushed to the side, exposing a pile of dirty T-shirts, jeans, and underwear.

"Chaucer, first we gotta find a disguise for you. Anybody can see you're a dog, which just won't work. It's a good thing Unca Jake and Felipe are gamers. They've got a lot of cool stuff we can use."

Chaucer stood in the middle of the room, tail wagging and tongue hanging down the side of his mouth in a doggie smile. Daphne rummaged through various costumes hanging in the closet.

"This will work!" Daphne pulled out a Darth Vader costume. Taking the costume's long, black cape off the hanger, she tied it around Chaucer's neck. After a moment of serious contemplation, she took one of Jake's belts and cinched the cape up around Chaucer's chest to shorten it. She tried to put the costume's helmet on Chaucer's head, but he kept backing away. Daphne gave up after the second try.

"Well, that'll have to do. Now it's my turn."

Nothing stood out, so she led Chaucer to Felipe's room. She found a toy lightsaber that glowed when she pushed its button.

"This'll come in handy if we run into trouble." She stuck the lightsaber in her belt and went to examine the closet next to the front door.

"Wow!" Daphne's eyes went wide as she saw what was in the closet. "It's Unca Jake's paintball stuff."

"Look at this!" Daphne dragged out a black, paint-smeared breastplate and laid it on the floor for Chaucer to examine. "And this!" An equally-distressed helmet, complete with goggles, joined the breastplate.

"Ooh." Daphne carefully picked up Jake's paintball gun. Chaucer whined and crept under the coffee table, tail tucked between his legs.

"Now this is what we need."

Chaucer whined again.

"Unca Jake showed me how to use this when he took me to a tournament last fall. It's easy, just watch!" Daphne hefted the gun, pointed it at the wall, and pulled the trigger. Nothing happened.

"Oh, yeah. Forgot to load it."

Daphne pulled the necessary supplies out of a gym bag that Jake used to store them. Working with exaggerated caution, she poured a pod of paintballs into the gun's hopper. Frowning, she poked her tongue out as she screwed the air tank onto the back of the gun. She smiled in triumph at the faint hiss of compressed air as the gun pressurized.

"See, it's easy!"

As Daphne held the gun up, it went off with a bang.

"Oops. Didn't mean to do that. You okay, Chaucer?"

Chaucer gave a quiet bark in response, but he stayed under the coffee table.

Daphne tried to spot where the paintball had gone. The gun had been pointing at Jake's room when it went off, so she looked in there first.

"Oh. Jake's not gonna like that." One of the supermodel posters now featured a bright yellow splotch covering the model's cleavage. Daphne got some tissue from the bathroom and tried to wipe it off, but only managed to make it worse.

"Maybe he won't notice," she said hopefully as she turned off the light.

Before heading out, she put on Jake's breastplate and helmet. Both were too large for her. She pushed up the helmet's goggles so that she could see, then went to the bathroom to check how she looked.

"Oh yeah, those bad guys better look out now!"

While she was in the bathroom, Daphne noticed a small shaving mirror hanging in the shower. That gave her an idea. Taking some duct tape from the kitchen, she fastened the mirror to the end of a toilet brush, creating a makeshift periscope.

"Perfect! Now we can watch 'em without being seen."

She left the house with a swagger, Chaucer following dolefully behind, his cape dragging on the ground.

Jake was disconcerted to see the state of his friend when Felipe was brought into the Northwood office where he had been speaking with Claire. Felipe was unshaven, his clothes were torn and soiled, and he was so unsteady that he had to lean against the wall to stay upright. *Dude looks like a train wreck! And smells like an old sock. What happened to him?*

As Felipe slumped to the ground, Jake rushed to his friend's side, with Claire following him.

"What did they do to you, man?" Jake asked.

"They jumped me when I got home."

"Jumped you?"

"Yeah, man. I opened the door, and then boom! These guys do this ninja thing, all dressed in black and coming at me from all sides."

"Are you okay? When did this happen?"

"I'm okay, I guess. Bruised a bit, and still a little woozy from downing my stash, and there's a sore spot on my arm like I got jabbed with a needle or something. Don't know how that happened."

"Felipe, did this happen last Wednesday? Daphne saw you fighting with some guys at our place that night."

"Yeah. The last thing I remember was Daphne coming into the room. She's okay, isn't she? Heh, she had Chaucer with her, and he took a chunk outta one guy's ass! Remind me to give that dog a steak next time I see him. Or a burger. I can't afford steak, not on what Northwood pays me."

"Daphne's okay, though she missed a day of school and got grounded by her mom."

"Well, that's a shame. Say, what are you doing here, bro?"

"Oh, well, I seem to have been arrested, like you."

"By who?" Felipe struggled to his feet. "I mean, have you got any idea what's going on? Or who these guys are?"

"They say they're with Military Intelligence, and they think we're spies."

"That's not funny. Seriously, what's going on?"

"He's right," Claire said. "Commander Nuance thinks you've been stealing some kind of defense secrets from Northwood."

"How do they figure that?" Felipe scratched his head in puzzlement.

"They got hold of a copy of a book that Jake wrote. Apparently, there's some sensitive material in there."

Felipe stared at Jake. "I told you, man. Didn't I tell you? Using that stuff in your book was a bad idea!"

"Hey, it was all public domain stuff. I didn't take any secrets!"

"Then why are we locked up? By the way, want to introduce me to your new girlfriend here?"

Jake glanced at Claire and blushed. "She's not my girlfriend, dork. Her name's Claire, and she's a literary agent who saw a copy of my book."

"So, what are you doing in here, Claire?" Felipe asked. "Are you under arrest too?"

"No, I'm…I was just…they made me…I'm sorry." Claire trailed off and looked away.

"Made you do what?"

"Spy on me," Jake said.

"Oh, like Mata Hari, huh? Cool!"

"There's nothing cool about it, Felipe." Jake turned to Claire. "Which reminds me, just how did that Nuance character force you to do this?"

"He knows things. About my past, my family."

Felipe's eyes widened. "Wow! So you were a hooker?"

"Dude! Shut it!" Jake exclaimed.

"It's okay." Claire's voice was quiet. "I owe you an explanation, and it's probably too late now, anyway.

"You see—" Claire paused. Jake waited silently while she gathered her thoughts. "My family fell apart when I was in school. My mom had cancer and passed when I was fourteen. After that, Dad changed. It was like he wasn't even there sometimes, he was so cold and distant. I tried to help, but no matter what I did, he was never satisfied. And it wasn't just me. My little sibs, Becca and Sam, he just ignored them. I tried to fill in, but it wasn't enough. It wasn't ever enough.

"That went on all the way through high school. My senior year, I tried to make a Thanksgiving dinner for us. I thought it would bring us together again as a family. But Dad…"

Jake put his hand on Claire's shoulder as she paused.

"Dad left the table and went into the garage. I heard a shot…"

Claire covered her mouth with her hand as she started to cry. Jake had little experience comforting anyone; all he could think to do was give her a hug. She was warm and smelled of lavender. After a moment, she continued.

"They took Becca and Sam away. Put all three of us in foster care. I never saw them again. I've tried to find them, but nobody will tell me where they are."

"I'm sorry to hear that," Jake said, his voice soft, "but what's that got to do with the mess we're in now?"

"Nuance, and that, that Dutchman guy. They have a complete file on my family. They said they'd tell me where Becca and Sam are if I helped them investigate you. But if I didn't help them, they'd make sure I never saw my sibs again."

Jake was stunned. "That's, that's—"

"Extortion. I know. But what else could I do? Jake, I knew it was wrong to help them, but it was a chance to find my family, to make things right again, after failing them so badly. I need to find them. I need to explain. I need them to forgive me."

Jake held her for several minutes, unsure of what to say or do. *She must think I'm a world-class creep.* All he could manage was, "I'm sorry. I shouldn't have yelled at you. I didn't know."

"It's okay." Claire straightened and wiped her eyes. "Not your fault."

Felipe coughed. "Uh, hate to break up a moment, folks, but do either of you know what they've got in store for us? I was pretty out of it when I was questioned, and nobody's spoken to me since."

"It doesn't look good." Jake let go of Claire so that he could walk over and check the door, blushing as he did. *She let me hug her! I wonder if she likes me?* "We're locked in, and I'm sure Nuance has some unpleasant plans for us."

"This is pretty unpleasant already." Felipe pushed himself to his feet. "What's he got in mind?"

"He mentioned something worse than waterboarding. I don't want to stick around to find out what that might be."

"Holy crap! We gotta get outta here now!"

"How? The door's locked and there's no window."

"Does that closet lead anywhere?" Claire asked, pointing to the door in the side wall.

"No, there aren't any side passages in this building," Felipe responded.

"True, but there might be something useful there." Jake rubbed his chin in thought.

"Like what?"

"If I remember correctly, we used a couple of the ground-floor closets to route cables to the servers last year. If this is one of them, we might be able to knock out the building's security system, maybe the power for the whole building. If we did that, we could get away before they even knew we were gone."

Felipe rattled the closet's door handle and frowned. "It's locked. Got any other bright ideas?"

"Could you jimmy it open?" Claire asked.

Jake frowned. "I could if I had a credit card or a bit of wire. These latches are decades old. Northwood never upgraded the interior units, so all we'd need to do is slide a flat piece of plastic or metal through the latch, and it would pop right open. But Nuance took my wallet, my belt, and my cell when he arrested me."

"Ditto." Felipe sighed as he squatted back down on the floor in despair.

"He didn't take my purse," Claire said. "I'm not sure why, but it probably won't do you much good. I only have one credit card, but it's kinda flimsy and already cracked. Would my belt buckle work instead? It's flat and thin."

"Let me see." Jake started to unfasten Claire's belt, then suddenly stopped himself, his face red. *Man, she must think I'm some kinda perv!* "Sorry, got carried away," he mumbled. "I don't usually take girls' clothes off in public."

"You don't do it in private either," Felipe smirked.

"Not a problem." Claire smiled as she pulled her belt off. "See what you can do with this."

It only took a minute for Jake to work the tang off the belt buckle, leaving a C-shaped piece of thin metal. He hooked it behind the door's lock bolt and then pulled it out, depressing the latch and unlocking the door as he did.

"Ta-da!" Jake gestured in triumph as the door swung open, revealing a small room filled with electrical cabling.

He rummaged around for a bit. "Well, I don't see any Ethernet cables in here, so we can't hack into the servers. I don't see any coax cable in either, so we won't be able to muck with the security cams. But there's a boatload of high-voltage cabling. I think this might be an access point for the building's main power circuit."

Peering in over his shoulder, Felipe said, "Those super-thick, gray cables might be for the circuit that goes to the welding units. If so, they carry over four hundred volts. Crossing two of those would take out half the city!"

"Be my guest." Jake stepped back to let Felipe into the closet.

"That doesn't look very safe. Are you sure you know what you're doing?" Claire sidled away, doubt evident in her voice.

Felipe pursed his lips in concentration as he pushed aside a ream of multi-colored wires. Using the silver belt buckle, he unscrewed one of the high-voltage cables from a black wiring bracket. "Yeah, I do have a degree in computer science, you know. Besides, what could go wrong?"

Snap!

Felipe flew backwards as the gray wire brushed against an exposed terminal. Sparks flew out of the closet as a loop of yellow electricity ran over his body, starting at his toes and ending at his hair.

The overhead fluorescent light exploded with a loud *pop*, scattering glass across the room.

By the glow of the overheated wires, Jake could see his friend smoking and shivering on the floor. "Dude! Are you okay?" Jake asked from a safe distance.

"Argh!" Felipe moaned as he lay twitching.

Jake helped Felipe to sit up while Claire patted at Felipe's smoldering hair, which had transformed from a loose pompadour into a credible afro.

"Did it work?" Felipe asked in a shaky voice.

Jake looked up at the shattered light fixture and nodded. "Pretty sure it did."

"Good. I don't want to have to do that again!"

"Let's try getting out," Claire said.

Jake helped Felipe to his feet, then picked up a small fire extinguisher that was attached to the side of the closet and sprayed foam on the wiring until the fire went out.

While Jake put out the fire, Felipe hooked Claire's belt buckle behind the bolt in the entry door's latch. A deft twitch depressed the pin, and the door swung open as he pulled.

A marine stood in the darkened hallway with his back to them, speaking into a microphone clipped to his shoulder.

"Don't move, or I'll shoot!" Felipe growled, shaping his hand like a pistol and pressing his finger into the man's back.

Looking over his shoulder, the marine said, "Seriously, dude? A finger?"

Clang!

The hallway echoed with the sound of a fire extinguisher hitting the man's helmet. The stunned soldier slumped to the floor.

"Let's go! The exit's this way!" Jake pulled Claire with him as he darted down the hallway. Turning a corner, he stopped by a door with a glowing exit sign above it.

Felipe examined the lock and said, "The buckle won't work here, the latch has a metal plate over it to prevent it from being jimmied."

Jake squatted down next to the door. "Let me see it."

"I wonder if we could get out this way?" Felipe opened a side door in the hallway, and then paused.

"Never mind, I've got it. It wasn't locked," Jake pushed the exit door open.

"J-J-Jake?" Felipe stammered, focused on the muzzle of an enormous pistol that was so close to the bridge of his nose that he went cross-eyed looking at it.

"What?"

"I have miswent."

"This is no time to quote Chaucer, dude, come on!"

"No, man, that's not what I meant."

Without rising from his crouch, Jake asked, "Well, what did you mean?" Then he noticed the dampness spreading down the leg of Felipe's jeans. Looking up at the pistol, he said, "Oh."

"Stay where you are!" a black-clad agent commanded as he followed Felipe out of the room.

"Stop them!" yelled the marine as he charged around the corner of the hallway, his helmet still askew from Jake's blow.

As the agent turned to look at the new arrival, he lowered his arm. When he did, Felipe tried to push the gun away, and it went off.

The sound of the gunshot was deafening in the hallway. For a moment, everybody stood still. Then Jake walloped the agent on the head with the fire extinguisher, more successfully than he had with the marine due to the man's lack of protective headgear.

Felipe fell to the ground next to the agent. Holding his thigh, where a dark red smear had appeared, he cried, "Run!"

Jake hesitated, then pushed Claire out the exit as the marine bulled into him. Jake tried to grab him, but the marine shouldered Jake out of the way and followed Claire through the door.

Jake picked himself up and followed, just in time to hear the soldier shout, "Stop! Stop or I'll shoot!"

Claire stopped, raising her hands in the air as she faced the man. As she did, Jake dove forward, wrapping his arms around the soldier's waist in a tackle that would have made a middle linebacker proud...if it had worked. But 150 pounds of out-of-shape geek didn't stand a chance against 240 pounds of combat-hardened marine.

The soldier looked down, annoyed.

Jake made a fist and hit the man in the stomach. Frowning, the marine slammed his rifle butt into Jake's solar plexus. Paralyzed and unable to breathe, Jake sagged to one knee. The soldier smacked him in the forehead, driving him to the ground.

"I said stop!" the soldier cried, firing a warning shot into the air as he spun back to face Claire.

Unable to move, Jake watched in horror as the man leveled his weapon at Claire. *No! Not Claire!* The snarl of gunfire was the last thing he heard before he slipped from consciousness.

31

Unaware that Jake, Claire, and Felipe were already in the process of trying to escape from Nuance, Daphne made her way up Merryman Street at a brisk pace, with Chaucer trotting at her side. After a block she slowed down, leaving the sidewalk and cutting through people's yards to avoid being seen. The night was clear, and the moon nearly full, so she had no trouble seeing the thick trunks of the oaks and ashes along her route. Likewise, she skirted the lilac and hydrangea shrubs with ease, though she tripped twice over garden hoses that had been left out on the grass, and once she stepped on something sharp that made her hop on one foot for a minute, biting her tongue to keep quiet.

At the end of the street, she turned right up Church Street, stopping two blocks later when she reached Main Street. The city's wastewater management system lay on the other side of the street and the Northwood office where Jake had disappeared was located behind that.

"Now you watch, and stay close, Chaucer. This street's dangerous to cross."

There was no traffic, the industrial end of town being deserted on a Saturday night. The dog stayed close on her heels though as Daphne darted across the road.

She cut through the wastewater plant's parking lot, then turned right, following Mann Street as it bent around toward the Northwood shipyard. When she reached the Northwood office building she dodged into a small patch of woods on the left side of the building.

"Shhh!" Daphne put her finger to her lips as she enjoined Chaucer to silence. "We gotta be quiet, so no barking, okay?"

Tiptoeing through the shrubs that clogged the woods, she found a blackberry bush covered in thorns and sat down behind it.

Holding up her improvised periscope, she tried to see the office building, but she was disappointed to find that it didn't work. Setting the periscope aside, she stood up and gave the building a good looking over. She couldn't see the front entrance from her hiding place, but she could see a couple of black SUVs and a pink one parked in the front lot.

Squatting down, she gave Chaucer the fiercest look she could manage. "The periscope won't work, so we'll need to get closer. Stay close, and let me know if you see anything."

Daphne lowered the googles on her helmet and stood up straight. As she did, a side door in the building flew open and a woman stumbled out.

"It's Claire! Chaucer, she might be in trouble. We got to help her!"

Daphne whipped out her lightsaber and switched it on. For one splendid moment it flared a brilliant red, lighting up everything within fifty feet, then it flickered and went out with a sizzle and pop. Daphne stared at her failed weapon in dismay.

"Rats!"

"Stop! Stop or I'll shoot!"

Daphne looked up in surprise. A soldier had followed Claire from the building and was pointing a rifle at the woman. He yelled again and Claire stopped, raising her hands in the air as she faced him. Then Jake came barreling out of the door and grabbed the soldier around the waist.

"Run!" Jake called out. Claire spun around and ran toward the river, but before she reached it, the soldier hit Jake in the head with the butt of his rifle, knocking him down.

"I said stop!" the soldier cried, leveling his gun at Claire.

Scared, Daphne took a step backwards. Her heel caught on a tree root and she fell down. As she did, the paintball gun slung over her shoulder rattled off a half-dozen shots, its hair trigger set off by the impact of the fall.

The soldier's response was immediate. He dropped to the ground, rolled over to face the line of trees, searching for whoever was shooting at him.

Daphne stood up, saw the soldier pointing his rifle at her, and immediately dove for cover.

"Cheese it!" she yelled to Chaucer as she scrambled away on her hands and knees. A moment later she heard loud footsteps coming up behind her. She looked back just in time to see Chaucer leap from the shadows and knock the unfortunate soldier face-first into the blackberry bush.

"Ow! Damn! Help! Ow!!"

"Come on!" Daphne waved to Chaucer and he sprang to her side, leaving the soldier tangled and helpless in the depths of the thorny bush.

Daphne ran until she was out of breath, stopping only when she reached the public library, about three blocks from the Northwood facility. Ducking under the white, clapboard building's raised wooden porch, she shucked her helmet and breastplate, wrapping them up with the defunct lightsaber and paintball gun in Chaucer's erstwhile cape. She tucked the bundle into a dark corner where it wouldn't be seen, promising herself that she'd come back in the morning to retrieve it. Then she headed for home.

"Chaucer, we need to act innocent. So walk natural. Like I do, see?"

They didn't make it a block before they were stopped.

32

When Claire hit the water, she forgot about escaping from Nuance's agents as she fought to keep from drowning. The concrete dock was much higher off the river than she had expected, nearly twelve feet. She went in feet-first, but she didn't go in straight, smacking her face on the water so hard that her mind went blank. Claire panicked. Thrashing her arms and kicking, she struggled to breathe, water burning through her sinuses and down her throat.

She surfaced for a moment, gasped, then went under again. Her hands were in the air though, which helped her to overcome her initial fear. One hard kick brought her back to the surface, and she was able to tread water while catching her breath.

She hadn't intended to jump in the river, not in the middle of the night. She'd planned to follow the shoreline away from Northwood until she reached safety. But the gunshots had terrified her, and she'd leapt in without looking.

Claire spit out water, sneezed out more, and then hugged her arms around her chest. Her teeth chattered as she flutter-kicked to stay afloat. Fifty-five degrees, Bob had said when she'd toured the river with him. The water doesn't get warmer until late August. She sneezed again, then got her first taste of the river. It was musty, tasting of earth with an overtone of diesel oil, and it felt greasy in her mouth. This puzzled her until she noticed the prow of the destroyer looming behind her. Bob hadn't had kind words to say about what the local marinas and the shipyard leaked into the river.

Now what?

She couldn't go back. Even if she had wanted to, the concrete dock was too high for her to scale. The destroyer blocked her path to the lake. Lights beckoned from River Park on the far shoreline, but she could see people gathering there under the lights on the piers. They were looking her way. *They're probably wondering about the gunshots. I can't go there. I need to stay out of sight.*

That meant her only option was upriver. Lights were coming on along the near shore creating pools of illumination under their sodium-yellow glare. Claire knew that people would soon be out on their piers looking for the source of the excitement. But Stephenson Island, which was located in the middle of the channel, was less than a quarter mile away in that direction. *If I can make it past the island, I should be able to slip ashore and find a place to hide till things die down.*

Claire slipped out of her jacket and let it drift away; it would only slow her down. Her purse was already gone, lost in the first wild moment when she'd entered the river. She kicked off her sneakers so that it would be easier to swim, bobbing under the water to wrench them off. She didn't want to lose them, but she had no choice if she wanted to cover any distance.

Then she felt something cold touch her foot. Claire shuddered. She looked down into the murky water, but she couldn't see anything. A moment later she felt it again; a slow, slithering contact as something scaly brushed against her ankle. She squeaked, trying to suppress a full-on scream as she pulled her legs up. Knees under her chin, she slipped below the surface.

A fish. It must be a fish. Snakes don't swim.

Claire held her breath, waiting for the next contact. She counted to ten, then let her feet back down into the water and kicked her way back to the surface. She felt a sudden urge to pee, a sensation that faded after a few minutes when the unwelcome contact didn't return. She was shaking all over, but it wasn't just the cold causing that.

Leaning forward in the water, Claire started swimming. She began with a front crawl, then changed her mind. The crawl was fast but tiring, and she needed to conserve her energy. So she switched to a breaststroke, frog-kicking forward and then gliding between breaths.

As she swam, Claire's waterlogged clothes dragged like a parachute, pulling her back, pulling her down. She didn't want to think about that and turned her thoughts to what her mother had taught her when she was a child. "Swim like an otter, relaxed, sleek, and graceful. You belong here."

Then she remembered how everything changed when it was just her father. Her stroke slowed as she recalled the day she'd tried out for the high school swim team. The feeling of disappointment when she'd failed to make the team. And then facing her father.

"Didn't make the team, did you?"

"No, sir."

"Figured as much." And then the look, his disdain squeezing the life out of her.

Claire realized that she'd stopped swimming as the memories flooded back. Closing her eyes, she cupped her hands and splashed her face. The river was cold and unfeeling, just like her father.

Lifting her face, she started swimming again. But it was harder. She could feel more than the weight of her sodden clothes holding her back.

She angled toward the middle of the river, hoping to circle the island and avoid being spotted by anybody ashore. But when she heard the thrum of motors behind her, she realized she'd never make it.

Claire looked back over her shoulder. Two boats equipped with spotlights were sweeping the river. The agents manning the watercraft raked the beams back-and-forth, searching for her. Claire took a quick breath and slipped underwater as a beam passed over her position. After it had passed by, she realized that the river was so black she couldn't see the surface. She fought against the feeling of disorientation, hanging on to the knowledge that she'd been upright when she went under. All she had to do was swim straight up to reach the surface. But she felt the chill numbing her arms and legs again as she hung motionless in the water. And the silence was absolute. She couldn't even hear the grumble of the boats' motors, just the hammering of her heart as it used up the last of her oxygen. *I can't see, can't hear, can't breathe! It's like being in a grave! I could die here, and nobody would ever know!*

Air began to bubble from Claire's mouth as she lost the battle to hold her breath. Two strokes of her arms brought her back to the surface. She sucked in air, making as little noise as possible, then ducked under once more as the spotlight flashed over her position again.

Claire repeated the process, but this time took a bearing on Stephenson Island before she submerged. Resuming her breaststroke, she swam underwater toward the island. She surfaced several times for air before she was spotted. By then, she was close to shore. Claire switched to a front crawl to pick up her pace. She could feel the burn in her shoulders. The island had a small spit of land pointing downriver, and she made for that. She arrived at the island a moment before the boat that was chasing her.

Claire surged out of the water and ran barefoot down a paved footpath. The hard pavement jarred her with each step. She was halfway across the island when the pursuing boat drove onto the shore right next to her path.

Claire cut to the left and ran past a log building that served as the park's visitor center.

"Stop! Stop or I'll shoot!"

Claire looked back and saw that the man wasn't carrying a gun, so she kept running. She dodged through the lilac bushes and ash trees scattered across the lawn and headed for a narrow channel of water that separated the island from the mainland.

As she neared the water, she heard the footsteps of the pursuing agent closing in on her. In the darkness, she failed to see the line of foot-high rocks bordering the shoreline until she tripped over one of them. She smashed the toes of her left foot as she tumbled into the water.

For a moment, Claire forgot the blinding pain in her foot as she watched the pursuing agent fly over her.

"Gotcha!"

Bong! In the uncertain light, the agent had mistaken the life-size statue known as the "Young Swimmers" for Claire. The statue depicted two boys who were about her size, one diving into the river and the other standing upright over where she lay. She winced as the agent hit the upright image head-first, his helmet ringing the bronze sculpture like a bell. He then slumped to the supporting granite boulder with his arms wrapped around the figure's legs.

Claire scrambled back onto the grass on her hands and knees. She bit her lower lip to keep silent, but the pain in her foot made her cry. She made it to the museum building, about thirty feet from the Young Swimmers, when she heard another agent splash into the water.

"Dawson! Dawson, are you okay?" Lying prone to avoid being seen, Claire watched as the agent dragged his luckless partner ashore. Tapping a radio clipped to the side of his helmet, the agent shouted, "Man down! Man down! I need a medic now!"

Moments later, another boat pulled up to the shore. Claire stayed where she was. She could see and hear everything clearly, but she was in too much pain to trust her ability to flee.

An agent jumped from the second boat and ran to the wounded man. "What happened?"

"Sir, we were in pursuit of the female when Agent Dawson went down."

"I can see that, but what *happened?*"

"We spotted the girl in the water and gave chase, sir. She ran ashore, and Dawson pursued her on foot while I pulled our boat up onto the beach."

"And?"

"I saw Dawson dive for the girl, but he hit that statue over there instead."

"Are you saying that one of our crack agents mistook a statue for somebody running across the grass?"

"Sir, the light wasn't good."

The officer sighed. "So what happened then?"

"The statue knocked him out, sir."

"How? Did it turn and punch him in the face?"

"No, sir. He ran into it head first."

"Wasn't he wearing his helmet?"

"Sir, yes, sir. But he was running flat out, and the statue is pretty solid. I'd guess bronze, being as it's in a park and all."

"But he was wearing a helmet?"

"Yes, sir. But in Dawson's defense, sir, that's one tough statue. I don't think it budged an inch. These folks up north here sure know how to work their metal."

"I see." The officer rubbed his face with his hands. "Agent, I want you to stay here with Dawson until the medics arrive. They were on standby for the operation, so it should only be a few minutes. Meanwhile, I'm going to search the island to see if the girl's still here."

Claire realized that she couldn't remain hidden any longer, so she limped as fast as she could toward the other side of the island. She made it to a line of birches near the water before she heard an agent shout, "There she is! She's going back into the river."

Being careful to avoid the rocks along the shoreline, Claire splashed into the water and then dove forward. She used a breaststroke so that she could keep her head above water and listen for pursuit. She could hear the man who was in charge shouting orders.

"Jenkins, bring the boat around and pick me up where she left shore. We've got her trapped between the bridge and the dam."

Claire felt fatigue return within a few strokes. Her arms grew heavy, and her legs felt like logs, doing little besides swirling the water. The cold pierced her as if making up for the brief moment of relative warmth she had enjoyed on the island and she began to shiver. Still, she pushed on past Boom Island, only to find her way blocked by the dam. She stopped to rest, then saw a floodlight from a pursuing boat. It was quartering the channel, working its way upriver from the bridge, and it was only a matter of time before it reached her.

Claire scanned the riverbanks, but they were too steep along this section of the river for her to climb them. And the dam was impassible. *Trapped! They'll shoot me, if I don't drown first.*

Despair washed over Claire, colder than the river's heart and more deadly than the black water that sought to pull her under. Then she saw a small light near where the Menominee dam met the shoreline. *It's the fish lift! If a fish can make it up that thing, I can too. And there's no way they can follow me in a boat!*

Claire began swimming again, this time with purpose. She fought against the current the whole way, and she reached the spot without being seen. The fish lift was a six-foot-square steel tub with a door on one side to let fish swim in from the river.

The low-power bulb lighting the lift revealed several fish floating in the tub, all of a size that would please an angler. But the sight of one of them made Claire's heart freeze—a torpedo-shaped giant that was as long as she was. It had scales the size of her hands, making it look like some kind of prehistoric monster. Claire swallowed and inched forward. *It's just a sturgeon. Got to be. And they don't have teeth. I'll be fine.* As she approached, the fish spun to face her, and she got a good look at its foot-long, tooth-lined bill. *Good God, it's an alligator gar! Eewwww!*

She'd seen such creatures in aquariums and had been frightened by them even with a glass panel separating them. Now, facing one in its own environment, and a big one at that, she felt her toes and fingers curl up as she pulled her knees and elbows close to her body.

A flash of light off the side of the building reminded her that people were chasing her. She ducked her head underwater while the light played over the buildings. When she did, the garfish glided closer until it was only a foot away. Its jaw was as wide as her head. They stared at each other. *I'm not good to eat. Go away!* The fish seemed disinclined to leave.

The light faded and Claire surfaced for air. The garfish rose to the surface with her and also took a gulp of air, it being one of the few species of fish able to do so. Its two-inch-long needle-shaped teeth glistened in the dim light when it opened its mouth.

Knowing that a boat-load of Nuance's agents were closing in on her, Claire took a deep breath and sidled around the fish. She found the aluminum maintenance ladder that ran up the wall next to the tub and scampered up it. She stopped halfway to look down. The gar was still watching her. Without warning, it lunged forward and grabbed one of the other fish in the tub, using a sweeping motion to impale the hapless bass on its sharp teeth. The motion reminded Claire of something. After a moment it came to her. *Tina.*

Claire swallowed, involuntarily counting her fingers and toes. After climbing the rest of the way up the ladder, she swung out of the fish lift and onto the concrete floor of the facility. The room she was in was forty-feet wide and about sixty-feet long. A few fluorescent tube fixtures provided a dim illumination to the room from the ceiling, which was three stories above the floor. Pipes of all sizes, some over a foot in diameter, filled the room.

Claire found a door, but it was locked. Using a fire extinguisher that was mounted on the wall next to the door, she smashed the doorknob off. The door swung open. As it did, a siren alarm went off and all the lights in the building came on.

Crap! Claire bolted out the door and ran right into a security guard who was running the other way. Both of them fell down, but the guard got up first, shining his flashlight on her.

"Hey! Who are you, and what are you doing here? This is a private facility—"

"That's her!" One of Nuance's agents who had been stationed on the bridge's catwalk yelled and waved as he ran toward the building.

Claire scrabbled away from the security guard and found herself facing the river. She had no choice, so she jumped in and swam away from the building.

Claire had second thoughts about her decision as soon as the river current grabbed her.

The spring thaw had raised the river level, boosting the flow, and though she fought the current, she didn't have enough strength to overcome it. The river pushed her along like a giant playing with a toy boat, driving her relentlessly toward the spillway that let water flow over the dam.

The top of the wall forming the spillway was about two feet below the surface of the river. Claire hit it with her hips. The water pressure on her upper body cartwheeled her over the edge to plunge into the dark waters fifteen feet below.

Claire landed flat on her back, knocking the wind out of her. For several moments, all she could do was float, battered and bewildered, but she was pretty sure that the awkward landing had actually saved her life. The back flop had kept her on the surface of the river; if she'd hit it head- or feet-first, she'd have gone under and might never have reached the surface again.

Treading water, Claire scanned for the boat that had chased her upriver. She spotted it about two hundred feet away in the middle of the river channel between Boom Island and the dam. The agents in the boat were still sweeping the river with their spotlights, but the river current had already carried her past them.

Claire didn't try to swim, letting the river carry her instead. She'd lost feeling in her feet from the cold, and her hands were numb. Her entire left side hurt where she'd hit the spillway, and she wondered if she'd cracked some ribs. She was so weak that she wasn't sure she could even make it to the shoreline now. But as she floated, her head cleared. *This isn't over. I'm not letting this damn river kill me!*

When she reached Stephenson Island, Claire noticed that the agents' abandoned boat was still on the shore. Nobody was in sight. *Finally, something's going my way!*

She kicked into a weak breaststroke, letting the current do most of the work until she reached the island. Claire crept up on the craft, crouching in the shallows to avoid being seen. She tried to pull the boat off the gravel beach but stopped when it made a grating noise. Peeking inside, she grabbed a life vest that had been left behind in the vessel.

Within seconds, she pulled the vest over her head and strapped it on. Then it was back into the water. With the vest on, she didn't have to swim and could conserve her strength. Letting the current carry her, she reached the mouth of the river in about twenty minutes. Best of all, Nuance's agents were looking for her in the opposite direction.

Claire used her last reserves of energy to kick toward the southern bank. As she followed the shoreline, she came upon the beach at Red Arrow Park.

When she reached shallow water, Claire tried to stand, but her legs folded beneath her. So she crawled out, the sharp rocks on the lake bottom cutting into her skin as she did so. She collapsed on the beach and tried to wipe the blood off her hands, but all she managed to do was rub sand into her open wounds.

She lay there for some time, cold, alone, and exhausted.

I can't stay here. Gotta move, or they'll find me. Claire forced herself to get up. She wobbled but managed to stay upright this time. Her left foot was still numb from hitting the rock on Stephenson Island, but she managed a hobbling limp that carried her inland.

As Claire made her way through the park, she tried to think of someplace she could hide. Nothing came to mind. When she reached the park's white, octagonal gazebo, however, she had an idea. It was raised a few feet off the ground and there was a wooden lattice covering the crawl space underneath it. Claire found a piece of lattice that had come loose over the winter. She managed to pry it back enough to slip under the gazebo, then let it snap back into place. It was filthy, dark, and musty under the structure. She was also pretty sure that some of the items she crawled across were the remains of dead and rotting fish. Even so, for the first time in hours, she felt safe. Curling up into a damp, shivering ball, she closed her eyes.

Nuance watched grim-faced as his men extricated their unfortunate comrade from the blackberry bush. The soldier was too deeply embedded to make it out on his own, and the other men were getting cut by the thorns as they tried to help him.

"Break it down for me, marine." Nuance leaned close so that he could be heard over the grunting and swearing. "How did a perfectly staged escape turn into such a complete, utter cluster-fuck? The wrong person got away, and now you're saying that an unknown intruder fired on you?"

"Sir, I followed orders and chased the woman out into the parking lot. But the man didn't make a run for it. Instead, he—Ow! Jenkins, stop pulling! Sorry, sir, as I was saying, the man grabbed me and I knocked him down by reflex. That's when—Damn it! Jenkins, I said st—Ow! Just stop! Sorry, sir. Anyway, the woman made a break for it while I was wrestling with the man. As soon as I was clear of him, I fired a warning shot to stop her. When I did—Yikes! Not there! Not there! Jenkins, don't pull! Ow! Sorry, sir. Anyway, right after I fired my weapon, there was a burst of machine-gun fire from these bushes. I hit the ground and turned to see who was firing at me."

"And you got a look at the intruder?"

"Yes, sir, the lighting wasn't too bad, but I couldn't make out a face. The intruder was wearing—Hey! Stop that, Jenkins! As I was saying, the individual was wearing a helmet with a full face mask. He had a breastplate on too, looked like black Kevlar armor, but I couldn't be sure. He was short and heavyset."

"And did the individual fire again?"

"No, sir. It looked like he was trying to escape after I spotted him, so I gave chase."

"And…?"

"He must have circled around and hit me from behind. Knocked me right into this damn thorn bush. I couldn't move, couldn't even turn my head to get a good look at him, and he got away."

"I see. And where was the woman during all of this?"

"Don't know, sir. By the time help arrived, she was gone."

"Do you have any idea which direction she went?"

"Oh, yes, sir. She was headed for the river when I stopped her. I think I heard a splash shortly after I landed in this bush."

Nuance waved for a group of agents waiting by the door to join him. "We need to get control of this situation ASAP. Set up a cordon of marines in a circle with a ten-block radius from here. No one gets in, no one gets out. Then I want every street and yard searched. If you spot the intruder, report in but do not approach until you have backup. This individual should be considered armed and dangerous. I also want a team on the river. Take a couple of boats and try to pick up the woman. Maybe we can salvage something from this night.

"Now go!"

As soon as his men were busy, Nuance hopped into his SUV to join the search. Lights off, he cruised down Riverside Street looking for any sign of the armed intruder who had helped Claire escape. As he passed the public library, he saw two small figures step out of the shadows and onto the sidewalk. He slowed to get a good look at them and then pulled the SUV over to the curb with a sigh. Circling around his vehicle, he stepped in front of the pair, stopping their progress.

"Daphne? What are you doing out at this time of night?"

Daphne took a step back. Chaucer growled and moved in front of her to confront Nuance.

"Easy boy." Nuance held his open hands out, trying to placate the dog.

"You stay away from me!" Daphne stood with her hands on her hips. "I know who you are. You're a bad man. But I'm not scared of you."

Nuance suppressed a smile. *Kid's got moxie.* "Daphne, I'm not a bad man. I just have the kind of job where sometimes I have to do tough things."

"Like arrest my Unca Jake? You did that, didn't you?"

"I'm sorry, but I can't talk about that, Daphne."

"That's what I thought. You can wear a disguise, but you don't fool me. You're a bad man."

"I'm not wearing a disguise."

"You're dressed up like a soldier, aren't you? But you can't be a soldier, cause my dad's a soldier and he's a good man, he protects people. You hurt people, so you can't be a soldier. They don't do that." Daphne's chin lifted as she made her point.

"Daphne, I really am a soldier. Actually I'm a sailor, but it's about the same thing. I'm an officer in the US Navy." Nuance took out his billfold to show Daphne his service ID, being careful to move slowly so as not to antagonize the dog.

Daphne squinted in an effort to make out the document. As she did, Nuance took a step closer so that she could get a better look, forgetting that Chaucer was on high alert.

With a growl from deep in his chest, the dog lunged forward and clamped his jaws on Nuance's leg.

"Ow! Call him off, call him off!" Nuance fell back against his car, dropping his billfold on the sidewalk as he did.

Daphne grabbed Chaucer's collar and pulled, but the dog wouldn't budge. He had a firm grip on Nuance's leg, although he had stopped just short of biting all the way down. Nuance could feel the creature's fangs pressing deep into the skin of his calf. He was certain that another ounce of pressure was all that it would take for them to penetrate into the soft tissue below.

Nuance took a slow breath to steady himself. "Daphne, please get your dog off my leg."

"Why should I? You'll just do something bad. That's why you stopped, isn't it?"

"No, Daphne, I stopped because it's late. Too late for a kid your age to be out by herself. And there are a couple of suspects on the loose tonight. One of them is dangerous. I was out looking for him when I saw you walking alone. I thought I'd better give you a ride home so you'd be safe. Your mom must be worried about you."

"Mom doesn't know I snuck out. And you better not tell her, or I'll sic Chaucer on you!"

The fact that the dog already had a firm grip on his leg reinforced Nuance's conviction that the child would do exactly what she said. The bandages on his backside gave mute evidence that things could get much worse for him, and quickly.

"Daphne, please. If you don't want to upset your mom, let me take you home. If you're worried, you can have Chaucer ride in the car with us. I'm pretty sure he won't let anything happen to you."

"Well…how do I know you're telling the truth?"

"I give you my word as an officer and a gentleman."

Daphne screwed up her face in thought. "Well, I guess that's okay. But Chaucer's coming too. And no shenanigans!"

Nuance felt the corners of his mouth twitch upwards. *Moxie isn't the word for it!* "That's fine by me, Daphne. Now let's get you home."

It took a minute for Daphne to get Chaucer to let go of Nuance's leg. After she did, he escorted both the girl and the dog into the back seat of his car. Retrieving his wallet, he got in and drove them to Daphne's house. He was surprised to feel a sense of relief that the house was dark and that the child's nighttime excursion would go unpunished.

"Here you are. Do you need me speak with your mom, or help you get in?"

"No. She'll worry if she knows I was out with Chaucer again. She was real mad when the Sherriff brought me home last week." Daphne paused, her lower lip pushed forward in resentment. "You know, it wasn't fair. I got grounded for that. But it should've been you. On account of you kidnapping me and all."

Nuance had no response for that, so he watched from the car while Daphne climbed into the house through an open window, followed a moment later by the hound.

He sat staring at the silent house for several minutes. *When did I become one of the bad guys? A boogeyman to scare children?* He thought about all the times he'd been deployed overseas like Daphne's father, and how his own house probably looked just like that while he was gone. He could picture his family waiting for every call, filled with hope that it would be his voice on the line, but also terrified that it would be a man they didn't know, telling them that something had gone horribly wrong.

Nuance looked down at his hands. *None of this makes sense. The pieces just don't fit together. Why's Dutchman pushing so hard for a quick resolution? Shouldn't we take our time and get this right, before any more good people get hurt?*

With that thought in mind, he drove to rejoin his team in their search for the mystery intruder.

34

Admiral Dutchman sat at his gray, metal desk in his office in the Northwood facility. His open laptop showed a particularly distressing email from the Pentagon. It was seven a.m., and it felt like a truck had dumped a load of dry sand into his eyes. Then it drove over his dress uniform multiple times, wrinkling and soiling it. The smell of diesel and steel from the shipyard contributed to the effect. The muffled tolling of church bells signaling the end of the early Sunday services whispered through the walls like an alarm clock forgotten in a suitcase.

Looks like I'm out of time. The Pentagon's got the Intelligence Oversight Committee involved. Three days, at best, to wrap this up before they send an inspector on-site.

Dutchman closed the laptop, turning his attention to Nuance. The officer had been standing at attention in front of his desk for the past twenty minutes. Dutchman was inclined to leave him there for the rest of his life. *After last night's screw-up, he deserves a court-martial. But I don't have time to bring a replacement up to speed.*

Leaning back in his chair, Dutchman folded his hands across his stomach and glared at his subordinate.

"Commander, I've spent the night reviewing your reports as well as the video of the botched escape attempt. Do you understand the ramifications of your failure?"

"Sir, yes, sir."

Dutchman held Nuance in his gaze for an uncomfortably long time. *Let him sweat a bit.* Careful to keep his voice neutral, he said, "Good. Now tell me what happened."

"Sir, the prisoners were put in a holding room with the Miller woman, as planned. My team selected the room based on an evaluation of the technical abilities of the prisoners to access the building's security system from within the room."

"And how did that work out for us?"

"Not as expected, sir. Whether by accident or design, the prisoners avoided the dummy access cables for the security system that my team had installed in the wiring closet. Instead, they cross-wired the high-voltage cables from the shipyard with the building's main circuit. The result knocked out everything."

"So? Wasn't that part of the plan?"

"Not exactly, sir. If they had cut the dummy cables, we'd still have had full monitoring capability, while they would had believed that they were free from observation."

"And that's why we have no video of the actual escape attempt, or of this mystery intruder who helped them?"

"Correct, sir."

"And while your team was rigging up the dummy wiring in the closet, nobody happened to notice the high-voltage cables?

Without actually moving, Nuance gave the impression of squirming under Dutchman's relentless gaze. "No, sir. But in their defense—"

"DEFENSE? WHAT DEFENSE CAN THERE BE FOR SUCH UTTER INCOMPETENCE?!" Spittle flew from Dutchman's lips as he leaned forward, slamming his palm down on his desk in anger.

"Sir, I can explain."

"Make. It. Good." Dutchman dragged out the words so that they slithered across his desk toward Nuance like vipers.

"Sir, the wiring in the closet wasn't labeled, and it wasn't up to code. Even so, we'd have known about the issue if the building's schematics were accurate. But Northwood's building engineers rerouted the wiring over the winter to avoid condensation from the cold. They've admitted that they forgot to update the diagrams afterward."

"And your people can't tell the difference between A HALF-INCH THICK CABLE FOR A WELDING SYSTEM AND A HAIR-THIN WIRE FOR A SECURITY CAMERA!?"

"Sir, we had to move fast. There wasn't enough time—"

"Time? Don't talk to me about time! We're running out of time, you cabbage-brained moron! The Pentagon put troops on high alert for this operation. Three companies of marines spent the night sitting on their hands, waiting for us to call them into action, based on your plan. The Pentagon would like to know why we didn't. I don't think they're going to accept a lame excuse like the one you've just handed me. Do you understand what this means for your career?" *And for mine, you meathead?*

"Sir, yes, sir."

"Then perhaps you could explain why you didn't have a contingency plan in place, in case things didn't go perfectly."

"Sir, I did, but there were unexpected difficulties."

"Isn't that what a contingency plan is for? To cover all those nasty little things that you DIDN'T anticipate?"

"Sir, yes, sir. But if I could explain?"

"Do. I'm all ears."

"Sir, when the lights went out, the marine stationed by the door to guard the prisoners thought that it was an issue unrelated to the staged escape. He was caught off guard when the prisoners jimmied open the door instead of sneaking out the panel we left loose for them in the back of the closet."

"So? He still knew what he was supposed to do, didn't he?"

"Sir, the blow to his head gave him a concussion and he wasn't thinking clearly."

"He's a US Marine, dammit, he's not supposed to think! Just follow orders."

"Sir, after being struck in the head, he reverted to his training, which was to apprehend any escaping prisoners."

"Which he failed to do."

"Sir, yes, sir. But when he was fired upon, he again reacted as he had been trained to do and confronted the immediate threat."

"And cold-cocked the prisoner who he was supposed to let escape. Tell me, commander, was that concept too complex for the young man?"

"Sir, no, sir. He was engaged with multiple threats and did the best that he could."

"And now we have two spies running loose, one of them capable of overpowering an armed marine and then eluding pursuit by a team of experienced agents. And, we're no closer to finding the alien base, are we, commander?"

"Sir, no, sir. We are not."

"What is the status of your search?"

"Sir, the Miller woman was spotted trying to escape upriver, but she dropped out of sight before we could bring her in. The teams have regrouped, and I'm confident that we'll find her before the end of the day.

"The other individual has proven to be far more elusive. This corresponds to the theory that we're dealing with trained alien operatives. Given the individual's facility with weapons and willingness to use them, I think that this must be the same person who made an attempt on Commander Solomon's life."

"Commander, didn't you tell me that the Miller woman would break when you applied more pressure to her?"

"Yes, sir."

"Would you say that her actions last night were the actions of a person in the throes of a psychotic meltdown? Based on your reports, it appears that she managed her escape quite capably."

"Sir, the psych evaluation indicated that she would experience a personality shift, retreating into a passive victim-state under stress. There was also a remote possibility that she might flip in the other direction. It appears that she did."

Dutchman leaned back in his chair.

"Commander, do you have this situation under control?"

Nuance paused before answering. "Sir, not entirely."

"Thought not."

After a few minutes of thought, Dutchman said, "Commander, we need to get this investigation back on track."

"Sir, yes, sir."

"First, find out how last night's armed intruder knew about the escape attempt. It can't be a coincidence that he showed up at the exact moment the spies made a break for it. There can only be two possibilities for how that happened. Either you've got a leak on your team, commander, or the Miller woman was not at all what she seemed and played you like a rookie, organizing the breakout."

"Sir, I'm confident that there were no leaks from my team. As for the Miller woman…"

"Yes?"

"Sir, her DNA tested human. She's also the person who sent the manuscript to Solomon."

"So?"

"Sir, I believe that she's in over her head with the spies. She got cold feet when she saw the manuscript and sent it to Solomon, hoping that we'd follow up on it. The alien that attacked us last night probably gave her instructions about what to do."

"Plausible. Go on."

"Sir, after the escape attempt failed, the Miller woman might have gone into hiding out of fear of the alien. She knows too much about their operation and she's proven unreliable. If she hasn't been terminated already, then it's only a matter of time. We need to find her before the alien does. I'm confident she's the key to cracking this thing wide open."

"And if she still won't talk?"

"The alien won't know that, and we can use her as bait to lure it within reach."

"Very well, then, commander. Use all available resources to locate the Miller woman. You also need to broaden the search for the alien to cover the entire county. He has to be close. With such a dangerous individual on the loose, I have no choice but to declare martial law. After you notify the local authorities, contact the assault teams we had standing by last night. Bring them onsite to assist with the operations."

"Sir, yes, sir."

"And commander?"

"Sir?"

"Resume your interrogation of the prisoners. Use whatever means you find necessary to wring the truth out of them. Understood?"

"Sir, yes, sir."

Dutchman glared at Nuance. The man's lack of expression hinted at some reluctance to take the necessary steps. "Commander, let me be very clear on this subject. So far, you've handled the prisoners with kid gloves. You should have initiated enhanced interrogation techniques long before now. You need to break them, and you need to do it fast. Start with stress positions and then move on to disorienting techniques. We don't have the equipment you'd need for sensory deprivation or over-stimulation, but their psych profiles should give you a good idea of what they fear and how best to use that to manipulate them, break down their defenses, and make them talk."

'Yes, sir."

"I hope you don't have any qualms about this, commander?"

"Sir, no, sir."

"Very well. Dismissed."

As Nuance turned to go, Dutchman stopped him. "Oh, and commander?"

"Yes, sir?"

"Twice now, these aliens have used deadly force to accomplish their objectives. First, the attempt on Commander Solomon's life, and then last night when they fired on one of our marines. I want them taken alive, if at all possible. But I don't want you to place any more of our people in needless jeopardy. You're authorized to use extreme force if needed. Am I clear?"

"Sir, yes, sir!"

Nuance left the room at a run. After he was gone, Dutchman opened up his laptop and reread the email from the Pentagon. *Even if we do catch the spies, I'm going to be in hot water. At least I can pin most of the mistakes on Nuance and his team. But my career's in the dumpster if he doesn't haul in the spies before the Pentagon's inspector arrives.*

35

When Jake woke after being knocked out during the escape attempt, he found himself lying face down on the floor of one of Northwood's offices. The actinic smell of hot steel and burning fuel oil precluded any other possibility, even if he hadn't recognized the dingy linoleum flooring.

Jake shivered as he looked around the room. Other than a folding chair, it was empty. There wasn't even a window to break the monotony of the faded green surface of the walls. Sitting down on the chair, he tried to think about what to do next, but his thoughts kept going back to Claire. Jake sat there for hours, berating himself over his failure to help her, then feeling guilty that he had thought of Claire before he thought of his friend, Felipe.

When the door opened and Nuance walked in followed by one of his men in black, Jake felt a surge of hope mixed with dread.

"Commander Nuance, is Claire okay? And Felipe? What—"

"Shut up," Nuance growled.

"But Claire—"

"You should be more worried about yourself at this point."

"Why? What's going on?"

"Get him on his feet," Nuance commanded. The agent rushed to obey.

As soon as Jake was standing, Nuance said, "Take off your clothes. You can leave your briefs on."

Jake stared at Nuance. "Here? In front of you?"

"Yes. Here, and now."

"Why?"

"That's a nice shirt. You wouldn't want it to get…soiled…would you?"

Jake swallowed hard at the implications of that statement. "Where should I put them?"

"Any place on the floor will be fine."

"What if I don't want to?"

"Then I'll have my agents remove them for you. After your partner took some shots at us last night, I wouldn't expect them to be gentle. Cooperation is your best bet right now, Andersen."

Jake took off his clothes, folding his jeans and T-shirt before placing them on top of his sneakers in the corner of the room.

"Socks, too. Then have a seat." Nuance gestured to the chair, which the agent had pushed up against a wall.

Jake complied and felt the hair on his legs lift as he sat down on the cold metal chair.

"Prep him." Nuance folded his arms, his gaze steady on Jake.

Jake watched, perplexed, as the tall, gangly agent approached carrying two shelf brackets and a cordless drill.

"What are you going to do with those?" Jake asked.

"Hold still, and tilt your head to the side. I'll try not to hurt you," the agent replied.

Positioning the bracket upside down on the wall so that its horizontal arm rested on Jake's shoulder, the agent tried to drill into the wall through one of the bracket's fastening holes.

"Can't you go any faster, Jenkins?" Nuance asked. "We'll be here all day if you can't do better than that."

"Sir, it's a bit awkward with his head in the way, and this isn't the right bit for drilling into cinder block. I can't hold the bracket and his head while I'm drilling. I'm doing the best I can, sir."

Jake watched Nuance fume, then step forward.

"Fine. I'll hold the bracket for you, Jenkins. You drill."

"Yes, sir."

Jake winced as Nuance pushed his head to one side, pinning it down with a forearm as he held the bracket against the wall with his other hand. The drill buzzed like a hornet in Jake's ear, accompanied by a grinding noise as the bit tore into the wall.

"Ow! Jenkins, watch what the hell you're doing!" Nuance dropped the bracket and jumped back, holding his hand under his armpit.

"Sorry, sir." Jenkins didn't appear to be sorry at all. "Forgot that the cinder blocks in these walls have hollow centers. When the bit broke through, I wasn't ready for it. Hope I didn't hurt your hand too badly when I mashed it, sir."

"Dammit, Jenkins! Just fasten the damn brackets to the wall so we can get to work."

"Yes, sir. It should go faster now, I know where to drill." Jenkins helped Jake out of the chair and stood him to one side. "Wait here, son, while I finish this." Jenkins half-grinned. "Unless you'd like me to drill holes in your ears for earrings?"

"No, thanks," Jake mumbled, puzzled. "What are you guys doing, anyway?"

Jenkins didn't answer, but the quick, furtive look that he gave Nuance made Jake uneasy. *Whatever they have in mind, it's not going to be pleasant.*

After the shelf brackets were fastened to the wall, Jake was again made to sit down. His shoulders just touched the bottom of the brackets. At a command from Nuance, Jenkins stooped and zip-tied Jake's ankles and knees together, then did the same for his wrists.

"Don't forget the tack strip." Nuance's eyes bored into Jake's.

"Sir, is that necessary?" Jenkins looked up, clearly reluctant to follow the order.

"Jenkins, if you don't have the stomach for this, then I'll bring in somebody else. And you can pack your duffel bag for cold weather because I'll see to it that your next assignment is some place that never sees the sun."

"Sir, yes, sir." Jenkins retrieved a three-foot strip of wood from the hallway, closing the door behind him as he returned to Jake's chair. The wood was shaped like a yard stick, with short nails protruding from one side to hold carpet in place and keep it from slipping. Bending over, Jenkins lifted Jake's feet off the ground and slipped the wood underneath them.

"Hey! That hurts!" Jake cried, as his naked heels came down on the sharp tack points sticking out of the wood.

"Lift your heels, and the pain will go away," Nuance said, stepping in front of Jake. "Jenkins, pull the chair."

"Sir..." Jenkins stood motionless, staring at his superior.

Nuance snarled, "Get the hell out of my sight, you coward! I'll do this myself!"

Jenkins slunk from the room, looking back over his shoulder at Jake as he went.

"What are you going to do to me?" Jake asked Nuance, afraid of the answer even as he spoke.

"Nothing permanent. But I warned you the last time we spoke that if you didn't cooperate and tell me everything I need to know, then things would get unpleasant. That time has come."

"But I don't know anything!"

"Wrong answer."

Nuance jerked the chair out from under Jake, leaving him standing with his back flat against the wall and his knees bent at right angles.

At first, Jake wondered what the point of the exercise was. His position was awkward but not overly uncomfortable. In less than a minute, though, his thighs began to tremble from holding his weight.

When Jake tried to straighten up to take the strain off his legs, the shelf brackets prevented him from doing so. When he let his heels down to relieve the pressure, the tacks in the wooden strip poked into his skin, forcing him back up on the balls of his feet.

The stress on his thighs soon grew unbearable, and Jake groaned in pain as his legs began to shake.

Nuance leaned over him. "Now then, Andersen, how many spies are in your cell?"

"I don't know! I'm not a spy! Please, God, this hurts!"

"I can make the pain stop, Andersen, just tell me what I want to know. How many?"

"I don't know anything about spies!" Tears ran down Jake's face as the pain grew, becoming the only thing in his universe, blotting out everything else.

"Last night, you had somebody waiting outside to help you escape. How did they know to be there?"

"I don't know! I tell you, I don't know!"

"Did the Miller woman give you your instructions? Was she the go-between with your alien masters? Where's the Miller woman now? Is she at your main base?"

"Claire? She's got nothing to do with this. And I don't know where she is. Please, God, stop!"

"Would you like me to stop, Andersen?"

"Yes, for God's sake!" As he spoke, Jake's strength failed, and his heels came down hard on the tack strip. When that happened, dark blood began to seep onto the floor around his feet.

"But you haven't told me anything, yet."

"I can't!"

"We'll see about that in a bit. This is just the beginning, you know. It gets worse for you after this." Nuance slid the chair under Jake's shuddering legs.

Freed from the stress position, Jake sank into the chair and then toppled to the floor, his legs quivering with the release of tension. After a minute, he managed to choke out, "I want a lawyer. I have rights, you bastard!"

"I thought we already covered that subject, Andersen. No, in fact, you do not have any rights at all. The Patriot Act allows me use whatever methods I deem necessary to break you. And I will break you. The only limit on what I do now is the fact that the scientists at Roswell need you alive and in sound condition for their vivisection."

"What are you talking about?"

"Vivisection? That's where they cut you apart to see what makes you tick. They've waited years to get their hands on a genuine alien. Looks like they'll finally get their chance."

"You're insane!"

"No, but I believe that your superiors must be. Your people could have approached us openly, like civilized beings. Instead, you sent spies into a key defense facility. And when we caught on to your activities, you tried to kill our people. First Solomon, then one of our marines. What did you expect us to do? Just lie down and let you compromise our ability to defend ourselves? Is that what your people have in mind, invasion?"

"I don't have 'people,' Nuance. I've got no idea what you're raving about."

"Pity. Well, perhaps your accomplices will prove more talkative."

"What do you mean?"

"As soon as the doctors finish digging the bullet out of your partner's leg, he'll get his turn in this chair. And more."

"But Felipe is innocent! And he's legal. He's got a valid green card, I've seen it."

"Son, we don't issue green cards to space aliens."

"What do you mean?" *Space aliens? This guy's stark raving mad!*

"One last chance to talk, Andersen. Where's your base? How many spies do you have on our planet? Where's the Miller woman?"

"Planet? Base? I still don't know what you're talking about. And I don't know where Claire is, but if she got away, then good for her."

"It won't be so good for her when we find her. And we will find her. We've let her off easy so far. Now that she's tipped her hand, she'll get the same treatment as the rest of your spy ring."

"No! Not Claire—you can't!"

Nuance gave Jake an enigmatic look. "At this point, I'm pretty sure that you know that I can. And will. Think about that while you wait for our next session." Then he left the room.

————

As soon as he was back in his office, Nuance slumped into his chair, resting his forehead on a palm as he stared at the floor. The thought of what he'd just done sickened him, but he felt trapped. Dutchman's orders were specific, and he could no longer avoid getting rough with the prisoners, not without facing a court-martial himself.

But what if Dutchman was wrong?

Nuance understood himself well enough to recognize that his growing reluctance to follow orders meant that his subconscious was trying to tell him something. Either these were the best-trained agents he'd ever seen, or they were exactly what they seemed to be, hapless nerds caught up in something they didn't understand. That didn't fit the physical evidence, but he was still shaken by Solomon's claims. Something about that man irritated Nuance like a tick in the ear, but he'd never known him to lie.

Nuance sighed, opened his laptop, and started reviewing the tapes of the interrogations. He went through them all again, looking for something he'd missed.

36

Daphne had trouble sleeping after her failed attempt to help Jake escape on Saturday night. She was still troubled when she went to early church service with her mom on Sunday morning. Afterward, she took Chaucer for a walk, rambling aimlessly around the neighborhood as she thought about the previous night's events.

The sky was overcast, and a cool breeze whispered off the lake, so Daphne threw on a gray hoodie over her blue-striped tee-shirt and jeans. The grass was still dewed, and most yards smelled sweet after recently being cut.

Chaucer was quiet and watchful, staying close to Daphne while giving every passing stranger the stink-eye.

Unca Jake's in trouble. But what can I do? I bet that mean Moo-once is behind it all. Or the empty-eyed man.

Daphne shivered, then sat down on the curb and started to cry. *I can't tell Mom. And the sheriff's in on it, too. I wish I knew what to do!*

Several minutes had passed when Daphne heard somebody call her name. "Daphne?"

Surprised to feel a touch on her shoulder, she looked up and then swallowed hard. "Ms. Eliot!"

"Good morning, Daphne." Her teacher eased down next to her. "Child, you seem upset. What's wrong?"

Wiping her eyes and nose on the sleeve of her hoodie, Daphne replied, "Unca Jake's in trouble, but I can't tell anybody about it."

"Why not?"

"Nobody would believe me. But it's true!"

"Daphne, you're not making sense. You say, your uncle Jake's in trouble? What's happened?"

"It's that Moo-once guy. He's got Unca Jake. And they're mean. They hit him, and he fell down."

"Hit him? Jake?"

Eyes wide, Daphne spoke in a rush, "Yes, ma'am. And he fell down, and he didn't get up. I ran away, and I think Miss Claire did too, but there was a bad guy with a gun, and he was shooting at everybody!"

"Daphne, please slow down. I can see that you're very upset. Come, let's walk for a bit, then you can take your time and explain everything that's happened." Eliot brushed off her brown tweed skirt as she stood up. She adjusted her green wool shawl, tucked her black purse over her arm, and then took Daphne by the hand.

"Would your mother mind if we walked down to the park? I like to go there when I have something to think about, and it sounds like you've got quite a story for me."

"Yes, ma'am. I'm pretty sure it'll be okay with Mom. And I like to go to the park, too."

"You do?"

"Yes, ma'am. I like the little round birds that run around on the sand. But they're shy, so I don't let Chaucer chase 'em."

"That's very kind of you, dear. Now then, start at the beginning. Tell me everything that happened, and leave out nothing."

"Yes, ma'am. Well, it all started last Tuesday night."

"That was the night before you stayed home sick, wasn't it?"

"Yes, ma'am. But I wasn't sick. Just real tired, on account of I was up all night, and the mean guys kidnapped me, and—"

"Slow down, please. Take your time and tell me everything."

By the time they reached Red Arrow Park, Daphne had managed to convey the gist of what had happened. She could tell that her teacher was upset by the story. Eliot's jaw was clenched tight, her face was red, and her nostrils were flared like she was having trouble breathing. Chaucer kept looking up at the teacher and whining, his tail between his legs as if he was afraid that a mighty storm was about to break loose.

When they reached the park's pavilion, Eliot sat down and patted the seat next to her for Daphne to join her. Chaucer slipped out of sight, although he could be heard snuffling around the base of the structure.

"Now then, Daphne, you keep mentioning a Miss Claire, but I don't understand what she's got to do with all this. Just who is she, and how is she involved?"

Daphne bit her lip and glanced sideways at Eliot. "Oh. Well, do you remember how I asked about getting a book published?"

"Yes…?"

"Well, I might have done something that I shouldn't have. Here's what happened…"

37

Claire's first sensation when she woke in the dark crawl space under the park pavilion was of a warm, soft, body snuggled against her back. It felt nice. She was still half-asleep when a fat, wet tongue slopped across her cheek.

"Hey! Stop that!"

She protested in vain. The face bath continued until she rolled over and pushed her assailant away. It was a dog—a large one, and a moment later it was back at it, except this time it was able to get her whole face.

Claire tried to push the dog away again, but paused at the sound of voices nearby. *I hope they didn't hear me.*

It was cold, and Claire thought briefly about hugging the dog to keep warm, but she already smelled like dead fish and rotting wood. Adding Eau de Fido to the mix was out of the question. Lying as still as possible, she listened as the nearby voices continued. It sounded like two people talking, an older woman and a girl. Their words were clear and loud enough that Claire realized that they must be sitting right above her.

Now what? I can't stay under here forever, but they'll see me if I try to leave.

Then Claire recognized the child's voice. It was Daphne, Jake's niece. *Daphne wouldn't turn me in. But what about the woman with her?*

The dog chose that exact moment to resume his ministrations, causing Claire to slide away from him until her back was pressed against the lattice that circled the pavilion's foundation. She didn't notice that the voices had stopped until she got a poke in the back. Claire jumped, banging her head on the underside of the floor of the pavilion.

"Young lady, what are you doing under there?"

Claire saw a mature woman dressed in a green shawl poking a stick through the lattice. Daphne crouched next to the woman and was shading her eyes to see who was underneath the gazebo.

"Miss Claire! Ms. Eliot, it's Miss Claire!" Daphne said excitedly.

"Hi, Daphne." Claire finger-waved, embarrassed.

Eliot pulled back a corner of the lattice. "Please come out where I can see you. It's uncomfortable stooping over like this to hold a conversation."

Claire crawled forward and was halfway out when Chaucer pushed past her to nuzzle Daphne, knocking Claire over as he went. Before she had a chance to get up, he rushed back to lick her face some more.

"Chaucer, you stop that and let Miss Claire up." Daphne hauled the dog back by his collar.

"Thanks, Daphne." Claire got to her feet, then wobbled and had to brace herself against the pavilion.

Eliot took Claire by the elbow and guided her into the pavilion. "Sit down before you fall down." Taking a moment to look Claire over, she exclaimed, "What have you been into, child? You look a mess!"

Claire looked at Daphne, who said, "She knows, Miss Claire. I told her what's been going on."

"She does?" Claire looked at Eliot. "You do?"

"I do." Eliot's lips turned down in disapproval. "At least some of it. If you don't mind, I'd like to know what you've gotten my pupil mixed up in?"

Claire sighed. "I'm not entirely sure of it all myself, but I'm stuck in the middle of it, whatever it is." She looked around at the overcast skies and then began to shiver. "Is there some-place warm where we can talk? I'm freezing."

"Of course. Do you live nearby?"

"Not really. My apartment's close to downtown."

"Well, my house is seven blocks from here, just about halfway to Daphne's. It's probably best to go there, given that you're soaking wet." Eliot wrapped Claire in her shawl and then led her from the pavilion, holding her arm to steady her as they walked. Daphne and Chaucer followed along behind them.

A chill drizzle began to fall as they walked. Barefoot, Claire kept to the grass as they trudged along, grateful for Eliot's supporting arm as she struggled to put weight on her left foot. Claire was shaking by the time she was inside Eliot's mint-green cape cod.

Eliot took Claire straight back to the bathroom, a cozy nook with a white pedestal sink and toilet next to a matching bath and shower stall. A brass light fixture, light-green fleur-de-lis wallpaper, and cream-colored tile flooring gave the room a warm, comfortable feel.

Claire stripped and then climbed into the shower, turning the faucet to the highest temperature possible, while Eliot threw her clothes into a washing machine. The spray of hot water soon filled the bathroom with steam. Claire washed as gently as she could, trying to clean the grit out of the cuts and scrapes on her hands and legs. The massive purple bruise covering her entire left hip was too painful to touch, but it was the pain in her foot that made her bite her lip to keep from crying out loud.

Sitting on the edge of the tub, Claire looked at her foot and then looked away. *Toes aren't supposed to bend that way. But how can I see a doctor when I'm running for my life?*

When she was done, Claire wrapped herself up in a towel and joined Eliot and Daphne at a round oak table in the dining room. The table sat on a russet and brown braided throw rug that was oval in shape. The rug was warm and cushioned the honey-maple flooring under Claire's feet. Looking around, she could see that the house had been tastefully decorated with wildlife paintings by local artists and porcelain display plates on beige walls.

A hot cup of green tea and a large blueberry muffin were on the table waiting for her. Daphne was already halfway through eating hers and appeared content to chew in silence while Claire told her story.

As she sat down, Claire eased her broken foot to the side. Chaucer came over and sniffed at it. Claire shooed him away in a halfhearted manner. "Chaucer, leave my foot alone. I just washed, and it doesn't need your ministrations. Nope. Not at all, please."

Chaucer laid down without touching it, giving Claire a reproachful look as he did so.

Eliot noticed and winced when she saw Claire's toes. "Young woman, I think your story can wait. You need to see a doctor."

"I wish I could. But if I do, Nuance's agents will find me."

Eliot looked at Daphne. "Is this Nuance the same person as the Moo-once character you told me about?"

Daphne nodded, her mouth full of muffin.

The teacher looked back at Claire. "Maybe I do need to hear some of your story first."

Claire took a sip of tea and a nibble from the muffin. Then she took a big bite, realizing that she hadn't eaten since lunch the day before. Between bites, she tried to explain what had happened, about the manuscript, and Jake, and being coerced by Nuance. *I must sound like an idiot. This doesn't make sense, even to me, and it's my story!*

When Claire was done, Eliot rose and said, "Wait here. I know somebody who can help you with this."

Claire huddled over her tea while Eliot called somebody from the next room. A few minutes later, the doorbell rang, and the teacher ushered a middle-aged blonde woman into the room.

"Doctor Simmons, this is Claire, the young woman I spoke about over the phone."

Claire tried to rise, but Simmons motioned for her to stay seated. "Just stay there while I take a look at that foot."

Claire shifted in her seat as Simmons touched her foot, unable to keep from whimpering when the examination focused on her toes.

"Could be worse," Simmons said, taking a seat. "You've got three broken toes, but the rest of the foot is intact. Near as I can tell without an X-ray, the breaks are clean, and there's good blood flow to the area. That means I can reset the bones and immobilize the toes without having to cut the foot open."

"Will it hurt?"

Simmons sighed. "Yes. I won't sugar-coat it. Toes are more sensitive than fingers, and it's going to hurt like the devil when I set the bones. If you can get to the E.R., I can give you an anesthetic to mask the pain, though to be honest, the shot hurts nearly as much as the procedure. But before I do anything, I want to take some X-rays. I don't like working blind."

Claire shook her head. "No, I can't go to a hospital. I've got some nasty people looking for me, and if I'm spotted, I don't know what they'll do."

"What kind of bad people? The sheriff hereabouts is a decent guy. If you're in trouble, he can help you."

"No law enforcement. They'd just turn me over to..."

"To who?"

"Federal agents. Dress in black, say they're from Military Intelligence."

"Any of them got a name?" Simmons asked, raising an eyebrow.

"Nuance, and Dutchman."

"Nuance? I know that one," Simmons said, scowling. "Thinks a lot of himself. Threw me out of my own clinic! Can you imagine that? Brought in his own doctor. Gives me this line that 'Commander Solomon has access to secret info' and that I'm not to be trusted around him in case he talks in his sleep. Balderdash!"

"Did you say Commander Solomon?"

"Yes, know him?"

"I do! How is he? Nuance told me that he'd been in a car wreck and that somebody tried to kill him."

"He'll be okay. How do you know him?"

"He's the naval officer that I sent Jake's manuscript to. That's what started this whole mess."

"Sorry, I don't know Jake or anything about your situation."

"Jake's an author who's been arrested for being a spy, but Solomon has to know that he isn't. Solomon could clear this whole thing up if only I could speak with him."

"Would that cause problems for this Nuance character?"

"Definitely."

Simmons grinned. "Then I think I can help you, young lady. And get your foot fixed properly at the same time."

"How?"

"Easy. I'll call an ambulance to take you to the E.R. When we get there, I'll sneak you in as a Jane Doe. We get them every once in a while, so nobody will think anything of it. After I fix your foot, I'll help you get in to speak with Solomon. When you're done there, I'll sneak you back out in the ambulance."

"I don't know what to say."

"Say you'll get dressed. I don't have all day."

"Miss Claire?" All three heads turned to face Daphne, who had remained silent throughout the discussion.

"Yes, Daphne?"

"I saw what the soldier did to Unca Jake last night. Is he going to be okay?"

"I don't know, Daphne. I hope so."

"Please!" Daphne started to cry as she leaned forward. "You've got to help him, Miss Claire! Only you can get him out of this. Please?"

Claire took Daphne's hands in hers and said, "I'll try Daphne. I promise. And I'll try to do better than I did yesterday." *I can't do any worse!*

"Thank you, Miss Claire!" Daphne jumped up and gave her a fierce hug, causing Claire to wince as her bruised side flared at the touch.

"Claire?" Eliot tapped Daphne on the shoulder so that she could speak with Claire.

"Yes, ma'am?"

"If you're hiding from law enforcement, have you given any thought to where you'll go when you leave the hospital? Nuance's agents might be watching your apartment."

"No, I haven't thought about it at all. I've been so focused on minute-to-minute survival that it hasn't even crossed my mind. But yes, they'll be watching. They have been for several days now."

"Then stay here."

"But, I don't want to cause you any trouble."

"Young woman, before I came to Marinette, I taught for a decade in one of Chicago's worst neighborhoods. I've had to face down drug dealers, gangs, and corrupt politicians. A few boy scouts dressed up like ninjas don't impress me in the least."

"Well, if you're sure?"

"I'm sure. Now sit still while I check if your clothes are dry. You won't want to visit Commander Solomon wearing nothing but a bath towel."

38

Solomon shifted in his hospital bed, trying to ease the ache in his left leg, then groaned as the bandages across his chest pulled tight over his cracked ribs. He was watching a Brewer's game on the room's wall-mounted TV but wasn't enjoying it, even though they were getting shellacked by his favorite team, the Cubs. It was the first game of a Sunday doubleheader. With the game's outcome clear, he decided to take half an hour for meditation to try and bring his pain under control, so he switched off the TV.

Solomon closed his eyes so that he wouldn't have to look at the ochre walls covered with an impressive array of the plastic and chrome implements used in what humans considered modern medicine. Then he slowed his breathing, calming himself, pushing away the pain as he reached for his center of energy. Sinking deeper into his meditation, Solomon suppressed all conscious thoughts, letting his mind drift with his surroundings.

The bedsheets felt cool and soft on his skin. The lemon tang of disinfectant filled the air, drifting down from the ceiling vent and mixing with the light, lilac-soap aroma of the sheets to form a pleasant floral scent-scape. Without the chatter of the ballgame on the TV, he could hear the beep of the room's monitors, and muted footsteps passing outside his door.

Floating in his meditative trance, Solomon felt the pain slough away as he relaxed his muscles.

"Commander Solomon?"

Solomon sighed at the intruding voice, then grunted as the pain returned.

A blonde woman wearing scrubs was standing in the doorway, looking in at him. A quick glance showed that Hansen wasn't in the room. *Must have stepped out for a cup of coffee, or to hit the can.*

"Yes, that's me. Who are you, and what can I do for you?"

"Hi, I'm Doctor Simmons. I treated you when you were first brought in to the E.R. a week ago. I just wanted to check how you're doing?"

"I'm fine, thank you. Look, I don't mean to be rude, but I was in the middle of something when you knocked. If there's nothing else…"

"Sorry, I didn't mean to interrupt. But there's somebody here to see you. She says that it's urgent."

"Who is it?" *I hope it isn't Nuance or one of his agents.*

"Claire Miller."

"Claire Miller? Claire's here?" Solomon forgot about his pain.

"Yes, and she needs your help. Can she come in to see you?"

"Yes, of course!"

Simmons gestured, and Claire limped into the room.

"I'll wait outside," Simmons said. "Claire, knock when you're ready to go, and I'll bring a gurney to wheel you out." Then she closed the door.

"Commander Solomon, thank you for taking the time to see me," Claire said as she eased into a visitor's chair.

"Of course, it's not a problem. From what I understand, you're in quite a pickle."

"That's an understatement! Have you heard of an officer called Nuance?"

"Yes, I have." Solomon clenched his teeth in anger. "And I'm well aware of how he operates. I'm sorry he's picked you to lean on. It's not right."

"It's not just me. He's got a friend of mine, Jake Andersen, in custody, along with another man, Felipe. Commander, they're being tortured. And Nuance won't let them see a lawyer. He claims that they're alien spies, if you can believe it?"

"No, I can't. This isn't an episode of Star Trek, for God's sake. Nuance is way off base." *And a little too close to home for my liking. Maybe Hansen was right and we should get out while we can?*

"But he says he has DNA evidence! And then there's the problem with the manuscript."

"I don't know about the DNA testing, but I can speak to the issue with the manuscript."

"Really?"

"Yes. It got mixed up with some other papers when I crashed my car. While I was unconscious, Nuance's team assembled the papers thinking it was all one document. The result looked pretty damning, but when I told Nuance what must have happened, he didn't seem to buy it."

"Commander, can you help me at all? Maybe try speaking with Nuance again, or with that other man…the Admiral."

"Dutchman?"

"Yes."

"I'm sorry, Claire. I've already spoken with Nuance, but if he's still after you, then he must not have believed me. Talking to him again wouldn't accomplish anything." *Except drawing attention to myself. The kind of attention I'd like to avoid.*

"And the other…?"

"Dutchman's a non-starter. He's above my pay grade, and he won't even talk to me unless I'm working on an assignment for him. And his reputation is, well, he's ruthless."

"That, I already knew. So you can't help me? Not at all?"

"Not directly. But if you can tell me more about your situation, then perhaps I can give you some advice. What's all this about DNA?"

Claire sighed and slumped in her chair. "Nuance has taken blood samples from everybody involved, even from me. He told me that Felipe's blood tested non-human. How can I argue with that? But it can't be right! Can you help me explain that to Nuance? Maybe he'll listen to you."

Solomon studied his hands for a few minutes. *If they're checking DNA, then Hansen and I could be in big trouble. I've got to stay out of this. But Claire's a good kid; she doesn't deserve what Nuance is doing to her. Damn!* "Claire, I have to be very careful right now. You see, I'm also a potential suspect because I was in possession of the manuscript. Anything that I say to Nuance would pass through that filter, and it wouldn't look good."

"Then I've wasted my time coming here." Claire's shoulders sagged in defeat.

"Not entirely. Look, Claire. Your best bet would be to convince Nuance of the truth and then to let him tackle Dutchman."

"How?"

"The key to convincing Nuance will be to disprove the two facts upon which he's built his case. The manuscript is already suspect. So if you can find a way to debunk the DNA evidence, then he'd have no choice but to close the investigation."

"You mean, that if I could get DNA tests proving Jake and Felipe are human, then Nuance would have to let them go?"

"Yes, there's an excellent chance of that. Nuance's techniques are brutal, but he is honest. He'll do the right thing if you provide strong enough evidence."

"So, how do I do that?"

Solomon shrugged. "I don't know. Nuance isn't going to let you just walk in and take blood samples from his prisoners."

"Do they have to be blood samples?"

"No, blood's only needed for deep DNA scans in research. What you need can be done with samples of hair. But I still don't see how you can get the samples."

Claire straightened and smiled. "That, commander, I think I can do."

"Excellent. But if I may say so, you need to move fast, today if at all possible. Based on my conversation with Nuance, Dutchman's under a lot of pressure to finish his investigation. Time's running out, and he's going to become more ruthless as his deadline approaches. You've said that your friends are being tortured. It will get worse for them with each passing day."

39

After her discussion with Solomon at the hospital, Claire returned to Eliot's house in an ambulance, the same way that she had left the place earlier in the afternoon. Whenever the vehicle approached one of Nuance's roadblocks, Doctor Simmons stuffed Claire into an empty cabinet in the back compartment. The white cabinet was labeled "Medical Waste" in large red letters above a yellow-and-black biohazard sign.

"We're in luck," Simmons said as she closed the cabinet door one last time. "This one's staffed by marines. They're more used to looking for bombs than people. If they had somebody from Border Patrol here, I'd never get you through. Now be quiet, I'll let you out as soon as we're at Eliot's."

Claire felt a pulse of fear as the door closed again, followed by the click of a lock. She was crammed into a space so small that she couldn't even move to scratch her nose, which began to itch the moment the door closed. With no ventilation and no light, it grew hot and stuffy in the cabinet. Her hip throbbed, but thankfully her foot was still numb from the anesthetic Simmons had used when setting her toes. A faint smell of lilacs lingered from her shower earlier. *At least I don't smell like swamp water anymore.*

She held her breath at the sound of approaching boots outside her hiding place. When they continued past, she let her breath out. *What if they arrest Simmons and just leave me in here?* Claire felt panic rising within her and fought the impulse to pound on the door and ask to be let out.

When the ambulance began to move again, she thought she'd cry with relief. But the door didn't open. A minute passed, and she was still trapped in the cabinet.

What's going on? Why hasn't Simmons let me out? I need to get out of here!

Claire's heart raced as the walls of the cabinet pressed in on her. She closed her eyes, but it made no difference in the dark. She began to feel dizzy, and no matter how fast she breathed, she felt short of breath, as if there was a hand gripping her throat.

When Simmons finally opened the door, Claire was wet with sweat.

"Are you okay?" Simmons asked, helping her out of the cabinet.

"No. Yes. No—I hope that's the last checkpoint. I can't take much more of this."

"It is. We've backed up to Eliot's house. It's clear at the moment. Are you ready to go?"

"I'm ready." Claire sat down on the ambulance's tailgate to get out, not daring to hop down on her broken foot. Wedging a crutch under her armpit, she hobbled as fast as she could toward the front porch. Simmons helped her up the steps to the door and then followed her inside.

"Sit!" Eliot commanded, pointing to an overstuffed, brocaded armchair near the front door.

Claire sat down, propping up her injured foot on a handy ottoman.

Eliot pulled a kitchen chair up next to her. "So, how'd it go?"

"Solomon can't help me. I could be wrong, but I think he's scared of something."

"Well, that Nuance character does sound pretty intimidating."

"I don't think it's that, but I can't see what else it might be. Anyway, he refused to go to bat for me."

"I'm sorry. What will you do now?"

"Solomon did mention one thing that's worth trying. He said that the manuscript could be explained away if it wasn't for the DNA evidence. If there was some way to test Jake and Felipe, to prove that they aren't aliens, then that might be enough to convince Nuance that we're all innocent."

"DNA testing?" Simmons asked, handing Claire a cup of hot tea as she sat down next to her.

"Yes. And I have an idea about how to get the samples for that. Solomon said that I wouldn't need blood samples to test for human DNA. Hair would be adequate. If I can sneak into Jake's house tonight, I should be able to get some from both of their hairbrushes."

"What then?" Simmons cupped her tea in her hands, leaning forward with her elbows on her knees.

"I'll send the samples to one of those testing services. They'd be able to test the hair for me, wouldn't they?"

"No. That's not something they would normally test for, though they might be willing to run a special request for you. Besides, it takes a month and a half to get the results back. Do you have that much time to wait?"

"No. Solomon said that it needs to happen within the next day or two. Nuance and his boss are under a lot of pressure to close the case. When Nuance questioned me yesterday, he told me that when they do that, he's going to send Jake to Roswell where they'll…they'll cut him up to see what an alien looks like inside." Claire felt tears start down her cheeks. "I can't live with that, knowing it was my fault."

"It's not your fault," Eliot said in her best brook-no-argument teacher's voice.

"Claire, maybe I can help you a little more," Simmons said, putting down her cup of tea.

"I can't ask that, doc, you've already put yourself at risk to help me."

"There's no risk involved. I happen to know somebody at the State Crime Lab who owes me a favor. I can give him a call and have the samples processed for you overnight."

"Are you sure?" Eliot asked. "I read in the paper last week that the lab has a six-month backlog."

"They do. But it only takes twelve hours to run a test, and like I said, this guy owes me."

"Do we want to know why?" Eliot raised an eyebrow.

"The jerk broke his leg while skiing with his girlfriend last winter. I covered for him. Told his wife, who's a manager at the lab where he works, that he slipped and fell on the sidewalk. Saved his marriage, and his job. You better believe the guy owes me. If you can get the samples to me before nightfall, I'll even drive them down to Madison so that he can run the tests tonight. I have to be there for a seminar at the university in the afternoon anyway. Might as well kill two birds with one stone."

"Doc, that's fantastic!" Claire said. "I'll sneak into Jake's after supper—"

"No, you won't!" Eliot said.

"But—"

"You're not sneaking anywhere with your foot banged up like that. You need to lie low, stay out of sight. I'll handle this."

"But—"

"I said I'll do it."

Arguing with Eliot, Claire realized, was like trying to convince a granite cliff to step out of your way. Giving in gracefully seemed like her only option. "Okay, but how will you get in?"

"Easy. I'll have Daphne open the door for me when she takes Chaucer out for his evening walk. Nothing more natural than a teacher walking with one of her students. After I get the samples, I'll drop them off at the good doctor's place."

"Are you sure? I don't want to get Daphne in trouble."

"Don't worry about that. What could go wrong, anyway?"

Daphne had just finished her evening meal and was clearing her plate from the table when the doorbell rang.

"I'll get it, Mom," she said, dashing to the front door.

When she opened the door and saw her teacher standing there, she caught her breath. "Ms. Eliot! Hi, um, my mom's in the kitchen. Would you like to come in?"

"That's all right, Daphne, I was out for a walk this way and wondered if you'd care to join me?"

"Sure! Let me ask my mom." Daphne poked her head into the kitchen and asked, "Mom, may I go for a walk with my teacher? I need to take Chaucer out anyway."

"Yes, dear. I'll finish up here. You go ahead."

"Thanks, Mom!"

Daphne grabbed her denim jacket and umbrella, and then slipped on a pair of pink vinyl galoshes. Chaucer was waiting by the door with his leash when she got there.

When she got outside, there was a pearl mist falling, drifting on a breeze coming off the lake that carried the smell of fish inland. Daphne's boots made satisfying *galumph* noises as she tromped through the puddles on the sidewalk. Chaucer stuck to the grass, and by the time they reached the end of the block, Daphne was sure that she would be giving the dog a bath when they got home.

They walked in silence for a few minutes before Eliot spoke. "Daphne?"

"Yes, ma'am?"

"I saw Claire a little bit ago, and I thought you'd like to know that she's safe for the moment. The doctor fixed her foot, so she can walk on it a bit now, too."

"Super! Did she talk with the man from the Bible?"

Eliot chuckled. "You mean, Commander Solomon, right?"

"Yes, ma'am."

"I don't believe that he's the same Solomon you're familiar with from Sunday school."

"Oh. I thought…"

"It's okay, Daphne. We should have explained it a little more to you. But I thought you'd like to know how things turned out with him."

"Yes, ma'am."

"Commander Solomon said that he can't help Claire himself. He did, however, give her a clue that might help her to clear her name."

"A clue? Like a detective sort of thing?"

"Well, sort of, yes."

"Cool! Do we need to sneak into the bad guys' hideout? Cause I've got a great disguise we can use. And Chaucer does, too!"

"I'm sorry to disappoint you, Daphne, but disguises won't be necessary. We're not breaking into anybody's hideout."

"Oh." Daphne scuffed her boot on the sidewalk in disappointment.

"It still might be dangerous, though, so I don't want you to get involved. I need to get into your uncle's house and get his and his roommate's hairbrushes. That's all. But I do need you to let me in because I don't have a key to his house."

"Sure! I can do that. But it'll be safe for me. It's my Unca Jake's house. Besides, Chaucer will protect me from any bad guys."

Chaucer whined as Eliot gave him a skeptical look. "I'm not so sure, Daphne."

"It's true! He saved me from a bad guy with a gun once!"

"I wouldn't count on that happening again. You were lucky."

"It wasn't luck! Chaucer saved me!" Daphne stuck her lower lip out and stamped her boots for emphasis.

Eliot rolled her eyes. "Well, I suppose it will be okay. With Jake and his roommate already arrested, there's no reason for Nuance or his thugs to hang out at their house. They must have searched the place a week ago."

"We should still wear disguises. Just in case."

"Oh, very well, Daphne. It can't hurt. We'll go back to your place so you can put on your disguise."

"It's not at home. I hid it so that Moo-once couldn't find it."

"Oh, that's right. You mentioned hiding your disguise earlier today. Under the library's porch, if I recall correctly?"

"Yes, ma'am."

"Very well, then. We seem to be headed in that direction anyway."

Excited at the prospect of another adventure, Daphne pulled her teacher forward as fast as she could walk. The library was closed when they got there. Daphne led Eliot around to the building's wooden porch and then handed Chaucer's leash to her.

Eyes wide, Daphne put her finger to her lips. "You wait here. I'll be right back."

Daphne crawled under the porch and dragged the bundle containing her disguise out. She took a moment to brush her knees, which had gotten wet and muddy from the rain-soaked blacktop. *Uh-oh. Mom's gonna be mad. These are my good Sunday clothes.*

She started to unroll the bundle, but Eliot stopped her. "Daphne, dear, perhaps you should wait to put on your disguise until we're at your Uncle Jake's house. Otherwise, people might see you and wonder what's going on."

"Gee, I hadn't thought of that. Okay!"

"And Daphne?"

"Yes, ma'am?"

"Is that a gun I see poking out of that bundle?"

"Yes, ma'am. But it's okay, it's not a real gun."

"Is it the paintball gun you mentioned earlier?"

"Yes, ma'am."

"Do you really need to bring such a thing with us?"

"Yes, ma'am. I need to return it to Unca Jake's. I'll be real careful, though."

Eliot sighed. "I hope so, child. I do hope so."

With her umbrella held high, Daphne carried her disguise under one arm as they walked back to Jake's house. Daphne led Eliot to the rear of the property. After a careful look around, she unrolled her disguise and put it on, sliding the defunct lightsaber into her belt and carrying the paintball gun in her hands.

"Do you have the key?" Eliot whispered.

"No, ma'am. Jake doesn't lock his doors."

Eliot scowled, but before she could say anything, Daphne went inside.

Chaucer followed Daphne in, then bolted through the kitchen to the living room.

"Chaucer!" Daphne chased after the dog, then stopped in surprise when she saw somebody sitting on the couch. Even though he was sitting down, she could see that he was a tall, gangly man. And he was dressed in black. *Just like one of Moo-once's agents!*

The man looked up from the video game he was playing and yelled, "Holy cow! Don't shoot!"

Grrrr! Chaucer leaped on the man, knocking him over and sending a jumbo bag of Cheese Puffs flying through the air, scattering golden bits of heaven everywhere as it spun out of the man's grasp.

Daphne backed away, bumping into Eliot just as the teacher entered the room.

"Watch out!" Eliot cried as she tripped and fell to the floor with a thud.

"Yikes!" Daphne dropped the gun as she fell. Then she winced and covered her ears. The gun went off when it hit the floor, emptying the two-hundred round hopper with a roar that filled the small room.

When the gun stopped firing, Daphne looked up from where she was huddled on the floor. The entire far side of the room was splattered with yellow paint, including the agent. Chaucer was the only thing present that was not covered in paint, having ducked under the coffee table in a suspiciously well-practiced maneuver the moment the gun went off.

"Are, are you okay, Daphne?" Eliot asked, looking around wide-eyed at the carnage.

"Yes, ma'am. I'm sorry, I didn't mean for it to go off."

Eliot sat up, brushing off her shawl and dress. "Well, let that be a lesson to you then. Guns are dangerous, and you should always assume that a gun is loaded until you know otherwise." Dabbing at some of the yellow paint spatter on her dress, she continued, "And you should only point a gun at something that you want to shoot."

"I'm sorry."

"It's okay, Daphne. Now let's check to see if this man hurt."

"But he's one of Moo-once's guys! He's a bad man!"

"Daphne, we don't know that."

"But he's all in black. And what's he doing here? He shouldn't be in here if Jake or Felipe didn't let him in."

"That's a good point," the teacher said, bending over the unconscious man. "Hmmm. He doesn't seem to be hurt. And I think you're right; he is one of Nuance's agents. Oh my God! He's got a pistol, child. Do you realize what would have happened if Chaucer hadn't knocked him out? He might have shot us both."

"So Chaucer saved us again!" Daphne pulled the dog out of his hiding spot and gave him a big hug.

"For once, I think you're right. I wouldn't have believed it, myself, if I hadn't been here to see it happen."

"Ms. Eliot?"

"Yes, Daphne?"

"What do we do now?"

"Oh! Yes, well, we're here for a purpose, aren't we? Let's get on with it. I need you to go into the men's rooms and get their hairbrushes. I'll tie this man up so he can't cause us any more trouble."

Daphne quickly gathered the hairbrushes and brought them back to her teacher. "What now, ma'am?"

"Now we need to get out of here. And you need to get rid of that disguise. And the gun."

"They're Unca Jake's. Can I just leave them here?"

"No, we're dealing with clever and suspicious men. They're certain to search the house again after this incident, so you can't leave any of it here."

"Should I take it home and hide it there?"

"No, Daphne. Just bundle it up and give it to me. I'll hide it at my place. Okay?"

"Okay. Will you give it back to Unca Jake later?"

"Yes. With a lecture about the dangers of leaving guns lying around where children can find them." Eliot sniffed. "He's a grown man, and he should know better than that."

Daphne took off her disguise and rolled it up around the paintball gun, being very careful to avoid the gun's trigger as she worked. "I can carry these for you, ma'am."

"That's all right, Daphne. I want you to take Chaucer home now. You've had enough adventure for one day. I'll hide your disguise, and then drop off these hairbrushes with my friend for testing."

As they were leaving, Daphne paused as she closed the back door. "Ma'am?"

"Yes, Daphne?"

"Will Unca Jake be okay?"

"I hope so, but I can't promise anything."

"And Miss Claire?"

"The same as Jake. Let's keep our fingers crossed, okay?"

"Okay."

41

Cheese Puffs crinkled and popped underfoot as Nuance strode into the living room of Jake's house. For a moment, he paused, speechless. Half the room was splattered with yellow paint. The chemical smell of the drying paint mixed with an aroma reminiscent of a food court. *Why me, dear Lord? Why me?*

Standing at attention in front of him, one of his agents was decorated like the room, albeit with the addition of several cheesy tidbits stuck in the gooey yellow paint in his hair and all over his body. One puff stood upright on the toe of the man's boot as if it too was standing to attention.

"Jenkins, what happened here?"

"Sir, I was attacked by a dog and an alien with a machine gun, sir."

"Can you describe them?"

"Yes, sir. It was the same dog we picked up last week. The alien was short and wearing black battle armor."

"And what happened?"

"Sir, I was sitting on the couch when the dog came flying at me."

"The dog flew at you?"

"Yes, sir. And it had a cape on."

"A flying dog wearing a cape attacked you?" Nuance closed his eyes, pinching the bridge of his nose. *God, give me strength.* "Was it also wearing blue leotards with a giant 'S' on its chest? Were you perchance attacked by Superdog?"

"No, sir. No leotards."

"Jenkins, do you understand how crazy that sounds?"

"Sir, yes, sir. But it's what happened."

Nuance eyed a video game controller lying on the couch. "Sure you aren't confusing what happened in the room with what happened in the game you were playing?"

"Sir, no, sir."

Nuance picked up the bag of Cheese Puffs and dumped the remains onto the floor. "Did you get the munchies while you were playing?"

Jenkins gave a despondent look at the cheesy debris on the carpet before answering, "A little, sir."

"I see. And your assignment here was what, Jenkins?"

"Sir, to monitor the premises and report any unusual activity or individuals attempting to gain entry, sir."

In a voice like an iceberg floating up to a boat during the night, Nuance asked, "And you performed that duty by playing games and eating snacks?"

"No, sir. I mean, yes, sir. I'm sorry, sir."

"Were you doing anything else, Jenkins?"

"Sir, no, sir."

Nuance toed the Cheese Puffs bag. "Sure you didn't take a quick toke of some wacky tobaccy?"

"Sir, no, sir! I would never do drugs on duty."

"I almost wish that you had. Jenkins, you are the most inept, incompetent, lazy, shiftless..." Nuance paused, unable to find adjectives with sufficient venom to convey his displeasure. "Do you know what you've done?"

"Sir, I guess—"

"Guess? We don't deal in guesses, Jenkins. We deal in facts. And here's one for you to consider. I'm writing you up for dereliction of duty."

"Will I be cashiered from the service, sir?"

"No, you won't get off so easy. I was prepping the prisoners for another round of interrogation when I got the call about this little farrago. Timing is critical in that procedure. Now, I'll have to wait till tomorrow and start it all over again. No, Jenkins, I've got something far worse than three months in a soft, civilian jail in mind for you. When I'm done here, I'm transferring you to Thule Air Base in Greenland. It's only a few hundred miles from the North Pole, and I understand it's so cold that people need to wear battery-heated underpants in the summer."

After another look around the room, Nuance shook his head and left.

42

Daphne stared at the clock above the blackboard in her classroom. It hadn't changed since the last time she looked. She tried counting, *one Mississippi, two Mississippi, three Mississippi* but the hands on the clock didn't go any faster. When she couldn't stand watching the clock anymore, she looked out the windows. They extended the full width of the room and reached from her waist up to the white ceiling tiles, offering a scenic view of the Menominee River. Yesterday's rain had faded to a light drizzle and drops inched their way down the window panes in slow motion. Daphne sagged in frustration. *Why is everything so slow today?!*

She kicked her sneaker against the chrome basket under her chair. Waiting for the results to arrive from the state lab was hard. She wanted to jump out of her seat, run to her teacher, and ask if she'd heard anything yet. But she couldn't. *I've got to keep this secret!* Holding it in made her feel like she was going to burst.

Daphne kicked the basket under her chair again, unable to concentrate on her lesson as she worried about her friends. Eliot was writing on the whiteboard, but Daphne's mind was elsewhere.

Monday mornings usually passed quickly at school. But this Monday morning had dragged on, with lunch offering no relief. Daphne was anxious to find out the test results for her uncle and his roommate. Eliot had promised to let her out of school to take the results to Claire as soon as they arrived. *I hope Miss Claire's doing okay. She'd be great for Unca Jake.*

Her white capris rustled against her chair as she fidgeted, twirling her brown hair in a loop.

"Daphne!"

Daphne jerked at her teacher's voice, and noticed that all of the other children were looking at her. "Yes, ma'am?"

"Daphne, did you hear a word I said?"

"Me? Oh…" Daphne blushed. "I'm sorry, ma'am. I guess I missed some of it." Some of the other children giggled, Timmy louder than the rest. She shot him a dirty look. *Someday it'll be his turn. He'll get caught. Then he'll be sorry he laughed at me.*

"Daphne?"

"Yes, ma'am?"

"Do I have your attention now?"

"Yes, Ms. Eliot, sorry."

"Very well, then. Please look at the sentence I've written on the board and tell me what's wrong with it."

Daphne twisted her lips as she stared at the sentence.

Eliot sighed. "What is the subject of the sentence, Daphne?"

"'Jane,' ma'am."

"That is correct. And the verb?"

"'Running,' ma'am."

"Also correct. Now, do you see what is wrong with the sentence?"

"Oh! It should be 'Jane ran home,' not 'Jane running home,' right Ms. Eliot?"

"Yes, that is correct, Daphne. Now please pay attention to the rest of today's lesson."

Daphne tried to pay attention, but she couldn't help herself. *I hope Unca Jake is okay. I bet that mean Moo-once still has him, but Miss Claire can save him if I can get the test results to her in time.*

Daphne kicked her desk some more. Every time the school's PA system made an announcement, she looked hopefully at the door, only to be disappointed.

Then the moment that she'd been waiting for arrived. Eliot paused in her lecture and picked up her cell phone, an uncharacteristic action. Daphne had never known her teacher to interrupt the class for any personal business.

"Daphne?"

"Yes, ma'am?"

"There's a message for you at the front office. You may leave class to attend to it."

"Thanks!" Daphne jumped out of her seat. Three steps toward the door, she stopped, ran back to her desk to gather her books, then ran from the room.

"Daphne!"

She poked her head back in the door.

"You need a note from me to leave class, Daphne." Eliot scribbled on a sheet of paper and then handed it to her.

"Thanks, Ms. Eliot!"

Daphne skipped down the hall to the counter facing the front door. When the blonde woman behind the counter looked up, Daphne passed her the note from Eliot. "Excuse me, ma'am. My teacher said to give this to you."

The secretary read the note and then went into a back room. She emerged a minute later with a sheet of paper. "Daphne, this just came in on the school's fax machine. According to your teacher's note, you're to deliver it to a nearby address. Is that correct?"

"Yes, ma'am."

"Do you know where to go?"

"Yes, ma'am."

"Very well, then. This is a bit unusual, but Ms. Eliot wouldn't ask us to do something if it wasn't completely above board. Now, don't be long!"

"Yes, ma'am!"

Daphne tucked the paper inside her denim jacket so that it wouldn't get wet and then scampered out of the school. As the door closed behind her, she looked up. The rain had stopped, but it was overcast and still cool. She took a deep breath. The air was fragrant with the scent of grass still green and moist from the recent rain. Over the hum of the traffic on nearby

Main Street, she could hear the waves from the lake breaking on the shoreline.

Her first stop was her house, where she picked up Chaucer. With Jake still missing, Daphne's mom had agreed to let her keep the dog at their house.

"You gotta come with me, Chaucer. It's part of my cover. Understand?"

Chaucer wagged his tail and snuffled, glad to take part in any activity.

Daphne hooked a short leash on Chaucer's collar, and then set off to Eliot's house, which was only a few blocks away.

————

Claire sat in one of Eliot's brocaded armchairs and peeked through the blinds of the front window, hoping to catch sight of Daphne. She had one of her host's thick woolen shawls draped over her shoulders but was otherwise dressed in her own clothes again. She squirmed, trying to get comfortable in her jeans, which had shrunk after her prolonged soak in the river. They were now skin tight, and though she secretly liked the way they showed off the curves of her legs, she felt that it was just a little bit much to be in good taste. *I'm not a hooker, for heaven's sake!*

Her blouse had shrunk too, but the shawl covered that.

Claire sipped from her mug of green tea. She'd finished lunch a while ago, nibbling on an apple and some cheese that Eliot had left in the fridge, but she was still a tad hungry. Missing a couple of meals on Saturday and Sunday had left her tummy in a mood to complain.

When Daphne showed up, Claire had the front door open before the girl had a chance to even ring the doorbell.

"I've got it!" Daphne said in a hushed voice, looking back over her shoulder to make sure that nobody was listening. As she slipped inside the house, Chaucer bulled past her to give Claire a shoulder bump in the knees, followed by a thorough licking of the hand, which made her giggle.

Daphne pulled the dog away. "Chaucer, you leave Miss Claire alone! We've got important business to discuss, and we don't need your help."

As soon as the door was closed, Daphne pulled the sheet of paper from her jacket and handed it to Claire. "Here's the test stuff you needed, Miss Claire. I hope it's good news!"

Claire took a moment to skim over the paper, then smiled. "It is, Daphne. It's excellent news indeed!"

Claire paused as her stomach flip-flopped. *I've got to take this to Nuance and convince him of the truth.* She shivered at the thought of confronting the man, of being skewered by his ice-gray eyes again.

"What's wrong, Miss Claire?"

"Nothing, Daphne. I'm…I'm just afraid of what I have to do next."

Daphne gave her a hug. "It's okay, Miss Claire. Mom says it's okay to be afraid. I was scared when Dad left to be a soldier. So was Mom, but she said it's a normal feeling. Things will work out."

Daphne hugged her again. "Don't let that mean Moo-once scare you. Unca Jake needs your help. And I think you're real brave!"

"I wish I was, Daphne." Claire swallowed, looking into the girl's trusting brown eyes. *I have to do this. For her.*

"Well, there's no point putting it off. Let's get you back to school. Then…" Claire looked down, searching for some inner strength. "Then I'll do what I can."

As Claire stood, Chaucer growled and ran to the front door. It swung open, and there was the snap of a Taser. Chaucer convulsed, then dropped paralyzed to the ground.

Three of Nuance's agents strode into the room. The first one in said, "You're a difficult woman to track down, Miss Miller. But we've been following everybody involved in this case. It was a bit of surprise when the girl led us to you. That's something that the commander is going to be quite interested in. Now, I hope you're not planning to give us any more trouble?"

"No, no trouble." Claire pulled Daphne behind her. "I'll come quietly. I was going to see Commander Nuance anyway."

"Really? That's a laugh. Now get on your knees and put your hands on your head."

Claire complied, though it hurt her foot as she knelt down.

One of the other agents gestured toward Chaucer, who was still lying on the floor. "Ensign, what do we do about the kid and the dog?"

"We bring them with us. Nuance is going to want to explore the connection between the girl and the Miller woman. And he'll have our hides if we let the kid go free so she can run around telling stories. Secure that dog, though. It's chewed up too many of our people already."

43

Claire and Daphne were separated during the car ride to the Northwood office building, but once they arrived, they were reunited outside a door guarded by two marines. Chaucer, restrained with zip-ties and a muzzle, growled in anger from his position on the floor next to them.

The agent leading Claire tapped on the door twice, paused, then tapped again. After a moment, they were let in. The room had the same dreary industrial look as all the others that Claire had seen in the building.

"Jake!" Claire stopped, her hand over her mouth. Naked except for a pair of white briefs, Jake knelt on the floor with his head in a small, round, wastebasket. His back arched as he puked, and the reek of his vomit filled the room. It seemed in keeping with the dull gray-green of the walls. At one of end of a nearby gurney was a puddle of water and two pairs of tubes, one set dripping water and the other hissing air. Nuance stood over him, arms folded, with a look of frustration on his face.

"Unca Jake!" Daphne tried to run to her uncle, but she was stopped by one of the agents. Rounding on Nuance, she screamed, "Stop it! You're hurting him! Let him go!" Unable to break free from the agent's grasp, Daphne stopped struggling and began to cry.

"What have you done to him?" Claire felt her face grow hot as she locked glares with Nuance.

"Nothing permanent. At least, not yet," Nuance replied, his gaze cold and steady. "Just a bit of warm water in the ears, followed by a shot of air. Harmless, really, and routinely used by the medical profession to test for vertigo. Most of the time, it triggers an acute attack of nausea, which lasts for about twenty minutes."

Claire was appalled. "Why would you do that?"

"Nothing breaks down a prisoner's resistance faster than physical distress. I must admit to being impressed with how long Mr. Andersen has held out. If I didn't have evidence to the contrary, I'd believe his claims of innocence."

"How long..."

"Going on three days now."

Claire shuddered, then felt something hot tiptoe up her spine like a stalking tiger. The look on Nuance's face reminded her of her father, and she remembered his cold disdain during her mother's funeral. An image of her mother's tombstone came to her; cold, hard, and gray, just like Nuance's eyes.

"Bastard!" Claire screamed and lunged forward. Twisting away from the agent holding her, she threw a punch at Nuance's face.

Nuance brushed aside the blow with ease, then grabbed Claire and threw her back to the agent. "Hold her."

"You'll never get away with this!"

Nuance sighed. "I hear that on a regular basis, Miss Miller, and I'm afraid I'll have to disappoint you on that subject. My actions are legal and sanctioned by our government at the highest levels."

"I don't believe it!" Claire panted, surprised by her own anger. *A week ago, I wouldn't have had the nerve to try that.*

"Miss Miller, since Nine-Eleven, America's intelligence agencies have been fighting an undeclared war against terrorists and spies. The courts have recognized this effort, and in cases like this, they have granted us broad latitude in terms of how we interrogate people."

Claire took a breath to calm herself. *Arguing isn't getting me anywhere. Solomon said I need to use facts to convince Nuance. Time to try.* "Commander, please listen to me. You've made a mistake. I have proof of Jake's innocence. And of Felipe's. We need to talk before this goes any further."

"Talk? All I want to hear from you, Miss Miller, is the location of your associate. You know, the one who assaulted two of my agents with a machine gun."

"I don't know anything about that."

"I find that hard to believe. Perhaps you'll feel more cooperative later." Nuance gestured at Jake, who was curled in a fetal position around the garbage can. "As you can see, I've been authorized to use enhanced interrogation techniques. You won't like them."

"You leave Miss Claire alone!" Daphne twisted free and stepped in front of Claire. "She didn't go anywhere near your guys yesterday afternoon."

Nuance shifted his gaze to look at Daphne, like a snake trying to decide which mouse to strike first. "Daphne, how do you know that one of the attacks happened yesterday afternoon? Did Miss Miller tell you? Or maybe her accomplice?"

"No." Daphne bit her lip.

"Then how do you know?"

"It was me."

"You? Impossible!"

"Is not! I can prove it."

"Daphne—"

"I had Unca Jake's paintball gun. And I didn't mean to shoot. It was an accident. The bad guy scared me, and I dropped it. It just went off."

Nuance stared at Daphne, then asked, "If that's the case, then what color were the paintballs?"

"Yellow. Now you gotta let Miss Claire go. And Unca Jake, too. He's no alien, and we've got proof."

"Yellow...?" Nuance looked down, apparently lost in thought, and then looked at Claire. "Proof? What kind of proof are you talking about?"

"This." Claire held out the fax from the state lab. "We had Jake's and Felipe's DNA run at the State Crime Lab. As you can see, they're not aliens. They're as human as we are. Like I said, you've made a mistake. A big one."

Nuance snatched the fax from Claire's hands, read it, and then tossed it back. "This could be faked. It probably is."

Claire could see that the man was shaken regardless of his bravado. "If you don't believe me, call the state lab. They have the full test results there. They'll confirm the data. And while you're doing that, take another look at Jake's manuscript. I've read it, and although I'm no expert on military tech, I'm pretty sure that there are no state secrets in the book. To make sure, I spoke with Commander Solomon yesterday—"

"Solomon?! How did you get in to see him?"

Claire smiled, sensing that she had Nuance on his heels. "Yes, Commander Solomon. And he confirmed that there were no secret documents in the original manuscript."

Nuance looked again at the fax in Claire's hands. After a long silence, he took out his cell and placed a call.

"Al, it's Fred."

Claire strained but was unable to hear the other side of the conversation. What Nuance said puzzled her.

"Yes, I know it's not secure. I'm past that now.

"Yes, I understand the risk. But I need to know, and I need to know now.

"Thanks."

Claire's curiosity grew as Nuance put his phone down on the gurney and paced the room in silence. He was clearly waiting for a callback. When it came, he snatched the phone up.

"Yes. You have them?"

"Good."

There was a long pause while Nuance listened to the voice on the phone. Head bowed, he rubbed his face with his free hand.

"Thanks." Nuance lowered the phone, his face whiter than Jake's underwear. Claire felt a surge of hope at the look of defeat on the man's face.

Gesturing toward Jake, Nuance said, "Clean this one up and get him dressed. Then bring in the other suspect." Confused, the agents shuffled around, exchanging looks as they hesitated.

Speaking into his phone again, Nuance said, "Al, I need one more thing. Contact the FISC and find out the status of our paperwork. The case number's on the test results you just gave me. Call me back on this line as soon as you learn something."

He hung up.

"Release them," Nuance said to the agents holding Claire and Daphne. Pointing at Chaucer, he said, "But keep that one restrained."

Being careful of her bandaged foot, Claire knelt down next to Jake and rubbed his back. "Are you okay to stand?"

"I think so." Jake lifted his head from the wastebasket and immediately went nose down in Claire's lap, retching.

Claire wrinkled her nose. *I just got these jeans clean.* She brushed Jake's hair back from his face and massaged his neck until his spasms subsided.

Daphne bent to watch, then straightened up. Lips pursed in a childish scowl, she took two steps and kicked Nuance hard in the shin.

"Daphne, no!" Claire cried.

"But he's a mean man! I hope..." While Nuance hopped away cursing, Daphne struggled to find the right words, settling on, "I hope he gets coal in his stocking for Christmas! That'd serve him right!"

Claire looked up at Nuance, who was perched on the gurney and rubbing his leg. "I wouldn't mind giving you a swift kick myself. But I'll settle for a ride home. My foot hurts, and Jake's in no shape to walk far."

Nuance glared at her. "Don't push your luck. You might be off the hook for being alien spies, but your new boyfriend here still has a lot to answer for concerning the use of secret information in his book."

"Not secret," Jake mumbled, his voice muffled by Claire's jeans.

"He's right," Claire said. "Solomon will back us up on that."

"Commander Solomon?" Nuance's lip curled. "He hasn't got the backbone to stand up for anyone."

Before Claire could reply, the door opened and a breathless agent stuck his head into the room. "Commander! Admiral Dutchman wants to see you ASAP!"

Nuance's Adam's apple bounced as he swallowed. Claire thought that he looked like a wolf with his foot caught in a trap. *Serves him right!*

"Did he say what he wanted?"

"No, sir. But he's furious."

Nuance looked around the room, then gestured to the agents. "Bring the suspects and follow me."

Daphne fetched Jake's clothes from the corner of the interrogation room and piled them next to Claire. Then Claire eased Jake onto his side and pulled his black jeans over his legs, hefting them over his hips while Jake made soft mewing noises like a sick cat.

"Can you sit up enough for me to get your T-shirt on?" she asked.

"Think so," Jake mumbled.

Claire helped him to a sitting position, then wiped his face with a paper towel provided by one of the agents. Jake wobbled but managed to stay upright as she pulled the shirt over his arms and head and then down over his body.

"Do you think you can stand yet?"

"I don't know. I've never felt this sick in my life."

An agent that Claire recognized as Jenkins knelt down next to her and said, "I'm sorry for all this. His vertigo should wear off in a few more minutes. If you can get him up and walking around, the nausea will wear off faster."

"Don't listen to him!" Daphne said. "He's a bad man too."

Claire looked at Jenkins and then thought about the trip down the Menominee River with him. "No, Daphne, I think he might be one of the good guys."

Jenkins helped Claire lift Jake to his feet, taking most of the load as she faltered, her broken toes screaming at the sudden weight.

"I've got him," Jenkins said.

"Thanks."

Daphne went over to Chaucer and picked up the leash still attached to his collar. An agent standing next to the dog cut off the zip-ties but refused to remove the muzzle. Chaucer got to his feet and growled at the room in general, before taking up a protective position at Daphne's side. She took off his muzzle, and every agent within ten feet took a step back.

Claire wrapped an arm around Jake's waist, and with Jenkins' help, got him moving slowly toward the door.

Felipe was waiting in the hallway. His right leg was bandaged around the thigh, and he leaned on a metal quad-cane. He was still wearing the faded blue jeans and navy polo shirt that he'd had on when first arrested, and both he and his clothes showed all the signs of being denied regular access to a laundry.

Jake roused at the sight of his friend. "Felipe! Dude, are you okay? I saw you get shot!"

"Yeah, the last couple of weeks have been kind of rough."

Claire wrinkled her nose. "What's that smell?"

"Might be me," Felipe said, taking a whiff of his shirt and then making a face. "I haven't shaved or bathed in...hmmm...not sure how long. Things have been kinda fuzzy since I got here."

"I guess none of us is in great shape at the moment," Jake said as the group limped down the hallway behind Nuance. When they reached Dutchman's office, they found the door open. Everyone filed into the room, and Nuance and the agents with him came to attention as they entered. Claire choked at the smell in the room and stopped breathing through her nose. The place was filled with the acrid scents of stale coffee, unwashed bodies, sweat, and fear.

From his station behind his battleship-gray desk, Dutchman glowered at the silent group, but his gaze lingered the longest on Nuance. A laptop was open in front of him and a short stack of manila folders sat on the corner of the desk.

He gestured at the laptop and snarled, "Commander, the internal surveillance team just detected a disturbing email coming into our system through an unauthorized channel. It's from Homeland Security's laboratory, and it's directed to you. Says something about re-checking our suspects' DNA tests. I don't recall authorizing that. Care to explain yourself?"

"Sir, I wanted to make certain of the data before we took irrevocable action with the suspects."

"Did you, now? And you didn't see the need to speak with me about that?"

"Sir, I didn't want to bother you with that kind of detail."

"That's just a fancy way of saying you wanted to go over my head to the Pentagon and take full credit for the investigation. Is that what you had in mind?"

"No, sir, nothing like that. I just—"

"Just WHAT? You mealy-mouthed weasel, I will not stand for this kind of insubordination!"

"Sir, yes, sir."

Claire studied Nuance. The man looked like a piece of wax fruit melting under a hot sun. *Solomon said that Nuance could help us with Dutchman, but I don't think he can help himself.* She almost felt sorry for the man. Almost.

Dutchman began tapping his fingers on his desk. "Commander, you've failed to deliver the alien spies in spite of almost unlimited resources, and you've dragged your feet on the interrogation of the suspects despite my direct order to 'take the gloves off.'"

"Sir, the techniques I used were effective—"

"Effective, my ass! A few bruises? A bit of dizziness? You call that getting tough with a suspect?"

Claire looked at Nuance in surprise. She hadn't realized that he'd shown restraint.

"Sir, there are aspects—"

"Silence!" Dutchman rose, his face mottled with rage. "I don't want to hear any more excuses!" Dutchman's voice dropped as he leaned forward. "But I would be more than interested to hear why you went over my head. Once again, would you care to explain that? Before I court-martial you?"

"It's the data, sir. There is some question about its accuracy."

"You derailed the entire investigation due to some piddling little detail? With our careers and the security of our nation at stake?"

"Sir—"

"Let me explain," Claire said, surprising herself as much as anybody.

"You?" Dutchman leveled his gaze at her like a spear.

Claire felt a wash of fear and took a step back. *How can I face this guy? It's like facing my father again.* Memories of past failures flashed through her brain as she faltered. *I'm such a loser. I can't do this.*

Then she felt a small hand in hers. Looking down, she saw Daphne, the girl's chestnut eyes liquid with trust. And she remembered her promise to help. She looked at Jake and saw the same look.

I've got to do this. I can do this. Swallowing hard, Claire limped up to the desk and handed Dutchman the test results from the State Crime Lab.

"Here are independent tests proving that Jake and Felipe are human. There are no aliens here. And unless I'm mistaken, that email you're talking about will say the same thing."

Dutchman looked at the paper, before throwing it down in disgust. "So what? Even if they're not aliens, you're still all spies."

"No, we're not spies either, and I can prove that, too."

"How?"

"Easy. The manuscript that Commander Nuance showed you that had confidential data in it was actually a mashup of a number of different documents. I spoke with Commander Solomon yesterday, and he assured me that the documents were originally separate. Nuance has admitted that his team merged the papers, with the resulting document giving the false impression that Jake had stolen secret information from Northwood."

"That's a far stretch, Miss Miller."

"It's true." Claire turned. "Isn't it, Commander Nuance?"

His armpits soaked with sweat, Nuance hesitated before answering. "Yes, it's true. I spoke with Ensign Johnson on Sunday, and she confirmed that the documents could have been mingled by our own team. In its original state, Mr. Andersen's manuscript does not actually contain any confidential data about the Eschaton system."

Claire rounded on Dutchman. "There it is. You've heard it from your own people. Jake is innocent, as are the rest of us. You have to let us go."

"Let you go?" Dutchman sagged back into his seat, a look on his face like a steer that had just realized it was in the line for the slaughterhouse.

"Yes. Let us go."

"But the investigation…"

"It's over, sir." Nuance seemed to have regained some of his composure. "There's nothing for us to investigate here, except for a bad car accident."

"But the Pentagon! What will they say? My career—"

Dutchman was interrupted by the loud ringing of Nuance's cell phone.

Nuance picked it up and said, "Yes, sir. I was—yes, sir—no, sir. Put the phone on speaker? Yes, sir."

Nuance placed his phone down on Dutchman's desk and said, "Can you hear me, sir?"

"Yes, commander, loud and clear." The man's voice coming over the phone was stern, and Claire thought that it could have managed a passable imitation of a gravel truck if the truck upped its game a bit. The man continued, "For the record, commander, please state who is present."

"Wait a minute! Wait just a darn minute!" Dutchman sprang from his chair. "Who is this?"

"This is Admiral Gunflint from the Inspector General's Office at the Pentagon. I have three of the Joint Chiefs of Staff in the room with me."

"Oh." Dutchman sat back down again.

Nuance quickly listed all the people present in the room for Gunflint.

"Admiral Dutchman," Gunflint said, "it has come to our attention that your investigation into an alleged alien spy ring at Northwood was based on false information. Is that not correct?"

"Well, I wouldn't quite say that…" Dutchman fidgeted, looking around as if seeking an escape route.

"What would you say?"

"Based on the evidence available at the time, the investigation seemed justified."

"And the torture of American citizens? How did you justify that?"

"It wasn't torture!" Dutchman's face grew red. "Nuance freelanced some enhanced interrogation techniques, totally without my approval, I might add."

"Is that true, commander?"

"Sir, no, sir. Admiral Dutchman gave me a direct order to, and I quote, 'take the gloves off' when questioning the suspects."

"Can anybody corroborate that?"

Claire saw Dutchman lean back in his chair, a smug look on his face. *He's going to get away with it! He set Nuance up to take the fall. I've got to do something!* Gathering her courage, she said, "Admiral Gunflint? This is Claire Miller."

"Yes, Miss Miller?"

"I can vouch for what Commander Nuance has just said."

"Were you present when the orders were given?"

"No, but just a few minutes ago I heard Admiral Dutchman castigate Commander Nuance for failing to be aggressive enough during the interrogations. There are other people present in this room who also heard him say it."

Claire blushed in response to the thankful look that Nuance gave her. *Just because I saved your hide, don't expect a card from me at Christmas.*

There was a brief pause, then Gunflint said, "Admiral Dutchman, it sounds like this whole mess is your responsibility. I've just conferred with the senior officers present, and we have reached a consensus. You have exceeded your authority, bringing injury to innocent civilians and compromising the security of our nation through your incompetence. You are hereby relieved of command.

"Furthermore, I'm ordering Commander Nuance to take you into custody, pending court-martial. Commander, you will escort the Admiral under armed guard back to Washington at the first opportunity. Am I clear?"

"Crystal, sir."

"Excellent. Now release the suspects, and shut down your operation. I want your team back at your home base by end-of-day tomorrow."

"Yes, sir!"

Nuance ended the call and turned to Claire.

"Miss Miller, please accept my apologies for your treatment. You and your friends are free to go."

45

Thick, mottled-gray clouds hung low in the sky as Claire and her friends left the Northwood office building. A brisk wind brought the clean scent of the lake to her, mingled with the aroma of freshly cut grass. A small flock of sparrows lurking near the doorway chirped their annoyance before flying off, while a family of goldfinches warbled after them.

Claire draped the green shawl that she'd borrowed from Eliot over her and Jake's shoulders to keep them warm. She held him tight around the waist, ostensibly because he was still unsteady on his feet, and he held her just as firmly so that she wouldn't have to put weight on her injured foot.

They had crossed the parking lot when Jake asked, "Where's Chaucer?"

Walking next to him with a firm grip on the hand that wasn't engaged with Claire, Daphne said, "I'm sorry, Unca Jake. I forgot and let go of his leash while people were arguing."

Jake looked around. "I don't see him."

"He's over there." Claire pointed at a rhododendron that was showing off its purple blossoms. "Looks like he's digging a hole."

"Oh no, not again!" Jake released his hold on Claire and stumbled across the lawn. When he reached Chaucer's pit mine, he chided the dog, "Chaucer, how many times have I told you not to do this?" After a brief tussle, he pulled a chewed-up stack of manila folders out of Chaucer's jaws.

"I think we're in trouble again," Jake sighed.

"What is it?" Claire asked.

"Looks like something from Dutchman's office." Jake handed the folders to Claire.

Claire opened the topmost folder, read a few lines, then stopped in surprise. "Oh, my God! This is Dutchman's file on me! And it's all here. Jake, it's got the addresses where Sam and Becca are living! I can find them, after all these years, I can find them!"

"You won't find them if we hang around here much longer," Felipe said, looking back over his shoulder. "As soon as Nuance finds out that this paperwork is missing, he's going to send out a search party."

"Good point," Jake said. "Let's get out of here."

When they reached Main Street, Claire realized that they hadn't decided where they were going. "Jake, before I take you home, would you like to stop somewhere and get something to eat? I'm getting hungry."

"Great idea, Claire! That agent was right, my nausea cleared up after we started moving around, and I haven't eaten since yesterday. Where would you like to go? Ethel's?"

Claire shook her head. "No thanks, bad memories of that place. How about Wilson's? It's my favorite spot to grab a bite when I'm out."

Jake grinned. "Mine too! Have you tried their black velvet grande? It's insanely good!"

Claire paused, and they exchanged glances. "I live on that drink. How come I've never noticed you in there before?"

Jake looked embarrassed. "I work nights, don't get out much otherwise."

Behind them, Felipe laughed. "He doesn't get out at all. And I'm totally on board with Wilson's. They have the best crème-filled chocolate Bismark I've ever eaten!"

"And he's eaten quite a few," Jake chuckled. "It's settled then."

As they made their way to Wilson's, they ran into a familiar figure headed in the other direction.

"Hello, Claire, Daphne," Eliot said as she approached. "I've been worried about you and decided to head down to Northwood after school let out to see how things were going."

Claire gave the teacher a hug, managing to do so without letting go of Jake. "They turned out well, thanks to you and your friend, Doctor Simmons. The investigation's been dropped, and our names have been cleared."

"That's excellent news! Where are you headed now?"

"We're all famished and going to Wilson's for a snack. Care to join us?"

"Of course! Lead on!"

A few minutes later, they were all huddled around a table at Wilson's with a pot of hot coffee and more pastries than it seemed possible to fit on the tabletop.

Daphne sipped a mug of hot chocolate and slipped donut crumbs under the table to Chaucer when she thought nobody was watching. This created a problem for the hound, who was actively soliciting tidbits from Claire at the same time.

"It's all here!" Claire exclaimed, leafing through the papers in the folder. "Their addresses, phone numbers, where they're going to school—everything!"

"What will you do?" Jake asked.

"I'm going to find them. We'll be together again." Claire paused to wipe her eyes.

"What about your job?"

"I'm not going back to that hole. I can do better than that. Maybe I'll start my own agency, like Gretchen keeps telling me to do."

"I lost my job, too. They told me while I was in my cell. So did Felipe."

"What will you do now?"

"Well," Jake paused as he tried to screw up his courage.

Before he could speak, Claire asked, "Why don't you come with me?"

"You mean that?"

"Yes. If you want to."

"Of course, I want to!"

"Uh, do you two need to get a room here?" Felipe said around a mouthful of donut. Unnoticed, he'd slid the platter of treats over toward himself while Jake and Claire had been talking. Without the pastries in the way, the two had started holding hands without seeming to notice that they were doing it.

"Huh? Geez, no!" Jake's face blossomed red, but he didn't let go of Claire's hand.

"Then it's settled." Claire smiled.

"But how will you start your own agency? Don't you need authors?"

"I've got a good start right here."

"Me?"

"Your book was good enough to send the US Military into panic. If I can't sell that to a publisher—"

"But nobody likes my stories!"

Claire sighed. "It's not your stories, Jake, it's your writing."

"She's right, young man," Eliot said, taking a sip of tea. "And that's something I would be happy to help you with."

'You will? I don't know."

From the expression on his face, Claire was sure that Jake had visions of repeating fourth grade. "It'll be fine," she said with a smile. "I'll help too," dimples appeared on her cheeks as she continued, "as long as you promise never to use secret info in a book again!"

"That I can promise!"

Felipe grinned and gave him a quick thumbs up before cramming the last Bismark in his mouth.

———

Standing across the street, Solomon and Hansen watched the group through the front window of the coffee shop. Both men were dressed in civilian clothes. Solomon's leg was in a walking cast, and he rested his weight on crutches under his armpits.

"Do you think they'll be okay?" Hansen asked.

"Who, the kids? Of course they will. They make a cute couple."

Hansen paused. "Jim, I did a lot of thinking while you were unconscious."

"Yes?"

"I want you to stop your hormone shots. I know that I was the one who dragged his feet on this, that you wanted to start a family a long time ago. But I'm ready now."

"Are you nuts? If I stop my hormone shots, I'll revert to my natural state and gender! How do you think the US Navy will react when my skin turns green and I grow breasts?"

"I can keep giving you melanin shots to mask your skin color."

"And my breasts?" Solomon laughed. "Target doesn't carry bras with six cups, and it's not the sort of thing I can ask a local tailor to fix up for me. Not to mention how the locals would react when a litter of half-a-dozen kits shows up for Kindergarten class. Try keeping that off social media!"

"We'll resign our commissions, so the military won't be an issue. After your car accident, I can issue a medical discharge for you with no problem at all. Then we'll move back to our surveillance post in Nevada. The AI units can help with the kits while we monitor human progress from a safe distance."

"Well, I like the safe distance part of the plan. But I must admit, I like the local folks. And these are good kids."

Hansen turned to look at his partner. "I like them too. What if they get into trouble again?"

"If things get out of hand, I expect that Daphne will help them sort it out. She's very advanced, you know. If there were more like her…"

"Then they'd be ready for contact. I don't need to read your report to Centauri Prime to know what you're thinking."

"After all these years together, I'd be surprised if that wasn't the case."

"So you're going to recommend another century of non-interference?"

"Maybe two."

"Do you think it will take them that long to advance to a state where they're ready for contact with galactic civilization?"

"No," Solomon grinned. "I think it'll to take us that long to get ready for contact with them!"